The Astronomer AND OTHER STORIES

The Astronomer

AND OTHER STORIES

BY DORIS BETTS

LOUISIANA STATE UNIVERSITY PRESS
BATON ROUGE AND LONDON

The following stories have been published previously: "Clarissa and the Depths," *New Campus Writing;* "The Dead Mule," *Red Clay Reader;* "The Proud and Virtuous," *Mademoiselle;* "Careful, Sharp Eggs Underfoot," *The Rebel Magazine.*

This book, like the others, is for Lowry,
and also for June and Robert Howard

CONTENTS

The Astronomer AND OTHER STORIES

THE SPIES
IN THE
HERB HOUSE

To be a child in the tall house where I grew up in Statesville, North Carolina, was to live marooned on an island. Along the front limit of the large yard ran a busy highway which—for several centuries—I could not grow old enough to cross. In back, the lot became a garden and fruit orchard before it stopped at the edge of railroad tracks where I was not allowed to play. Twice a day the last surviving steam engine in that part of the state puffed slowly by toward Taylorsville, and twice a day I stood in the limits of a honeysuckle bank to wave to the engineer. Sometimes he put out a hand the size of my head, and waggled the fingers inside his striped denim glove.

On both sides of our old-fashioned house lived old-fashioned couples who trained roses over white arbors, and were forever setting seedbeds between us like barriers. I had no brothers and no sisters. Most of the girls I knew at school lived close together in a cluster of brick cottages, miles away from an old house in a bypassed part of town.

I did the things marooned children have always done. I made society ladies from kitchen matches—impaled grapes for their heads, inverted morning-glory blooms for ball-gown skirts. An apple tree became a team of horses, its crooked limbs saddled with old newspapers and bridled with lengths of clothesline. At the beginning of World War II, there was enough soot inside the house chimneys to blacken the faces of a thousand commandos, and there were sharp kindling pieces in the pile to carry sheathed in the belt. There were godlike games to be played with the black ants living at the base of the oak; I blessed and cursed them indifferently, sometimes sprinkling bread crumbs near their hills, sometimes flooding their tunnels with vinegar water. And I fell in love with books.

In that large yard there were also three cement ponds for goldfish (two of them dry) and a tiny back-yard golf course my father had built by embedding tin cans in the turf at regular intervals, with a painted broomstick stuck in the earth alongside.

The summers were very long. Most summer Sundays I stood by the only pond which held fish and water, and kept ready a garden hoe to lift out the golf balls when they plopped among tangled water lilies. In the drowse of the afternoon the sequence was *Plop,* and "Oh, hell," from my father, and a warning called through the kitchen screen by my mother. "It's Sunday," she would say, making it sound like a threat. She really felt God changed gravity around for Sundays. God had made six other days suitable for swatting balls into holes but on the seventh He sent them neatly into the water; and swearing only made things worse. Every week I dragged them up from the silt, and every week the pattern was as even and dependable as the drone of bees: *Plop,* and *Oh, hell* and *It's Sunday.*

The trouble with my father was that, though he was only five-feet-eight and small of bone, he could never learn to play on the tiny course he himself had made. The stocky muscle in his arm treated such delicate distances with contempt, and often the ball would arc away truly and "home" into the pond, scattering a dozen goldfish toward the shadows. Those Sunday afternoons had a bad effect on me, watching him try to cramp his stroke and constrict his vision. I grew up flawed in exactly the same ways.

Winters there was school, and from September to June I broke the rules and walked the two miles, not by sidewalks but on the forbidden railroad tracks. That awkward stride from crosstie to crosstie jolted the hipbones. But if I watched the mysterious reflected light which traveled in front along the edge of the black rail, the body would balance along that line and one foot would follow the other as easily as breath goes in and out. I thought this strange, receding light was some form of glue, and had guided Jesus over the water to where St. Peter stood.

One path to the train tracks was made through back yards and under fences. Just as at our house, back yards were always more interesting than front. I thought about who might be eating breakfast behind all those kitchen doors. All this time Statesville's ten thousand souls went on about their business, including breakfast, with no apparent knowledge of the uniqueness of me, no speculating about my obvious royal blood. Night and morning they let me go by; and I was afraid when they were old (any minute now) they would have failed to save my face for recollection, my gait, my black bangs, and all the little hints of excellence to come.

So when I passed them near their garages and woodpiles and trash cans, I wanted to catch their arms and look up into their faces and say: *Remember me! Oh, do remember me!*

Yet it all went backward. And it is I who remember them.

The very grass which eventually reclaimed my father's practice tees was itself practicing for the time when it took him as well. The lilies won out over the goldfish pond. I am the only one who goes back now to look and wonder if golf balls are rotting underneath.

Yes, it went backward; and all the time I cried to the world: *See me!* the world slipped by and around again. And, striking an attitude that ought to be imprinted on the eyeballs for all time, I only saw them; and could never stop seeing. To be marooned this second way was not what I had wanted at all.

I would prefer it to sound like an elegant home where I lived in Statesville, with pools and golf greens, but it was only a shabby old house on Front Street. My golfing father worked in a cotton mill, and we rented three rooms in a house which, as it stood near the train, stood also near the mill. Golf was one of my father's protests. He never in his life played a real game and the club he used—one club—was another painted broomstick with a slab nailed to one end.

Another of his protests stood inside that tall house, a corner bookcase in the shape of an ascending pagoda holding a ten-dollar set of an encyclopedia. A depression encyclopedia, bought in stubbornness, for me. Probably I was some kind of protest, too.

"Now *read* these!" he'd say, glowering, although I was only seven at the time. "They cost ten dollars; read them!" I began to read them.

Even skipping around, it took some time to reach the volume marked SAL-TIM and learn from it that Statesville, hitherto drab and unremarkable, was listed as the "herb center of the world." It was a shock to find this little town where all the sidewalks were cracked had some distinction already, prior to the hindsight which was to come from knowing me. I was proud. I was disappointed.

To my father I said, "What are herbs?" (And that word started, always will, with a good strong *h,* except at Grandmother's, where they were "yarbs." If it isn't pronounced correctly in the herb capital of the world, what authority is there?)

Herbs were, my father said, plants and roots and bark used to make medicine or flavor food. "Around here it's medicine," he said, and he named some things which came from Iredell County and from all the way up to the Blue Ridge: elder flowers, truelove, wild cherry bark, blackberry and pokeweed roots, sumac berries, ginseng, sassafras bark, catnip, balm of Gilead buds. "Haven't you seen the Herb House right here in town?"

No, I had not. They would not even let me cross the street.

"The really big one," he said, "is right uptown. They don't use it any more, but you've passed it a hundred times, walking to town with me. There's a smaller herb house near the depot." He promised to show me next time we went by.

When it was shown, I could hardly believe it. Across from the county jail stood a big, black, ugly building, like a shack thrown up for some shiftless giant, never painted, the width of a city block and half its depth. Around it in grass and on concrete, like wooden dandruff, lay chips and splinters where the roof shingles were flaking off. The boards of a three-sided porch were warped and splintered and rounding at the ends. If this was how the world picked its centers, even for herbs, I thought I could lower my standards. If this was all it took to get into the encyclopedia, I thought I would make it.

"Empty," my father said. "They don't use it." He walked ahead at a slow pace, giving me time to shout words through the cracks between wall boards and send my voice flying into the darkness. The wide porch ran between the sidewalk and sills of the broad doors; it would have been easy to roll laden wagons in and out of the Herb House, if anyone ever had.

"Built out of heart pine," my father submitted as I swooped back to him again. I clattered across the sloping porch. Heart pine sounded ever so splendid, and not like these planks which wind and water had worn so dark.

I saw that the pine had reacted in the Herb House as in my grandmother's home; left unpainted, it had given off occasional yellow crusts in horizontal streaks or in a golden aura surrounding each knothole. All children learned to scratch names, arrows, egg faces onto these yellow resin spots. I found a stick and in one patch of gold wrote my crooked name in tall white letters upon the Herb House. Disappointing though the building was, some part of the world came to a center here; it was like poking the earth in its navel to mark on the very spot. In loose-jointed letters I scrawled the name D O R I S, a dot over the *i* the size of a small apple. Afterward I skipped around the three-sided trembling old porch and called out the names of medicinal herbs. I felt ceremonial, like an Indian dancing home the buffalo.

The next time I saw Betty Sue, I told her all about the Herb House.

Betty Sue was the closest thing I had to a playmate. She lived across the railroad tracks and down a dirt road in a line of houses backed up to the cotton mill; she was allowed to walk to my house at will, without permission, without promises of when she would be home. Very rarely I was allowed to walk to hers.

Already Betty Sue owned almost everything I valued, which may be why she held no convictions of a startling future. Just as I fell like a panting runner over the line to Age Eight, she was on the verge of being Nine. She wore long hair in twin plaits which, combed out, fell forth in ripples. It was the color of weak lemonade but someday, she said calmly, she would dye it to match Rita Hayworth's. Her three older sisters had breasts and wore stockings and high-heeled shoes; on Saturday nights they went out to beer places with paratroopers. I hung on the edge of her family, smoothing my bobbed and jealous hair, eying the *True Love* magazines so casually dropped in the living room, envying the chinaberry trees in her front yard. Once she had even tried on a paratrooper's boot, which felt as big as a closet.

Betty Sue did not care much for my Herb House or the ginseng and balm of Gilead buds. It is hard to impress the rich of this world.

She wrapped the tail of one plait around her entire wrist. I hated that. "That big old black building uptown? It's the *ugliest* thing!"

"I guess it's the biggest in the world or it wouldn't say so. Right there in the encyclopedia." Betty Sue didn't have an encyclopedia at her house—but then, she didn't want one, either.

"I guess it is." She threw the plait over her shoulder. Indian princess stuff. "Marge got a V-mail today. It's a little bitty thing. They do it with a camera."

I lowered my voice. "Where's he stationed?"

"Secret."

I wasn't about to let her V-mail give her the upper hand. "We're the herb capital of the whole world. It says so in the book." Sometimes it helped to tell Betty Sue something twice.

"I guess so. Listen, when you grow up would you rather be Sonja Henie or Hedy Lamarr?"

"Joan Crawford," I said, "because her mouth is like a box. But *you* listen!" Here I stripped off leaves from a limb of her silly old yard tree. "Listen, it doesn't matter so much what it *is* as it does being biggest or best! Or the Only. Just think about that!"

Betty Sue did not think of it. She tried to look as if she did, but it was no good with me. I knew how the proper excitement should have mounted in her face.

"Never mind," I sighed, pretending not to care. She climbed to sit in a nest of chinaberry branches; she flicked twigs for switches and made a roaring noise; and from far below I watched the plane of my brave Air Force husband scream to the ground in flames. I had real tears in my eyes. We hadn't been able to find a game yet that could make Betty Sue have tears.

The year I was eight, Mother made me join the Silver Circle at our church. The group met on Wednesday afternoons and I talked Betty Sue into joining with me.

"You can stand by me in the Christmas pageant."

"What good is that?" Betty Sue seldom went to church. Her sisters needed their sleep on Sunday mornings.

"The preacher turns out the church lights and we shine. All of us stand in a circle on the stage holding this special string of colored lights. Hands folded, you see, like praying; and hiding this little Christmas bulb inside your fingers." I demonstrated. "And we light up."

"What's it for?" she said, already bored.

I said it was for serious young Christians. It was a youth group. In the *church*. Didn't she understand anything?

She understood the lemonade and cookies to be served each Wednesday while the leader read Paul's Epistles. My mother was very pleased to hear I had gained a new member for the Silver Circle; and she felt better knowing I would not walk home alone from the meetings.

Always it was up to me to find new routes and short cuts (Betty Sue would have walked exactly the same streets forever) so she did not question the way I selected to head home from Silver Circle. We read the signs at the theater, took the street by the jail so we could wave at the barred windows and make some poor soul feel better. I was stuffed full of the thirteenth chapter of First Corinthians and wanted to sing some cheerful duet as we walked by, but Betty Sue wouldn't.

Then we turned the corner and I pointed a finger at the Herb House.

She swung her head the width and length of the building. "It *is* ugly," she breathed, and I heard the beginnings of awe.

I directed her to the uneven porch and sought for the testament of my name but it was gone. Does rain do that? Betty Sue didn't know and I never could find out; but this time I saw the same patch of yellow was unmarked so I wrote my name again, harder. Betty Sue didn't write her name, of course.

She had flattened her face against the wall. "I can see through this crack. It looks empty."

"On the right," I said. "Boxes of something."

She sucked in her breath, making that noise the goldfish made in the pond at home. "They're big. They could have dead people in there."

"Lions," I said. "Tigers and guns."

"Or bombs."

Until she said that, I think it was just another game, a reaching for time-tested terrors which had already begun to lose their power. But it was different with bombs. This was a terror from our parents' world. We had seen in newsreels the big planes letting them fall, like birds laying eggs into the wind. Bombs made headlines; an old classmate of my father's had been killed by one.

"You could get a bomb in there," I said soberly, looking through the crack. "One bomb in each box." Defense workers sometimes chalked a message on the bombs they made: "Hello, Hitler!" I thought about writing my name on a bomb instead of the pine board, so that death would come out of the sky with a signature. My right hand began to hurt.

Silent now, Betty Sue and I continued around the huge porch. The dust on both sides of the window glass was so dense we could not see in, and there were iron bars vertically over each, six per window.

"The bars?" said Betty Sue, whispering. I shook my head.

There was one pair of padlocked doors, wide enough for a loaded wagon to roll through; and where the halves did not quite meet a bigger crack caught our eyes. Betty Sue placed her shoe against one door and leaned hard into it; I caught the edge of the other in my fingers and pulled out. "You're closer," I said, lying.

She bent to look. Suddenly she gasped and leaped two feet away.

At this the door which had been braced against her shoe sprang back and pinched my fingers. I felt as if the Herb House, angered, had bitten me on my writing hand.

"TINKER'S DAM!" I yelled, an oath my father was allowed because the preacher had finally admitted it was not exactly profane. I flailed the sore hand in her direction but she dodged. "What did you do that for!"

"Oh hush!" moaned Betty Sue. "It moved. One of those boxes moved!"

I left off sucking my fingers. "Moved?"

"Toward the door. Toward me. They've seen us!" She grabbed my sweater sleeve and shook it. "We better run!"

The throbbing fell out of my hand, through my arm, into my stomach. I did not ask who "they" might be. And I never doubted for one minute that one of those bomb-sized boxes had taken a step toward where we stood. But I muttered, "Let me look," and put my eye to the door crack. Naturally I could tell right away the boxes were not where they had been, and it seemed to me there was a high humming sound coming out of the dark and maybe, just at the corner of my view, a flicker like the gleam of eyes.

Then, while I watched, I saw the nearest box move. I tell you, I *did* see it! It lurched awkwardly in my direction. Two nights later, out of a sound sleep, I was to remember that Frankenstein came at his victims in just that blind, threatening way.

But when the box moved I did not pause to make comparisons. I leaped backward, caught a heel on the edge of the porch, cracked my head against a post, and hit the sidewalk running hard. Even so, Betty Sue was ahead of me. Wildly we ran from the black house, now one slightly in front and now the other, until we were hurting for breath and I thought my appendix would come out by the roots.

When we slowed to a walk two blocks away, neither could talk. We puffed and drew sweeping pictures in the air with our hands. Often we twisted back to look, half expecting a sea of dark boxes in pursuit.

I managed to pant, "They don't know where we live."

She was making groans and whimpers. "They'll find out! Oh, they can find out anything!" And she made that piteous noise all the way home.

Now we kept vigil over the Herb House. I remember that time as a solid lump of terror, a block of days pulled into shape by the Silver Circle on Wednesday afternoons and the awful duty of walking by the Herb House. Fright lay in my throat like a . . . like a golf ball. Even the thought of the Herb House made me shiver and Mother was always sending me needlessly to the bathroom on account of it. I hated the Herb House. I hated the encyclopedia which had trapped me into this awful knowledge. I hated Nathan Hale for the kind of example he left in the history books, and the thought of St. Paul martyred for his beliefs made my hair crackle. Each Tuesday night I was unable to fall asleep, and my parents had a long talk about bad radio programs which preyed on the minds of children.

For all our fear, Betty Sue and I were faithful sentinels. We knew we would have to watch the Herb House until we had *proof*. If parents were hard to talk to, the F.B.I. was likely worse.

So as often as we could we slipped away, running from school in the afternoons and then running two extra blocks to arrive home at the usual hour, taking a quick brave look at the Herb House. And on Wednesdays we forced ourselves to inspect more closely, holding hands and whispering about whose hand was really *wet*. Sometimes we hid behind a small garage which went with the house nearest the Herb House. The garage was built entirely of tin roofing. When our legs became so weak that we leaned against it, the tin wall would bend in and pop back again with a deafening noise. It sounded just like a pistol shot—and wouldn't the enemy shoot any child in the back without a qualm?

One day we spotted something marked on the wall of the Herb House in light chalk or crayon. We crouched against the tin garage until we could pass the Herb House walking behind a woman, disguised as her two daughters. Normally and light-heartedly we passed, our eyes sliding off to examine the cipher. Was it an "X" scraped by a schoolboy or a drawing for tick-tack-toe? It hardly matters now, for on that day we knew exactly what it was. We caught damp hands and marched stiffly on, eyes front, behind the woman.

At the next corner we broke and ran. There was no need to compare what we had seen. There was a swastika marked in chalk on the wall of the Herb House!

The Evil Swastika! Already I had written a poem in my notebook about that which began: "Hitler and Hess, Are full of wickedness."

Now Betty Sue and I had to admit in words what we had already known. There were Nazi spies headquartered in the Herb House. We hardly discussed it all the way home, just parted at the corner and took the awful secret separately to our two houses.

Our meetings now became secret, elaborately arranged. We barely spoke in public. At school we pretended there had been some serious quarrel between us and we would never be best friends again.

"To throw them off the track," said Betty Sue. "In case they're watching us."

I only nodded. I *knew* they were watching. How recently I had believed the glances of strange adults were fond and tolerant! They were enjoying the sight of me going by. They were storing me up to remember. Now I caught like a knife in the breastbone the sharp stare of a man in a passing car. I saw the cruel woman pretending to wait for a pretended bus. I did not believe half my marble collection had disappeared by accident.

Betty Sue and I left notes at a spot along the railroad track nine crossties east from Gander Street. They were always cryptic, signed by Z-6 or X-271. For together we had figured out what the Germans were doing in the Herb House in Statesville, North Carolina, in the spring of 1942.

The Herb House stood just across the street from Iredell County Jail (COVNTY, it was carved in the arch above the door) and from time to time the sheriff would pour bootleg whiskey into the street drain from the curb in front of the jail, making a great ceremony of it. If it was a large supply, the Salvation Army was notified and came to sing hymns to cover the sounds of splashing. All our lives Betty Sue and I had heard that the colored people learned of such occasions in advance and came up through sewer passages right underneath that drain, and caught in fruit jars the stuff the law poured out.

Once we understood this, we knew the earth was honeycombed with mysterious passages most people never thought about. The Nazis came in and out of the Herb House through some such concealed passage. Perhaps they were even building a tunnel to the sea.

"Submarines!" we whispered, shocked. Statesville was—by the way—hundreds of miles from the Carolina coast.

Yet that must be it. There were submarine parts inside the wooden boxes. Was it not typical of Hitler's audacity, to build a war factory right inside America, in a little town nobody would suspect? Betty Sue and I began to take a desperate interest in the daily newspapers. Every U-Boat we read about had probably been shipped out under the sheriff's nose, or under his feet at least.

"Could we write the White House?" asked Betty Sue.

But I said who would listen to a couple of eight-year-old girls? ("I'm nine," she said. Naturally she would say that.) I said when we had seen enough to prove everything about the spies, then we would simply cross that street and knock on the door of the jail. . . .

"Can you do that at a jail?" interrupted Betty Sue. "Just knock?"

Just knock on that door and tell whoever came.

Her eyes were round. "Even if it's a prisoner?"

I sighed. Sometimes this undercover work didn't seem to come as easily to Betty Sue as it did to me.

We had two other dreadful discoveries to make. On a late spring day when the German Twelfth Army had just driven back the Russians and we figured the spies in the Herb House would be celebrating and off their guard, we tiptoed across the broad porch and peered through a different crack. We were looking into what must have once been a main office for the herb business. There were a roll-top desk (our fingers itched for all those secret documents) and two dusty chairs; but most unbelievable of all were two long glass cases against one wall. They were about as high as the glass counters which held candy at the dime store. By taking turns, by twisting our necks, we could see they were lined with velvet. Against that dark field stones on display caught splinters of the dim light.

We ran toward the Post Office because it was owned by the government, and that made us feel less isolated. "Diamond smugglers!" I announced flatly. We sat weakly on the Post Office steps and began to fool with our shoestrings.

But Betty Sue frowned, and for one minute I thought the tight plaits pinched her face and—in ten years—I might be as handsome as she even when she had matched her hair to Rita Hayworth's. The moment passed.

Deepening her frown she said, "Why would the Germans do that?"

"Submarines cost money!" I spluttered. "For all we know they're tunneling into the jewelry stores right here in Statesville." And I waved an arm at Bradford's store, which had probably never housed an uncut diamond in its life.

"We've got to do something," she said. "This is too serious! We've got to get help."

I did try. That very night, offhand, I said to my father I had seen two glass cases in the Herb House.

He didn't even lower his newspaper. "Seems to me the fellow used to run that thing was a geologist on the side. Collected all kinds of rock samples."

Rock samples! In my scorn I almost let him glimpse the cool brain now locked in mortal combat with Hitler's Secret Service. "And just left them in an empty old building for anyone to take?"

"They wouldn't be valuable. It was just a hobby. And the building's locked." Now he let the paper droop. "It *is* locked, isn't it? You've not been messing around inside that place?"

"Oh no!"

"If you're going to start doing things like that, we'll ask the Silver Circle lady to ride you home on Wednesdays."

I hated to hear her called that—Silver Circle lady. But I could see I would get no help from him, not even if I had pulled up a hundred of his golf balls to safety. I blamed him, too. It was *his* encyclopedia! "To give you a bigger world," he'd once said; and who knew that could be dangerous?

For a long time I blamed him. Sometimes I'd slip outdoors and lift handfuls of water out of the fish pond and slop them inside his tin-can golf holes. I got so I couldn't find half the balls when they fell beneath the water lilies. Just as he got ready to stroke the ball, I'd slide my hoe blade over the water and ask, "How deep can a submarine go?"

"Oh, hell," he'd say and Mother, through the kitchen screen, would call, "It's Sunday."

That was the spring my father lost interest in golf. One day every ball headed for the pond as if it were amphibian and he growled toward the kitchen window, "What's the use!" Between his shifts at the mill he went back to blackjack and rummy with the men in the filling station across the street from our house.

Now that he had quit his golf, I could sometimes get permission to go see Betty Sue on Sundays. We talked about the Herb House. I said, "Maybe there really were rock samples at first. And the Nazis took them out and put the diamonds in. And nobody would suspect!"

"Clever!" cried Betty Sue, just the way they did in the funny books.

Our second discovery was worse than the swastika or the diamonds. The Nazis threatened us—right out in the open. The message was in code, of course, but so public that anyone could have figured it out! How brazen they were! How sure of themselves!

The Wednesday we first saw their message, printed neatly in chalk on the black wall of the Herb House, right by the door, Betty Sue and I knew it was directed at us. There were only four capital letters so we suspected code right away. Those four letters stood for something. I pondered them in order.

F? *F* for Fuehrer? Or Fatherland?

And *U.* Could the *U* stand for United States?

Then the entire message hit me. I almost screamed aloud. It was for Betty Sue and me, no one else. It was a personal threat. It was an indication of the terrible slant of the Nazi mind.

"Those letters! Don't you see what they stand for? What it means?"

She did not see it. Long plaited hair is not everything.

I read the four initials in order and translated what they meant. "Fight Until Children Killed. Fight until the children are killed!"

At first she doubted. "There's nothing for 'the.' I don't see that 'are.' "

I was impatient. "They're understood, like those sentences at school. Fight Until Children Killed—that's what the letters stand for! And they mean us, Betty Sue! The children are you and me!"

A minute longer we stood, hoping one of the four letters might fade, making the threat less deadly. But the *F* was for Fight. Then the *U. C* had to be children. . . .

We caught hands and ran from the Herb House for the last time; we walked awhile, ran some more, skulked and redoubled on our tracks. We took turns crying. Doom seemed certain and we could not prepare for it, we two small girls against a whole nation of fanatics. A speeding car—and police would tell our mothers it was an accident. Perhaps the sheriff himself would tell them, never noticing the strange, harsh accent of the driver. ("Ach Himmel," the driver would have whispered under his breath, or "Schweine!" We had not read all those comic books for nothing.)

Or we might be kidnaped. Pushed into a well. Shoved under the wheels of the last steam engine left in that part of the state and mangled half the way to Taylorsville. Drowned in a fish pond. Thrown from an apple limb or a chinaberry tree. Poisoned in the school cafeteria. Perhaps held in the Herb House while we slowly starved, our noses full of the sweet and tang of dried and ancient leaves. Nailed into one of those wooden boxes. Carried screaming down a slimy tunnel to the Fuehrer's fleet.

"Oh," sobbed Betty Sue, "we should have left it all alone!"

For once she was right. Now I saw the whole thing had always been too big for us and, facing my certain death, I hastily forgave my father. He had not *dreamed*. He had not known that a world opened up could be dangerous.

Still I could not tell him about the spies and the threat. Even that boldly chalked warning was no proof; dozens of adults must have seen those four letters scrawled on the Herb House without understanding what they meant. Even while Betty Sue and I panted toward home, adults were passing that wall and glancing up and wondering briefly about that funny word.

By now I was crying as loud as Betty Sue, for I did not want to die! This was not how I had planned to startle the people of Statesville. It was not for this I had struck memorable poses up and down these streets.

By the time we reached the corner where Betty Sue would turn her way and I would turn mine, I had scraped up what little courage was left. "Well," I said, "that's war." I would not look at her. I tried to hold my lips in a cool, straight line, the way they did in the R.A.F.

Betty Sue went on crying so I shook her. I said if she told her mama now, the spies might kill her whole family. They might kill the three sisters and burn all the V-mail! She was shocked into silence.

"We've got to be careful, that's all. It's all we can do now. We have to watch out every minute."

Finally she said, "All right."

So Betty Sue, still sniffing, turned glumly home; but I stood on the corner and watched her, and every few steps she would turn to wave and I waved, and she grew smaller and smaller down the hill till she was little-finger-size and it hurt my eyes to see her.

Then I walked away, too, full of grief and exaltation.

There was so much I understood that day—valor, and patriotism, and the nature of the enemy. Even my fear was specific. The war had come to me and I did not have to go to it. I was one with all the innocent victims of history. The German High Command across the sea had taken an interest in my life and in its termination. Oh, do you see that in the days when the spies were in the Herb House the world was still comprehensible to Betty Sue and me?

THE
MANDARIN

Mrs. Applewhite, outwardly sedate, sat on the garden bench trying to coax her mind into forming strange and shocking thoughts. *Try it,* she said to herself like someone offering medicine to a child. *Just try it.* But her mind, girded round by years of discipline, withstood her.

It sat sanely in her skull as within a walled tower. Not that it mattered. Not that Allie would ever know the difference.

At this depressing thought Mrs. Applewhite sighed and plowed the tip of one finger along the furrow time had worn in her forehead. Allie looked up and asked quickly, "Tired already?"

"Eighty years tired," snapped Mrs. Applewhite to that. She hunched her brows forward, letting her finger measure that bulge and the wisps of hair. She had always hoped this made her look forbidding.

But Allie gave a cheerful laugh. "You're as young as you feel, I always say."

"I know you do," muttered Mrs. Applewhite. She put that finger with the others under her laprobe.

"What's that?"

"I said I know what you always say. I ought to know it. It never changes one day to the next."

All she got was Allie's usual smile. Someday Mrs. Applewhite was going to hold a ruler to that smile. Mondays to Sundays it would be the same width and thickness. Allie held up the skirt she was now hemming on her lap. "Such a lovely blue," said Allie pleasantly.

Mrs. Applewhite made an ugly sound in her nostrils which, she thought happily, was hard to do through a patrician nose.

"It would be nice with your eyes," Allie finished. She returned carefully to her hem, darting the needle in and out, and out and in. God Himself could not have taken more pains when first He seamed the firmament. For a while Mrs. Applewhite watched until she felt as though she were ducking her head and burrowing each time the needle dipped in and under. She turned away firmly, feeling a bit giddy.

For one wild moment she thought, I wish I were Allie.

But she pushed that notion quickly away and said aloud, "I'd rather be dead!"

"What's that?" said Allie. "Than wear this lovely skirt? How you do tease!"

How I do tease, thought Mrs. Applewhite bitterly. I ought to go on television.

And, spreading her surface to give room for more sunlight to fall on her thin skin, she went back to her original intention and wondered what she might now remark that would sound utterly mad. If someone would even commit me to an asylum it would break the monotony, she thought. The lunatics can't be as dull as Allie.

So with careful diction Mrs. Applewhite said, "Did I ever tell you I once saw Jesus Christ walking in this very garden?"

"Never did," said Allie calmly. She spread the hem with her palm to see if it had puckered.

Mrs. Applewhite leaned forward confidentially. She cleared her throat to make Allie lift her head and frown. "Plain as I see you now. He was tearing the hearts out of all the fine roses!" she ended, magnificent.

"Tch, tch," said Allie. She frowned but did not lift her head.

She directed her needle into the cloth and took it out again.

"He was very tall," Mrs. Applewhite persisted, shifting in the lawn chair. "I didn't know He would be so tall."

Allie poked at the blue material spread on her lap like a tiny sea. "This thread's a little dark," she worried, smoothing it again with her hand.

In a loud voice Mrs. Applewhite said, "He didn't look a bit Jewish."

"I should have bought the lighter blue."

At this Mrs. Applewhite raised both her own fine hands in the air like two pale flags of surrender. There was no way to bother Allie Martin. Six months now she had been trying everything: snobbishness, ill temper, stupidity. She had been ill; she had been slovenly; and today she had been insane. But there was no touching Allie. She was a piece of furniture. Where do they get the Allies of this world? thought Mrs. Applewhite. How in the world do they ever find them? Maybe the government breeds them especially for jobs like this. Mrs. Applewhite had a great contempt for the government.

"Allie," she began seriously, "tell me about your mother."

Allie looked surprised. (Wouldn't you know a question so simple could make her look surprised? If Jesus tore out every rose in town, Allie would sleep through the whole affair.)

Allie said, "She was a fine woman. Fatter than me. She worked all her life. Lived to be seventy-two."

This seemed to tie up Allie's dead mother in the right paper and string and store her away like a package. The poor old soul, thought Mrs. Applewhite.

While she watched, Allie bit the thread between her front teeth, delicately, and lifted it with thumb and forefinger off the tip of her tongue. She began to form the knot which would hold the hem invisibly in place for generations.

That was more than Mrs. Applewhite could take. Irritably she said—since Allie was only a paid companion and could be treated irritably—"Go away now, Allie. I'm going to walk."

And Allie, whose politeness and obedience were among her worst traits, rose immediately and walked away at a comfortable pace between the clipped bushes and the two terrible old fountains which had come all the way from France.

When Allie was out of sight, Mrs. Applewhite cleared her throat and pretended to be a miner with silicosis and spat hackingly into the tulips.

Allie, well-trained, reappeared. "You all right, Mrs. Applewhite?"

"Of course I'm all right! And I'm surely rich enough to be able to spit in peace on my own flowers!" She turned her back and walked down the sandy path herself, very straight, very small, very old.

Mrs. Applewhite hated the gray stone house where she lived, and she believed if for one rebellious year she failed to pay its mammoth tax bill half the American government would collapse. Washington would return to sending mail by clipper ship and the President would turn army camps into orphan homes if Mrs. Applewhite once failed to attach her spidery name to that outlandish check. In her latest of many wills, Mrs. Applewhite—childless—had left the stone house to an orphanage. Maybe a flock of children in those dark halls would improve the architecture.

But she loved the gardens surrounding the house. She loved the very rigidity with which plants were permitted to exist here—the hedge so exactly square, the flowers hemmed into narrow, rocked-up beds, the precisely round bush which grew neatly behind a stone bench like a large green sausage.

She liked to watch the gardener go up and down the labyrinth of paths, pouncing on weeds as on trespassers, spraying for bugs, pruning a limb to the proper size above the very bud which next year would inherit his command and leaf out in the proper direction.

Watching the gardener work, or walking alone as now, Mrs. Applewhite would say aloud (she liked to discuss things aloud with herself), "I have coped." By this she meant she had taken a great untidiness of being and imposed on Nature a certain form, steadily, day by day, the way one must constantly shear and train formal gardens.

When I am dead and the orphans come, Mrs. Applewhite would think, this garden will go to rack and ruin. The contemplation of that pleased her. She had made this particular order; it would end when she ended. The beautiful evergreens would hang full of broken kites.

Flowers would escape through chinks in their careful borders and vines would run rampant to engulf the unyielding benches and the fountains. All the shrubs would put out wild, rebellious limbs in every forbidden direction. And the insects would come in droves as though they had heard Mrs. Applewhite had died, and the beetles would lunch on the leaves and birds would leave droppings all up and down the wall with no one paid to hose them off. I will forget all about the garden, she thought, and by next spring the garden will forget about me.

Walking now in the well-ordered place, thinking these things, Mrs. Applewhite laughed aloud because she had this secret pact with Destruction.

Mrs. Applewhite was eighty years old. She was not frail. Each time she visited the safety deposit box, her hovering attorney would try to support her thin arm; she always jabbed him with the point of her elbow as if it were some umbrella stick. She kept a paid companion half for superstition—no one had midnight heart attacks unless he tempted fate by living unattended. Often Mrs. Applewhite wished she could slide into her death like Sleeping Beauty, prick a finger, blink, collapse quickly. Lacking spindles, Mrs. Applewhite thought a rose thorn might serve.

"Just my luck it'll be a long sickness and I'll have Allie and oxygen tents to contend with," said Mrs. Applewhite aloud. She pricked one thumb on the nearest briar but nothing happened. It didn't even bleed.

Mrs. Applewhite was the end of her family line. In her the

Farnsworths (railroads) and the Applewhites (pharmaceutical houses) met like two mighty rivers joining, and through her they were ebbing quietly out to sea. She had not yet decided what to do with the rest of the money there would not be time enough to spend. The orphanage was definite. Beyond that she sometimes left large sums to charity or endowed colleges; in the next will she would pick new charities and new colleges. Once she had impulsively bequeathed everything equally to the first sixty names in the New York telephone directory.

At such times she excused herself by telling her lawyer everyone needed some hobby. Wincing from some recent thud of her elbow, he would roll his eyes. It pleased Mrs. Applewhite to think that whenever a cool young secretary sent in her name the man must go pale and long to be in Bermuda.

For all her money, for all the dead illustrious family which had been lieutenant governors and symphony sponsors, and for all the ordered and lovely gardens, Mrs. Applewhite was lonely in her grim old house. She no longer glanced at the rare vases set into hall cubicles. Years ago she had stopped noticing the paintings or the chairs which had once graced European castles. The only improvement Mrs. Applewhite had ever made in that house was to donate a suit of armor for scrap iron during World War II.

She had no one to talk to except servants who had been trained against real talking, or Allie—as if she were anybody. The gardener could only say, "Yes, ma'am," and "No, ma'am," and "Paris green." The servants had come with the house like the French fountains. Most of them were as invisible to her eyes as the other antiques.

So Mrs. Applewhite spent lonely days walking up and down the paths of her garden, took some amusement from acting deliberately strange in front of Allie. She had always longed to be known as that "eccentric Mrs. Applewhite." She knew it was all wasted on Allie; but perhaps she had succeeded with the family attorney. One could hope for that much.

She also pursued one private hobby, the one discovered by accident that time she chose telephone subscribers as heirs to her fortune. Since then, Mrs. Applewhite had been playing games with strangers she never expected to see. Her favorite was conducted through the city library, and she had been playing it for seven years.

Dismissing Allie, Mrs. Applewhite would change to a shabby dress she had frayed against her own window sill, and make the chauffeur park a block away from the library. There she would check out some unlikely volume—*Tales of the Crypt,* or *A Taste of Love,* or *Murder Stalks the Gamewarden.*

Before she returned that book, Mrs. Applewhite would slip a $20 bill between its pages. She measured each book and put the currency exactly three-fourths into the volume, because she was not interested in people who failed to read on to the very end.

In the seven years Mrs. Applewhite had played this game, only twice had the next patron returned book and money to the library. The librarian called Mrs. Applewhite, who had admitted the cash was hers. "I'm forgetful and eccentric!" she barked into the telephone. "Just add it to your book fund." Twice this had happened. You couldn't get much reputation for eccentricity over forty dollars.

One reader who sent back the cash was a beautician named Stella Jones (*A Taste of Love*) and the second time a barber who read nothing but science fiction. It gave Mrs. Applewhite the feeling there might be something virtuous in hair.

Now when she visited the library, Mrs. Applewhite each time would read (aloud) from the library cards the names of all the other people who must have kept her money. She shook her gray head at their dishonesty. The government, she was not surprised to see demonstrated, was ruining the nation's character.

It's the Chinese mandarin all over again, she would think. That very old dilemma. *If by pushing a button you could kill some unknown aged mandarin in China and his death would be no loss to anyone and would make you rich beyond your wildest dreams; and no one—including the mandarin himself—would ever know you did it, would you push the button?*

These people, Mrs. Applewhite would think, pronouncing the names on the library card in an accusing tone, would push the button. If it were left to them, the mandarin would die.

She would feel gleeful. *I am realistic about people. My money hasn't really protected me from anything! I live in a big stone house, but it was never an ivory tower!*

Grinning, Mrs. Applewhite would nod at the polite librarian as she left. For all she knew, that old biddy at the desk kept some of the money for herself. For all she knew, that forty dollars never even *saw* the book fund.

But on the library steps in the sunlight Mrs. Applewhite would feel suddenly depressed. She dismissed this as the familiar reaction of any champion; it's boring to win all the games. It's boring.

Underneath her breath she would suggest that she might be getting old. And if anyone, passing by, should smile at her standing on the library steps in her poor dress talking to herself, Mrs. Applewhite would glare at them fiercely, like an old hawk.

Now, walking alone in her garden, Mrs. Applewhite raised both shoulders and pulled her brows down and darted toward the boxwoods as though she might surprise them full of beetles. Then all the starch went right out of her and she sat abruptly in the center of the sandy path. The surface was white as sugar and had been hauled to her estate in dump trucks for three hundred miles. She thought, sitting stiff-backed and aching, on the bleached sand, *I hate this place.*

And after that she thought: *I really am old. And bored. I'm very bored.*

One red ant crossing the path climbed over the black mountain of her shoe. "Make yourself at home," she cooed. The ant had paused and sent a level look along the length of her shoestring. One tiny feeler examined its texture.

"Next year you can have it all," announced Mrs. Applewhite.

She waved one of her blue-veined hands at all the flowers and the fountains and the tall stone wall. "The whole blooming mess," she said. The ant crossed the black river of her shoelace and slid to sand again and crawled away. Ungrateful thing. Mrs. Applewhite wrapped both hands around her thin ankle, lifted her foot like a giant club and set it down hard upon the ant.

"That's what the orphans will do," she said.

She heard the sound of Allie coming steadily in search of her and she sat very still and waited to be complained about. She kept her fingers clutched at the top of her shoe.

When Allie caught sight of her sitting there in the middle of the path, she gave one scream of just the proper tone and volume. "What are you doing there!" cried Allie after the tiny scream.

Mrs. Applewhite said grimly she had broken a leg.

Allie's tongue came and went against her teeth (steady, steady, like a metronome) and she lifted Mrs. Applewhite to her feet, brushing sand from her dress with an efficient one-two swoop. "What in the world were you thinking!" she scolded.

"Ants," said Mrs. Applewhite. "Ants and desolation."

But Allie did not really hear. Allie heard only the words which came in on the frequency for which she was set, and Mrs. Applewhite knew what was on that frequency. It was the I'm-Fine-How-Are-You channel, the Let-Sleeping-Dogs-Lie and Stitch-in-Time station. When anything fell outside the wave length of such ordinary falsities, Allie was turned off. Allie did not receive.

"They built you without an antenna," Mrs. Applewhite said now, seeing it clearly at last. "That's what it is."

"What you need," Allie said brightly, "is some good hot soup."

A dish of warm lava, she thought. A cup of molten steel.

But she followed along the path to the huge house without objection, her ears closed firmly against Allie's chirps. She turned off her own frequency, but somewhere inside her head she could still hear all the things Allie must be saying. By now they were tape-recorded on reels which rolled forever.

"You'll feel better after a good sleep," Allie was probably telling her. "Things always look better in the morning. Every cloud has a silver lining. Tomorrow is a new day."

It might not be, thought Mrs. Applewhite stubbornly. Maybe God would decide to be eccentric. Maybe He would send in an old one, just for the hell of it.

In the morning things did not look better, and although it was *another* day nothing seemed either new or old about it.

Mrs. Applewhite believed she had been too busy to feel tired until this very moment, the way a man can work so late night after night he forgets even to yawn until one morning he falls asleep standing waiting for a bus. At least people used to work like that, she thought. The government might have ruined it.

Though Mrs. Applewhite had been lonely and bored before, she seemed now for the first time to grasp the size and proportions of both. They were vast. She was inside her loneliness and it was bigger than the stone house. Even her breathing made echoes.

When she woke that next morning she looked at the brown landscape which had hung in its gilt frame on her wall for forty years. It was a country river without a bridge. For the first time in all those years she saw the omission of a bridge. She clambered out of bed and turned the thing to the wall.

She thought her ears were humming until she spotted rain running noisily down her window glass, making a wavy world. Grunting, she placed her hand flat against the pane, letting the storm pass just beyond her palm. Most rainy days she thought of her garden and hoped the fertilizer had been spread in time to wash down to the roots. Today she thought: Sad.

Just then Allie bustled in and said it was fine weather for ducks, Mrs. Applewhite, and breakfast was ready; and why didn't they read aloud afterward since it was such a stormy day?

"Don't want to read," she snapped. She did not like the petulance she heard in her own voice. For me, even sadness is trivial. That was the morning's worst discovery. Dear God, she thought suddenly, if *I* could have had Job's boils to suffer, I would have been a noble creature.

"I really would," she swore to Allie.

"Fine, we'll read whatever you like," the woman agreed.

Following breakfast, over more coffee served in the downstairs library, Allie read from Matthew Arnold, then William Blake. After a while the postman pulled the bell and left two circulars and a bill.

This visit made Mrs. Applewhite feel oddly desperate; she found herself standing in the drafty hall asking in a high, strange voice, "Allie, call that man in from the rain! We'll give him a cup of this coffee!"

"You know he can't stop," said Allie soothingly. "He has mail to deliver." She told him thank-you and closed the carved walnut door. "Here's something from National Casualty Insurance."

"I'm already a National Casualty."

Summoning that much irritation left her quite tired. She scuttled back to her chair and put her feet on a stool, and clutched at the fragile cup to warm her fingers.

Again Allie began on the book, running through lines of poetry like a water tap. "Weary of myself and sick of asking what I am and what I ought to be . . ." until Mrs. Applewhite was so exasperated at the sameness she thought she might scream. If I had more energy today, I would. I'd scream something eccentric. I'd make her slam shut the book.

Suddenly the thought burst in her like a silent scream: Here I sit, another rich old mandarin anyone might kill by pressing some button half a world away.

She dropped her coffee cup and the flowered china split on the parquet floor. Allie began to gather up the pieces.

"I'm getting a headache."

"You drink too much coffee. I think I've found all of it. How about an aspirin?"

"I believe I'll just lie down," said Mrs. Applewhite. A chill passed over her. "I'll lie down with a blanket, that's what I'll do."

Allie helped her climb the curving stairs and left her in the bedroom. Mrs. Applewhite frowned at the back of the picture frame she had turned to her wall. Clarence had bought that picture, she recalled. Some present. Knowing she liked gardens, he had thought the scene of hills and river suitable. Clarence Applewhite. He had been dead two dozen years; she hardly thought of him at all. He had been nice, plump, smiling, a good husband, dutiful, financially skilled. He had never forgotten birthdays, or complained that they had no children. Once they had gone on a boat to Europe and waited all the way over and back for seasickness which never came. She could hardly remember the crossing. I stood at the medicine cabinet most of the way, making certain we had brought everything we'd need.

I did not know Clarence very well, she thought.

Then (and a little grunt escaped her at the effort of remembering) she fixed her mind on their wedding day. It was when? She had looked . . . how? What swam into view at last was confusion and many attendants and a marquee to the touring car. . . . Clarence . . . she could barely see him in that picture. Pink but calm. Full of Farnsworth punch and champagne. And after that?

Mrs. Applewhite shook her head. It was too hard to remember fulfilled desire when desire itself had gone. Had she really desired? It did not seem important to remember. And Clarence, had he been—well—satisfied? She did not know. She knew the year they put in the row of Lombardy poplars. She remembered the greenhouse and the first cyclamen and Cymbidium orchid.

In a fit of sudden anger she jerked the landscape all the way off her wall, dragging the hook half out of the plaster, and stood it in a corner.

She tatted awhile, making thin lace for the edges of nothing. Finally she went over and dropped a great wad of it behind her washstand.

There is no need, she thought grimly, pretending I am any *use* in the world. Even Allie has her uses. Mrs. Applewhite touched the mirror to make certain her image was really there.

Allie brought tea and an aspirin (Mrs. Applewhite despised tea) and advice about a long nap. Mrs. Applewhite accepted all three. She did not feel up to arguing.

When Allie had smoothed the linen pillowcase for the fifth time and drawn the window hangings, Mrs. Applewhite relaxed and closed her eyes. She could hear Allie refilling the silver pitcher by the bed. After the door closed at last, Mrs. Applewhite got out of bed immediately and padded barefoot to the window and opened the curtains. It was like looking into a waterfall.

When the sky cracked brightly with lightning Mrs. Applewhite saw the storm had cleaned every twig from the rock wall. The lonely old fountains lit up briefly in her garden, adding their own supply of water to the overflow. Near them she could see all the wet benches without anyone sitting on them.

She put her face against damp glass and said aloud, "There is nobody that I love."

Rainwater seemed somehow to be getting in her eyes. Mrs. Applewhite stumbled across the room and flung herself in bed as if she were a bag of clothes. She pulled the sheet across her face. "I've got to stop talking to myself," she said, muffled against the fabric.

The roar of the rain began to fade. She felt herself dozing. Once she roused to be angry at sleeping through such a day of discoveries. To be old was an indignity. In the face of the terrible thing she had told the window glass, she should have lain wide-eyed a hundred nights.

"If I had a hundred nights," she whispered.

Her anger was too slippery to hold; she lost it somewhere in the warming folds of the bed. Lightly she slid away from it and into a dream:

She was a child left in a world where no one else was. She ran up and down long corridors which never turned and never ended.

In the dream she said (aloud) in a frightened prayer rhythm, IF I CAN ONLY GET OUTSIDE THIS TIME, I WILL NEVER DO IT AGAIN.

Suddenly she was outside. She ran through a field of daisies taller than her head with butterflies like eagles and three sparrows which passed overhead like a roaring echelon of planes. She pushed her way through tangled flowers, absurdly happy. She laughed aloud and her own voice was more beautiful than bells.

Skipping and laughing she breathed deeply until her whole frame hurt from consuming the world. She was filled up with it— the smell of flowers, the unbelievable blue sky and giant birds which cut through it like a formation of bombers.

She said to herself in a musical voice, There is nothing better than this in all the world, not even to be a seashell.

Too quickly Mrs. Applewhite woke from her dream. Like Alice falling down the rabbit hole she tumbled breathless out of the daisies and into her canopied bed. She lay there regaining the feel of herself—that face loosely wrapped now on her bones, one arm aching in the damp air, the little lost breasts that hung on her without purpose.

She did not believe the dream, or that she had ever been a child called by the name of Ruth. All she could believe was rain, her wrinkles, and that a ball of lace was getting dusty on her floor.

She would not believe any dream, or any longing, which turned out to be so ordinary. She turned her face into the pillow and said—but not aloud this time—I wish I were young! I wish it were all new!

Nothing happened, of course. She could not claim any single day out of time which, on second chance, she would have passed differently than she had already passed it. She would not even say her life had disappointed her, or consider if she had disappointed it.

She struggled halfway out of bed, this time calling in a furious voice, *"There's not enough of it!"* But she slapped her own hand over her own mouth. If Allie should hear, she would soon arrive with more blankets, more tea, more aspirin, more water, more Matthew Arnold. Mrs. Applewhite cocked her head but she heard no approaching footsteps.

There was nothing but silence all across her room. The wall-paper and the carved frames and the polished Martha Washington mirror were undisturbed. A brown landscape stood crazily in the corner where she had dropped it. The lace behind her washstand gathered dust and did not stir. And outside her tall old windows the flowers in her garden grew their lives away, carefully, and with precision.

CLARISSA
AND
THE DEPTHS

Clarissa had a really frightening feeling that things were always dropping off into holes, automobiles and people and things.

It was hard to say now when she had first thought of that, when she was a child probably, living in the house with her daddy and uncle and granddaddy, listening to their endless arguments, having her hair braided tightly every night so she would look like a white girl. It was during those years that Clarissa first got the notion that out-of-sight things had somehow slipped over the edge into an unforeseen abyss. Now that she had become a woman and had gone to cook and clean for Miz Sullivan, she realized it was all nonsense, of course. It had to be all nonsense or other people would have mentioned it too.

The whole idea had begun when she was still a bony little girl (with eyes like coffee cups, The Terrapin said) living in that old white house that had been in her family for sixty-two years, ever since her granddaddy built it and tenanted for Mr. Morrison. Mr. Morrison was dead now and Granddaddy had gradually paid for the house himself; he told everybody he had owned it for sixty-two years, although it was only twelve, really.

The house sat just back from the highway and over the years it had begun to lean forward as though trying to get across to the other side. On Sundays everyone would sit in dark green rockers on the slanted front porch, and watch the cars go by in front of them. Sometimes they would say to one another with pleasure, "Lots of traffic today," as though they had done something them- selves, and sometimes when only a few cars passed, they watched them gloomily, as if so small a number were vaguely insulting.

When a man drove by in a brand-new automobile, everyone would sit up straight and watch him all the way out of sight. By squinting the eyes against the sun some of them could even read the license plate as the shiny car went up and by and over the hill.

"Well, looky there!" they would cry in sharp pleasure.

"Black, wasn't it?"

"Navy blue, I think."

"Naw. It was black."

"It had a Georgia plate."

"That's five I've seen today. Coming from Georgia."

And sometimes a car would pass with the wheels screaming around the far turn and be gone before you could blink your eyes one time or get any look at all at what state it was from. This seemed to please them, too.

"Well, did you see that!" They would ease back in the chairs placidly and rock a few times, looking at one another out of satisfied faces. "I say, did you see that!" The porch would creak under the rockers like an echo.

"He'll never get there like that."

"Like a bat. Drives just like a bat."

"How fast you reckon that was?"

"Oh, sixty mile, easy. It was sixty mile easy enough."

"Shoot!" Granddaddy would spit out into the rosebush. The rosebush had been planted by the front steps years ago when Grandma was alive, but now it was a bedraggled sight, splotched all over from his tobacco juice. Grandma ought to have knowed better than to set it in his spitting place.

"Shoot!" yelled Granddaddy now, spitting angrily at the rosebush, which always quivered a little. "Shoot, that man was going seventy if he was going a mile!"

"What do you know about it?" This would be from Harmon, who was Clarissa's daddy. "How much you ever rode in a car, Old Man?"

"Don't be uppity!" Granddaddy would order in a roar, his sunken little eyes gleaming. "Just don't you get uppity with me!" And Uncle Terrance, who had all his life been called The Terrapin, would break in nervously, because he could not stand to hear people shouting at one another. "Well, it don't matter *how* fast it was. It's gone now, over the hill."

That was where Clarissa first got her idea. All cars came around the far bend and passed briefly in the level place right in front of the house and drove on and up a hill, and then seemed fairly to fall over it, out of sight. The top of the hill was too far for her to walk all by herself, so Clarissa began to think maybe there was a great big hole over there, where thousands and millions of wrecked cars were lying, all in a crumpled heap.

Everyone was very careful about letting Clarissa walk anywhere (even to the top of that hill) by herself, because her mama was dead and the rest of them had to look after her. Looking after her seemed to be a great burden on her daddy, who would sit around and pop his big brown knuckles and look at her worriedly.

"You got to be careful about things, Clarissa," he would say finally, as though this were very difficult to say and had called up all his courage. "You watch out for men, now, white *and* colored."

So on Sundays Clarissa sat on the leaning front porch and "watched out" for them as they rode by in the gleaming automobiles. On Sunday, too, the woman cousins came over and sat with Granddaddy and Harmon and The Terrapin in the green rockers and watched the traffic. Every now and then one of them seemed to notice Clarissa as if for the first time, and then she would rare back in her rocker with pinkish palms uplifted, clattering her tongue against the roof of her mouth.

"Poor child!" the woman cousin would cry, raising and lowering her palms and making the noise in her mouth. "All alone but for menfolks."

"We do all right," Clarissa's daddy would say shortly.

"Don't you be uppity about things that don't concern you, Winnie-Faye," Granddaddy would snap irritably to the woman cousin. Then Winnie-Faye might lean forward and take Clarissa's shoulder blade between two fingers and pinch it lightly.

"Looky there, how thin she is!"

"It's in the family," Harmon would growl. "I'm thin, ain't I? Her mama was thin!"

"Oh," the woman cousin would groan, "but not *that* thin! Nossir, not *that* thin!"

"You hesh your mouth," Granddaddy would scream, getting into one of his quick rages and clambering up onto the bony little legs that made him look like an old grasshopper. He would turn and spit out into the rosebush, sometimes twice, to give them all an idea of how mad he was.

"Listen, honey." The woman cousin would lean forward so that Clarissa could see her gold filling, which was supposed to be very handsome. "Listen, honey, I knowed your mama real well. She was a fine upstanding woman. Don't you be a disgrace to her."

"No'm," Clarissa would say quickly, drawing back and trying not to stare at the gold filling. "No'm, I wouldn't do that."

"Let her be," Harmon would say. He would be stiff all over by now and Clarissa could hear him popping his knuckles until it sounded like sticks breaking.

"Hey," The Terrapin would put in quickly, "ain't that a Buick? Ain't that a new Buick?"

And all of them would turn back quickly to the highway, forgetting about Clarissa and how thin she was, and even Granddaddy would sink back into his chair again and squint out at the road. "Red, ain't it?" he would wheeze.

"Naw. They calls that maroon."

"Red's red," he would grumble, hating to be corrected, yanking with yellow fingernails at a stubble on his chin.

They had been living there, Clarissa and the three menfolks, ever since her mama died, which was on Easter in 1942. Everybody talked about that when they came to visit on Sundays, about how it had been on Easter morning when Bertha passed on to her reward. That was something special. It wasn't everybody could die on Easter.

"She always were a religious woman," the woman cousins would say, almost every Sunday they talked about it. "It was right fitting, it being Easter and all."

That made Clarissa's daddy mad. "Well, I don't think it was fitting!" he'd come back at them. "I don't think dying's ever fitting, no matter what day it was!"

The woman cousins would roll back in the green rockers and look at one another with sad, wet eyes. "You never was a religious man," one of them would accuse him. "I allus said so."

"That's a fact. You never even went to meeting except when Bertha made you."

"That don't concern you," Harmon would tell them angrily.

And Granddaddy, who could not bear to stay out of any argument, especially when it concerned his family, would reach over for the fly mop and bang the handle up and down on the floor. "Snooping females!" he would screech bitterly. "If we could rid the worl' of snooping females!"

But everyone ignored his outburst. The woman cousins were never offended. "You bring this girl up right, hear?" they would say to Harmon, even though Clarissa's mama had been dead now since 1942 and they had never helped out with anything yet. "You give her a good Christian raising. You two ever go to meeting?"

"Never," Clarissa's daddy would say firmly.

At this the woman cousins would clatter their tongues behind their teeth and lift their palms.

"Uppity!" Granddaddy would be yelling all this time, banging and banging the fly mop down against the floor. "Uppity, snooping females!"

Granddaddy loved to scream; he said that it cleared his head and that people that never made a racket were prone to snuffly noses.

During all this, The Terrapin would get up and walk around the side of the house and lean up against the chimney until things got quiet on the porch. Sometimes Clarissa would follow to where he stood with his arms folded, looking at grass, trying not to hear Granddaddy screaming and banging the fly mop.

"We ain't got time for that stuff," The Terrapin would say sadly, waving his hand in the general direction from which he had come. "Ain't none of us got time. Going to be dead tomorrow anyhow, and got to hurry."

Clarissa, embarrassed, would go back to the porch after a while because she didn't like to hear The Terrapin talk either. He made her backbone wiggly, always telling her there was dignity in race. She didn't know where he'd learned to say a thing like that, much less what it meant; but he'd say firmly there was dignity in race and she must be a credit to her people. So, because The Terrapin was strange, Clarissa would leave him propped up against the chimney, looking sadly in the weeds; and she would go back and sit on the edge of the porch. Everything would have quieted by then.

"That ain't no Ford. That's an old Hudson," Harmon would say happily. "That's a 1938 Hudson."

Clarissa didn't go to school much when she was a little girl. There was lots to do around the house with nobody but menfolks so that she was usually at home canning or picking cotton or boiling out clothes in the yard. She made soap twice a year out of all the fat she had saved up, and the pale brown cakes were stored down in the cellar until they were needed.

Then sometimes she would stay home from school just because she wanted to make the house beautiful. She would go out along the ditches up and down both sides of the highway and pick the Queen Anne's lace and blow the little black bugs away, and carry a handful into the dark kitchen. Here she would dip the white blooms into food coloring until she had a bright bouquet to put in a water glass in the middle of the table.

Only The Terrapin noticed. He would touch the flowers with the end of his finger and tell the others to "see how Clarissa is prettying up the place."

"Uh," her daddy would grunt, giving the flowers a glance.

"It's bad to get too fancy," Granddaddy would wheeze, bending his old face down to peer into the cooking pots on the stove. "You'll get depending on it."

"No, no," The Terrapin would protest in his soft voice. "It's a sign, that's what it is. A sign Clarissa wants something better."

Granddaddy would lift his face from the pots and flash his son a look of dark suspicion. "Better than what?" he would rasp, all on the defensive.

Clarissa just liked the looks of the flowers. The Terrapin didn't need to be making things out of it. "Let's hush and eat," she would say, just like women have always said to men who won't sit down to table.

When Clarissa was eleven, she quit school altogether. She told them one day at breakfast.

"I don't b'lieve I'll go to school any more," she said.

"Well, whatever you say. Whatever you want to do," her daddy said, glancing up. "You can go if you want to, now."

"No, I don't think I want to any more."

Only The Terrapin was disturbed. "I wouldn't do that," he said in a voice that showed his distress. "I'd keep on at it, Clarissa. I wish I'd gone on to school."

"That's no cause for *her* staying," Harmon interrupted, "just because you didn't."

"I know that. But there's where the future is, with book learning. If niggers ever get to be anything better than just niggers, it'll be because they had book learning."

Granddaddy, who had buried his mouth deep in the grayish coffee, now blew into it like a child so that it burbled up about his face. He put the cup down. "Uppity talk," he said dryly. "What matters is how strong a back you got and how big a hands."

"No sir," said The Terrapin, respectfully but firmly. "No sir, that don't matter too much any more. It's what you know."

Granddaddy snorted. "And what you know, uppity nigger? Go on, tell us that."

The Terrapin looked sad. "Me, I just knows what I don't know," he said.

Harmon laughed and banged the table. "Ain't that a crazy thing to say?"

"A crazy thing!" Granddaddy yelled, whooping and wheezing with laughter.

The Terrapin hung his head and turned his spoon in his coffee, around and around. "I reckon it is," he said sheepishly. "I reckon it is at that."

"Listen," said Clarissa's daddy in a halfway angry voice. "I told her she could go if she wanted to." He glared at The Terrapin. "You heard me say that, didn't you?" The Terrapin only nodded.

Granddaddy cackled. "*I* heard you. I sure did."

"Well, I won't have you saying it's on account of me she quit. Or that I wouldn't let her go on."

"All right," said The Terrapin mildly.

"All right, then," said her daddy. He looked pleased with himself for having gotten the whole thing settled. "It's up to Clarissa."

"Of course," said The Terrapin, watching her rather hopefully. "It's what Clarissa wants to do that counts."

"Well, I don't b'lieve I'll go," said Clarissa. She did not look at The Terrapin.

"Well, then!" Harmon was very gay.

"Whatever you want, Clarissa," said The Terrapin sadly, watching the surface of his coffee as though he expected something to rise from it.

Granddaddy looked up at Harmon with a sly little grin. "Your brother," he said scornfully, "he's feebleminded. Nothing in the worl' suit him."

Clarissa felt ashamed. "Oh, let him be," she said.

So Clarissa did not go back to school, and when the truant people came to see about it everybody swore she was fourteen already. The man got real mad because he said they had on all the school records that she was just eleven, and how had she got to be fourteen all of a sudden?

"She's fourteen and I can't help your records," said Harmon firmly. "She's done turned fourteen and we got it in the family Bible."

Clarissa knew this was a lie because the only Bible they had ever owned had been buried with her mama in 1942. The women cousins were always talking about that, how Bertha was probably leafing the pages in Heaven, reading again the things she'd marked. They had a feeling the Lord would directly resurrect a thing like the Scriptures, and think what a comfort it would be, they said. Your own familiar Bible!

But the truant officer was suspicious about the whole thing and Clarissa was afraid he might ask to see the Bible.

"Little girl, you come over here," he said. He was a big white man with a reddish beard that he never shaved very close, and he always smelled of machine oil. He drove a Forty Ford and wouldn't let anybody else touch it, because he said the Forty model was the best car Ford ever made. Granddaddy and Harmon were always talking about how they wished they had that car, because it was took good care of, they said.

Clarissa stood in front of him so that she could smell the oil and see the face hairs that weren't shaved down far enough. He looked at her suspiciously.

"You getting fat in the chest?"

Harmon was indignant. "Sure she is!" he said, coming to stand behind her and touch her shoulders. "I done told you she's turned fourteen."

"Oh, all right then," shrugged the truant officer. "You can't do nothing with niggers when they get that age. I know what they want then." He got a notebook out of his pocket and wrote down that Clarissa Johnson was fourteen and was quitting school of her own accord.

"I think you got to sign something swearing it," he said, putting the book away. "They'll send it around."

"That's all right with me," said Harmon proudly. "I can write. Me and my brother can both write."

Behind them Granddaddy cackled. "I can't," he called out delightedly. "I can't write a line."

That night at supper, as though the truant officer had reminded him of something, Clarissa's daddy asked The Terrapin questions about her, even when she was in the same room. It was as if it didn't matter whether she heard or not, as if hearing wouldn't tell her much.

"What will I do with Clarissa?" he said, turning rather desperately to The Terrapin. "What will I do now?"

The Terrapin looked both puzzled and embarrassed, glancing at Clarissa with his eye corners where she was serving the food at the end of the table. He cleared his throat. "You mean since she's out of school? That what you mean, Harmon?"

Harmon sighed and, picking up his plate, turned it all the way around and put it down again. It was a gesture he had kept from boyhood; it kept him from losing his temper, he said, to bring something full circle. "Did you hear that?" he asked the plate and the table, looking down at them both. "Did you hear what The Terrapin just said?"

"I heard it," said Granddaddy, looking up from his food. "It's just like him. He's got no sense."

Clarissa, spooning out the food onto the other three plates, tried to look as though she were not listening although of course she was. But it was like she had thought; you listened and heard all the words but it didn't help much.

"That's certainly not what I mean," said Harmon finally, turning to The Terrapin.

Granddaddy interrupted before The Terrapin could say anything. "He means since she's nearly come a female. Anybody would know that's what he means."

"Oh," said The Terrapin in real surprise. He ducked his head a little, humbly. "I don't know," he said. "I don't know what you ought to do about that." He shot his eyes toward Clarissa and then away, quickly.

"Her mama ought to be alive," grumbled Harmon, as though this were an inconvenience Bertha might have thought about.

"There's Winnie-Faye," said The Terrapin. "Winnie-Faye loves to talk about anything. Winnie-Faye might talk to her."

"Yes," said Harmon, sighing. "I suppose it'll have to be Winnie-Faye." He looked up at Clarissa and frowned. "Next week some-time, we'd better."

So, on the following Saturday afternoon, Clarissa went to Winnie-Faye's house in town, where she had lemonade out of a peanut-butter glass and sat stiffly on a store-bought sofa while Winnie-Faye did the talking. Winnie-Faye first read to her out of the Bible, about Mary and the Holy Ghost and conceiving. Winnie-Faye was very religious. She always said you oughtn't to come at anything serious till you looked up the Scriptures.

When Winnie-Faye finally finished reading and put the Bible down she began to shake her head back and forth so that the gold filling flashed when her mouth went by. "Only that's not the way it is," she began matter-of-factly. "Conceiving. Not for ordinary women. Conceived in sin and in sin my mother bore me." She went on shaking her head about it, winking the gold tooth like a now-seen, now-hidden lantern.

And after that she told Clarissa how it was for ordinary women and how she would be sick every month because of Adam and Eve. Clarissa really didn't understand that part of it, except maybe it had something to do with Eve and a serpent and that was the reason women were sick every month. Clarissa thought maybe it was like having a tapeworm.

Winnie-Faye also told her what made women have babies; and then she gave a long sigh of relief. "So much for Bertha's sake," she said, sighing. "I hope I did it as good as she would."

"Thank you very much," said Clarissa politely.

Winnie-Faye gave her a cookie with the second glass of lemonade and after a while her daddy came and drove her home in a car he had borrowed from another cousin. He looked worried, but he wouldn't look anywhere except out the front glass. "You got everything straight now?" he said, staring at the highway as though it were something strange.

"I don't know," said Clarissa.

"What is it you're not sure about?" asked Harmon gruffly. He gave the highway a downright murderous stare.

"When will it happen to me?" she said.

"Oh," said her daddy nervously. "Part of it will happen soon because you're getting fat in the chest. The rest of it . . ." He cleared his throat, sounding a little like The Terrapin. "The rest of it won't happen for a long time. Not until you're married, maybe." He added, giving her a fierce glare, "If you do right."

Clarissa was both glad and disappointed. "Then what's she telling me now for?"

"Just so it won't happen," snapped her daddy. He seemed angry. "So you'll know to be careful and do right like I said. You watch yourself."

That was what they were always saying. Clarissa was confused. "All right," she said vaguely. "I'll watch myself."

"And listen here," her daddy went on angrily. "Don't you take no money from anybody to do nothing. Not even a white man. White men are as bad as the rest. And there ain't nothing you can do if it's a white man."

"I'll watch. I'll be careful," said Clarissa again.

"All right, then," said her daddy furiously. They drove on home in silence and The Terrapin met them in the yard.

"Is it done then?" said The Terrapin quickly. "Is it all been said?"

"I hope so," Harmon said shortly, getting out of the car. "I hope it don't have to be done again."

Clarissa got out on the other side. She felt suddenly embarrassed and did not want to look at The Terrapin. She didn't want him to look at her either, because it seemed to her she must have

changed and looked funny all over; she crossed her arms tight
on her chest to mash it down.

"Poor thing," said The Terrapin suddenly in a softer voice than
usual. "Ain't nothing the same now, is there?"

All of a sudden right there is the middle of the road, Clarissa
was afraid she might cry. "Oh, let me alone!" she snapped, turning away from him and pretending not to see the hurt look on his
face. "Why don't you all let me alone!" She wanted a bath. She
wanted the cookie and the two glasses of lemonade out of her
stomach and lying on the ground all around the rosebush. She ran
to the porch and Granddaddy was waiting there in the rocker,
wearing a crooked smile with all his brown-stained teeth showing.

"You knows now, don't you?" cackled Granddaddy. He spat
out into the bush almost gaily, as if he were including it in their
fun. "I guess it's all come home to you now."

Clarissa was already inside the door where she could not see
the brown roses. "Oh, let me alone!" she cried again, really
wailed this time; but softer, almost to herself, not really aiming to
change anything. "I'll fix supper," she said, again to herself. And
louder, firmer, "I'll go in and fix the supper."

Clarissa was thirteen when she went to work in town, but she
was a grown girl already. That's what everybody said. They
would all look at her and then at her daddy and say, "She's shoot-
ing up mighty fast, Harmon. You want to watch that."

"I'm watching it," her daddy would say irritably.

It seemed that even though he'd said she was going to grow
into a female like Winnie-Faye told her, he got mad when he saw
it happening under his very eyes. He kept acting as if it were
something she could have stopped if she had only closed her eyes
and counted to ten, or pressed down on the top of her head to stay
small.

But there Clarissa was, getting tall and pushing out the fronts of
her blouses as a botheration to him, his look said. All of this made
Clarissa feel strange; she hunched her shoulders forward to flatten

her front and dropped them down a trifle, as if that might leave her an inch or so shorter.

But The Terrapin noticed this part of it, and he didn't like it any more than her daddy did the other.

"Here," he objected, "don't stand like you got no starch in you."

"I'm all right," Clarissa muttered.

"You got to have pride this day and time," The Terrapin said. "You got to hold that head up, good as anybody. You got to look folks in the eyes. You got to . . ." Here he paused, looking a little desperate for the right words, and then finished forcefully, "You got to stand there like you got something burning in you. Like a candle. Like you had a candle lit inside!"

Clarissa was embarrassed. "Where you learn to talk like that?"

The Terrapin would drop his eyes. "Things just up there in my head," he would say apologetically.

"Granddaddy says you crazy."

"He's old," said The Terrapin, as if he were forgiving it. "He thinks different."

"Well, me too," Clarissa burst out. "I'm like him and Daddy. I'm not like you, Terrapin!"

The Terrapin looked a little stunned at this. He said in a little while, "All right."

"I mean it. Do you hear?"

"All right," said The Terrapin again. "I heard you."

What Clarissa really wished most of all was that everyone would let her alone, let her do things herself. Grow up and find out and be somebody like *she* wanted, not like *they* wanted. But people seemed to be always after her, and when it wasn't The Terrapin talking about candles, it was her daddy worrying about how big she was getting.

"You need them dresses cut longer," he'd grumble. Or another time, "You got on a petticoat, Clarissa? Don't you let me catch you going anywhere without a petticoat!"

The Terrapin tried to help a little, but he seemed embarrassed by the way she looked, too, in spite of what he had said about the candles. They had, before, always slept all together in one long room, but now The Terrapin wouldn't come to bed until she was in and covered up. He wouldn't touch her any more either, wouldn't pat her hand or spank her behind when she bent over.

Once he said to her, "It's all ugly. The flesh is all ugly."

"What do you mean?" said Clarissa.

"It gets in the way," he said vaguely. "It gets in the way of things."

"What things?" Clarissa felt impatient with him, the way her daddy did sometimes.

The Terrapin did not exactly explain what he meant. "Laziness and eating and sleeping and loving," he said. "They take up so much time. They use us all up."

It was things like this that made Harmon say The Terrapin was just a little bit crazy. That was supposed to be why he had never married, although he would go here and there with different women. Women seemed to like The Terrapin because he had a soft voice and mingled-looking eyes, not like the eyes of most of the colored men they knew, and now and then he would talk like a pretty book.

"Where you get them eyes?" they'd say to him, even the woman cousins.

"I scrambled 'em," The Terrapin would answer mysteriously. "When I was born I reached up and scrambled them with my finger."

In May, Cousin Lacey Thorndyke came to see Clarissa's daddy and said she was quitting her work with the Sullivans because she was having another baby.

"I aimed to stay on," she said, "but Miz Sullivan's afraid the children gonna notice and ask her something about it."

"That's too bad," said Harmon Johnson. "It's a good place."

"I come to see if Clarissa would like to take it. It's time she took a place if she's going."

Clarissa's daddy looked worried. "I don't know," he said. "She ain't but thirteen."

Lacey Thorndyke snorted, which she did well because of her broad nostrils. "She's a growned girl and you know it. And don't tell me you folks couldn't use the extry money. The Sullivans pay good and gives away clothes. Can she cook and clean good?"

"Sure she can," said Harmon defiantly. "Sure she can! What do you think?"

"Well then," said Lacey firmly, as if that settled it. "Well then, you send her in tomorrow and I'll show her things before I leave."

"I don't know," said Harmon. "I just don't know about it."

"She got to learn," said Lacey. "I know what Bertha would a done if she was living. Clarissa got to learn her place, and being around that Terrapin ain't good for it."

"All right," said Harmon. "I guess I'll send her."

"I guess you will," said Lacey.

So the next day, which was a Saturday, Clarissa went into town to the Sullivans' house, and Cousin Lacey showed her where the china was, and what silver to use, and told her what she could and could not do. It turned out she would sleep in a room over the garage. Clarissa had never had a room to herself before, and she liked that best of all.

"On Mondays and Thursdays the garbage got to go out front," Lacey told her. "On Friday nights the Sullivans goes out and you got to mind the children. Sometimes you'll have Saturday nights free if the children goes to their grandmama's. On Sundays you can go off anywhere because they eats at Old Miz Sullivan's. And you suppose to keep the flowers watered."

"All right," said Clarissa. She wasn't interested in all this. She wanted to go back and look at her room again.

Clarissa thought how nice it would be to set some Queen Anne's lace on the table where the bowl and pitcher were, and how at night she could think anything she wanted to. You had to be careful thinking things with somebody in the same room; they might could tell it somehow. But now she could do just what she pleased, and nobody but Clarissa Johnson would be there to know.

Lacey showed her how to operate the vacuum cleaner and where the dust cloths were and how the iron worked.

"You got to set it for the kind of material," she said. "Can you read these things here?"

"I been to school," said Clarissa indignantly.

"That ain't what I ask you. Here, read them off for me."

Clarissa read them loudly. "Rayon, silk, wool, cotton, and linen."

"All right," said Lacey. "See you mind them."

Lacey was big and fat and it seemed to take her a long time to show everything to Clarissa, and when that was finally done Miz Sullivan had to talk to her.

"Do you think you have everything straight now, Clarissa?"

"Yes, ma'am, I think so."

"Now you just come and ask me if there's anything you aren't sure about."

"Yes, ma'am."

"We're really going to miss Lacey," said Miz Sullivan, smiling. "She's practically one of the family."

"Yessum, I'll sure miss you all, too."

When Lacey had finally gone and Miz Sullivan had finished talking to her, Clarissa went up into her own room and closed the door. She looked around her, thinking she had never seen any place so elegant.

The iron bed was painted very white; it was the whitest thing she had ever seen, like eggshells. And the sheets were sparkling clean ("They goes out in the regular Sullivan laundry and don't cost you nothing," Lacey had told her proudly) and they were freshly ironed, and a quilt was turned back. The quilt had every color of the rainbow in it, every tint of Joseph's coat; Clarissa sat on the bed and touched the bright squares timidly with one finger. She put the finger slowly onto red, and green, and stripes, and triangles of flowers; and then she drew a long breath. This was something! This was the way to live, in spite of all The Terrapin said.

On the wall just above the bed hung a magazine page of Jesus on the cross. Lacey had cut it out of the great paintings section of one of the Sullivans' magazines, and she said she was only leaving it behind because Clarissa might need it.

"It's for comfort," Lacey had told her happily, gazing up at the half naked and contorted body in the painting. "Let it soothe your spirit in trouble."

"All right," Clarissa had replied awkwardly, glancing up at the picture and looking away quickly.

She thought now she would take it down because it made her arms and legs feel they were being pulled from their sockets. It made her want to draw them back up into herself again.

A little table with a bowl and pitcher stood against one wall and on the other two shelves were nailed up. One was for your cosmetics, said Lacey, and when Clarissa looked puzzled she explained about soap and sweet lotion. And the other you could use for magazines. You were allowed to have all the magazines after the Sullivans had finished with them.

There was a blue linoleum on the floor which Lacey said had once been in the kitchen. Sure enough, if you looked at it awhile you could see where the refrigerator had sat, and where the stove had been, and the little holes where the children had reared back in the kitchen chairs.

Clarissa sat quietly on the bed, touching the bright coverlet and looking around her with shining satisfied eyes. She was going to like it with the Sullivans. She could tell she would like it.

After that first awkward week, there was no question at all in her mind; she liked everything about her new job. Things were completely different from the way they had been at home, where she had a constantly "pulled about" feeling, as though they were all battling over her. Nobody cared about her at the Sullivans', really cared. Oh, they wanted her to eat enough and feel well and not be unhappy, but none of them really cared about what went on in her head. Nobody picked or pulled at her to think this way or that; sometimes she didn't know whether the Sullivans were quite sure if she thought or not, that perhaps they talked to her as if she were some awkward brown puppy, asking each other incuriously afterward, "Do you suppose it understands at all?"

And even though she knew how The Terrapin would feel about it, it was for these very reasons that Clarissa most liked her life at the Sullivans'. Her whole mind felt rested; she was aware of only a quiet, steady motion up in her skull, like a machine with most of the switches cut off.

Sometimes, pausing in her work, she would put her fingers to her temples gently, as if she were supporting something precious; and she would say to herself (sometimes aloud), "Everything all right, ain't it, Clarissa? Everything all right now."

She liked other things about being with the Sullivans. She liked working in their gleaming kitchen with the new refrigerator and she liked polishing the bright oak floors in the hall or catching sight of herself in the full-length mirror while she scrubbed the bathroom tile.

"Hello, Miss Clarissa," she would whisper, seeing herself in the mirror.

"And hello yourself," she answered after a while. This would strike her as so ridiculous that she would sit back on her own calves and giggle; and seeing herself laughing there in the long mirror made her laugh even harder.

"Oh my," she would sigh happily to herself, going back to the tile. "Oh my, Clarissa."

The Sullivans didn't call her Clarissa. Mrs. Sullivan said it was too long a name for the children, but you could tell she just didn't think much of it. So everybody in the household called her "Clarie," which she hated. She would repeat it under her breath whenever any of them called her by that name. "Clarie," she would repeat angrily. It sounded like a hen squawk.

She was a good housecleaner and the Sullivans seemed well

satisfied with her. They told Cousin Lacey she was almost as much a treasure as *she* had been, and, being younger and little, she did things quick. Lacey repeated this to Clarissa in an angry voice, obviously a little jealous; and added to Clarissa that she ought to watch out because haste sometimes made waste.

"One job done right is worth a dozen half done," Cousin Lacey counseled grumpily.

"That's right," said Clarissa.

The Sullivans paid her fifteen dollars a week and board, which her daddy said was very good. Besides, having the little room to herself was almost as good as the fifteen dollars, since every week she mailed twelve of that to the farm.

"Dear Daddy," she would write painstakingly. "Here is the money. Clarissa."

She could picture them taking her letter out of the mailbox (they hadn't even bothered to put up a mailbox until she came to town because there hadn't been any need of that; nobody sent them any mail) and reading the address and carrying it to the porch to open.

"What does she say?" The Terrapin would probably ask, leaning forward hopefully.

"Oh," Harmon would answer, studying over the message to make sure he had gotten it all, "nothing much."

"Is she feeling good? Does she say she's feeling good?"

"Of course she's feeling good! Here's the money, ain't it?" her daddy would answer sharply.

"I hope she ain't letting them break her spirit," he might say sadly.

"Shoot!" Granddaddy would snap, spitting.

"Clarissa's gonna be all right," Harmon would insist.

"Well," Granddaddy would scream triumphantly at them from his rocker. "Well, I maybe can't read but I can see the green stuff. I guess that's good enough for me."

"She don't write very long letters," The Terrapin would complain.

"They'll do," her daddy would say shortly. "What's to write?"

Once The Terrapin came all the way into town to visit her and sat uncomfortably in her little bedroom over the garage. He didn't even seem to notice how elegant it was, or that lacking Queen Anne's lace she had made paper roses and stuck them in the pitcher.

"You doing all right?" he said nervously, not even looking at things. "They treat you all right here?"

Clarissa was very angry because he hadn't said anything about the clean white sheets, or the quilt, or even about Jesus dying up above her bed.

"Of course they do," she said impatiently. "What did you think?"

"You can't tell," he said vaguely. "Sometimes they don't. If anything goes wrong, you just tell me. People got to stick together in this thing."

"What thing?" said Clarissa impatiently.

"Oh, the war," The Terrapin answered, waving a brown hand. "The war for freedom."

"You been going to some of them political meetings again."

"They're not political," he protested. "Just colored people talking to other colored people. About the future."

"Hah. What kind of future you got, Terrapin?"

He would not answer that. "They say, these men, they say the future belongs to them that always looks toward it. They say we all got to look toward it."

"Look toward it how? I'm doing all right. You're doing all right, ain't you?"

The Terrapin ducked his head, his voice losing the ring he had imitated from the political meetings. "What's gonna become of us?" he asked her sadly.

She was not moved. "I tell you what. We gonna eat steady and stay healthy, that's what. We gonna have clothes on our backs and roofs on our heads. What more do you want?"

The Terrapin shrugged in genuine bewilderment. "I don't

know . . ." he said. "It just seems like . . ." He paused, frowning. ". . . like there ought to be more. I don't know. It just seems like . . ."

"Wasn't your eyes you scrambled," Clarissa told him good-naturedly. "Was your brain."

She looked up at her cosmetic shelf where she now had one bottle of Apple Blossom perfume from the dime store, a little yellowish bottle not as long as her thumb. Poor Terrapin, Clarissa thought, almost imagining she could smell the strong sharp sweetness that rose when she unscrewed the bottle (it had a little glass rod inside for putting drops just behind the ears). Poor Terrapin, Clarissa thought affectionately. He's so mixed up.

"There's one more thing," said The Terrapin, picking nervously at a knot in his shoestring.

"What's that?" asked Clarissa, smiling. He didn't really bother her any more with his wild talk, now that she knew about things.

"Your daddy . . ." The Terrapin swallowed loudly. "Your daddy says to ask you if . . . if you still all right. If you . . . if you been bothered."

Clarissa tossed her head. "Course not. You tell him I said to get that out of his mind."

The Terrapin looked quite relieved by her answer and got to his feet. "Well," said The Terrapin, smiling vaguely, "I know he'll be glad about that." When he got to the door he turned around as though he had suddenly thought of something. He said awkwardly, "Don't let 'em humble you."

Then he was gone out the door and down the steps before she could answer.

Once a month Clarissa got on the bus and went out to see her daddy and her granddaddy and The Terrapin. They would all be sitting on the front porch because it was Sunday, and when the big bus stopped in front of the house they would lean forward curiously and in some amazement, even after she had been home half a dozen times.

"Clarissa, is that you?" her daddy would call, before the bus had even gotten started again.

"Sure it's me. Who you think?"

"Getting uppity with her town ways," Granddaddy would yell, spitting out into the yard. "Outgrowing her raising."

The Terrapin would defend her proudly. "No, she's not. Just changing, that's all. Just learning things."

"Not learning anything but work," she'd tell him quickly, not wanting him to expect things of her. "Just dishes and cooking and mopping is all. Same as I did here."

"But it's a different place," he'd insist. "You learning white people's ways. That's how we got to do it; we got to take up all the white people's ways."

"Shoot!" Granddaddy would say viciously, and a long brown stream of juice would spatter onto rose leaves. "Shoot, I say."

"Everything all right, Clarissa?" her daddy would say. "You not having any trouble? You know. You know the kind I mean."

"Course not," she'd tell him impatiently. "That's all you think about."

"That's all *most* men think about!" her granddaddy would cackle. Then he would begin to wrinkle up his nose. "Fah!" he'd snort. "You smell, girl."

"It's perfume," Clarissa would explain happily. "Apple Blossom."

And her daddy would scowl.

Everything went smoothly for Clarissa at the Sullivans' until July. The children, whose names were Bert and Sue, liked her even better than Lacey.

Some days she took them for long walks and on others she showed them things they could do in their own back yard, like making dandelion curls and plaiting certain weeds.

And she taught them about sourgrass, the little plant that grew wild in the yard that you could chew on. The leaves were sweet and sour at the same time, and sometimes the tiny stems held little pods which Clarissa called pickles. They were very tiny and very sour and held almost invisible little seeds, smaller than pinheads.

"Is this a sourgrass, Clarie?" Sue would ask, holding up a clover.

"Naw, silly, that's a plain clover leaf. Here it is. The little light green one." She was surprised at how ignorant they were. She thought everybody knew about sourgrass.

Or they would point out the small red berries that grew along the wall of the garage.

"Clarie, look at the baby strawberries."

She would draw back. "Them ain't strawberries. Them's snake berries. Snakes come up at night and eats 'em."

Or, pointing out the wine-red clusters which they sometimes mashed in their mud pies, Clarissa would say, "And don't you be eating *them,* either. That's polk, and the berries will poison you."

It seemed to Bert and Sue that nobody in the world knew as much as Clarissa, except maybe their daddy. He was nearly always at work, or eating, or reading his paper, so it was hard to tell about him.

But in July they changed deliverymen down at the grocery store. Miz Sullivan had always done her own shopping and everything was delivered late on Saturday when she and Mr. Sullivan had already gone out for the evening. Sometimes Clarissa would have to mind the children, but usually they went to stay with their grandmama, who thought they were much too thin and fed them lots of cookies.

The groceries had always been brought before by an old colored man who had only one eye, and wore a plaid patch on the other like a pirate; but the first Saturday in July a younger man brought them, a young light-skinned, sharp-nosed colored man with very white teeth and both his eyes. The eyes were as black and as shiny as marbles.

"Where you want these, girl?" said this new man insolently, still sitting in his truck in the back yard and staring at Clarissa.

"Just put them on the kitchen table," said Clarissa. She was out back watering the flowers in the cool of the evening, because the children were at their grandmama's and it was a good time to get it done without them messing in the mud.

"I might and I mightn't," the new deliveryman said. He got out of the truck and came over to stand in front of her. "What's your name?"

"My name's Clarissa," she said. She stood there with the hose dribbling down at her side uselessly, she was so astonished at being asked.

"That'll do," said the young man with the black eyes. "Clarissa will do."

"Clarissa ain't going to do nothing," she said sharply, remembering her daddy and Winnie-Faye. "You just leave them groceries for Miz Sullivan like I said."

"How old are you, girl?"

"A hundred," she said.

"Old enough, I bet."

"Go put up them groceries before I hose you down."

He laughed, a warm rich laugh that seemed to come up from his middle so that involuntarily she dropped her eyes to it, saw the firm chest and the belted waist and the hard flat stomach.

He said, still laughing though more softly now, "Look close, girl. Look close and tell me what you see."

Clarissa turned her back and watered the flowers wildly, flinging the water up and down in wide arcs. Behind her she heard the young man's rich laughter again.

"O.K., Miss Clarissa," he said. "I'll be seeing you, Miss Clarissa."

"Not if I see you first," she said shortly.

He laughed at that. "Maybe you won't," he said.

Still, Clarissa didn't think too much about him until the next Saturday when he was back again. This time she was in the kitchen and both children were there, licking out of an icing bowl and quarreling over who was getting the most.

"Well, howdy, Miss Clarissa," said the young man politely, flashing his white teeth.

"Goodness," said Sue. "That's not Miss Clarissa. That's Clarie."

"Clarissa will do," he said, keeping his eyes on her and not looking at the two white children.

"I got no time for your foolishness," she said.

He began to unload the grocery boxes with exaggerated slow motions. "When you reckon you gonna have time?" he asked slyly.

Clarissa said nothing. "You through with that icing bowl?" she demanded irritably of the children after a while.

"Not yet," said Bert in surprise.

"Well, eat it up," she said. "I'd like to wash it with the others." To the deliveryman she said, "What happened to that other fellow?"

"He quit."

"Here's the icing bowl," said Bert, handing it up to her. She began to soap it under the hot-water faucet.

"Hey, Miss Clarissa, you live out over the car shed?" asked the deliveryman, looking at her all the time his hands were setting the groceries out. "You live up there where I see the chimney and the window shades?"

"No," said Clarissa quickly. "Don't nobody live up there."

"Why, you do, too!" said Sue.

"Of course you do, Clarie," added Bert, still standing by the sink and looking up at her curiously.

The groceries were all out on the table by then. "Then I'll be seeing you, Miss Clarissa," the man said softly. "I'll surely be seeing you."

That night she put a chair under the doorknob and sat on her bed pillows all night, fully dressed even as to shoes, but he did not come.

When she found out Miz Sullivan had ordered some extra groceries on Wednesday, Clarissa was nervous all day. And sure enough, about sundown there he came in the store truck, his uniform looking clean and starched so that she wondered for a minute who did his laundry. Some shiftless woman that hangs after him, she thought contemptuously.

"There you are, Clarissa," he said, nodding his head to her. "It's a hot day."

"Not so hot," she said sharply, running the water in the sink although there was nothing there to wash. She said it wasn't hot just to be disagreeable with him, just so he wouldn't feel so big.

"Bet it's hot up to your place," he said, eying her.

"That's so," said Clarissa quickly. "Nobody could stand it up there."

"Oh, I don't know. You look healthy enough."

"I don't sleep up there in hot weather. Nobody could stand it at night."

"That so?"

He had moved around the table while he was setting out the things until his back was directly to her back, and now he brushed her very slightly. It might have been an accident. She told herself it might have been an accident.

In a few minutes she said sullenly, "You got a name yourself?"

"I surely have," he said. "My name's Philo. My name's Philo Mingle."

Clarissa turned and stared at him. "Whoever heard of a fellow named Philo Mingle?"

"I never did," he said. "Not no other."

"I don't see how you keep your job. You talk back too much."

He laughed. She had never heard anybody else laugh like he did. "I don't talk back down at the store," he said. "I'm careful. I'm mighty careful about everything." He stepped to where she was facing him and looked at her. "Careful and easy," he added.

"Well, don't be telling me," Clarissa returned quickly, ashamed that he could see she was running water in an empty sink. "It's none of my concern."

Philo Mingle went back to unloading the groceries and she stole a look at his back. He had big shoulders, and the light skin along his neck prickled from the curly hairs. And he had big hands. He could circle her arms easy, she thought, and then quit thinking it.

"I got to be going now," he said.

"High time," Clarissa told him quickly. "It takes you longer than the other."

"He was old," said Philo Mingle. "He was too old to be distractible."

"You go on home," she said.

"All right. Sleep well, Miss Clarissa. It's a mighty hot night, but you sleep well."

This time Clarissa did not stay up all night, but she slept restlessly, waking off and on thinking she had heard feet on her stairs, or the doorknob turning, or the bedsprings creaking quietly beside her. But of course none of these things actually happened; it was just that she was afraid they were going to.

When morning came, she was as tired as the night before, and all her bones felt pulled. That made her look up at the picture of Jesus, but his face wasn't turned outward to look at her. He seemed to be looking down into a crowd of people, as if he were talking to somebody in it. Talking to Mary maybe, thought Clarissa dully, who had conceived without sin.

She thought maybe she ought to go see Cousin Winnie-Faye about it, or at least Cousin Lacey Thorndyke. But she didn't know what she would say if she went. It was just a feeling she had that she couldn't describe to them, a lazy feeling at the bottom of her stomach as though things were tightening up and loosening, tight-and-loose, tight-and-loose. She thought sometimes it was like having a hand inside her stomach that closed and unclosed gently.

Or maybe, she thought, maybe that was the way a flower felt, opening and closing with the light and the dark.

Then she thought how ridiculous that would sound, and wondered if she might be getting crazy like The Terrapin.

On Friday, Miz Sullivan said she thought Clarissa didn't look well.

"You look tired, Clarie, like you're not getting enough sleep. Is it too hot up in your room?"

"Well, it gets pretty hot sometimes," said Clarissa, scraping one foot nervously.

"I'll give you a fan. Bert can take it over for you."

"Thank you, ma'am. That'll be nice."

So on Friday night she had the fan, but in its own way that kept her awake too. The feel of wind blowing on her would wake her up and set her to clutching at the bedclothing and at her nightgown, as if they had all been stolen. She kept touching them to assure herself that they were still there, and then drifting back off into a restless sleep again. Being cool bothered her; it was too much like being naked.

Toward morning she dreamed she was tied to a tree in the back yard at home. Her daddy came out of the house and stooped down and put a knife between her feet and said hollowly, "Cut if you have to." But her hands were tied and of course she couldn't reach the knife.

And The Terrapin would come out of the house a few steps behind him and take the knife away and put a candle in its place. "A light and a fire," he would tell her grandly. But of course her hands were tied and she could not take up the candle.

This went on and on, her daddy with the knife and The Terrapin with his candle, one after the other, over and over. "Cut," her daddy would say sometimes. "Burn," The Terrapin would tell her.

"Cut and run."

"Burn and stand your ground."

"Cut and remember your mama."

"Burn and remember your people."

And then, after a while in the dream, her granddaddy came out and leaned forward and pinched the inside of her thigh and laughed.

"I've come to plant a rosebush," he said, cackling at her through the stained teeth. "The old one's no good any more."

Clarissa woke from her dream quite cold and, leaning over, turned the fan all the way off.

On that day, which was Saturday, Philo Mingle brought the groceries but he didn't have much to say. He just came into the kitchen where she was and began to take things out of the big boxes.

Clarissa couldn't resist it finally. "You've quieted down," she said sharply, half fearful because of it.

He shrugged, silent.

"You got a worry?"

He shook his head and gave her a brief smile that showed the strong white teeth. "Everything going to be all right. Going to be fine."

"What's going to be fine?"

"Everything," he said. "You'll see."

She turned her back to him while he finished unloading. I won't even look around until he's gone, she thought. And she heard the last things set down and the crates lifted off the table.

Then, as quickly as a snake striking, Philo Mingle flicked his fingers up beneath her arm and caressed her; it was only a second, it was only as soft as a bird lighting.

"I'll surely be seeing you," he said softly. And, since he did not laugh, she knew he meant it this time.

By the time she had turned with the wooden potato masher uplifted, he had already gone out the kitchen door.

"Goodbye, Miss Clarissa," he called.

"You get away," she screamed, running to the back screen and feeling she was going to burst into tears. "You get away and stay away, do you hear?"

He waved at her from the truck and drove off.

That night, Clarissa waited up for him, as sober and solemn as death. She pulled the straight chair to where it would be hidden when her room door opened, and she sat there with the butcher knife laid across her knees. It was as sharp as she could get it and she had sharpened all afternoon in the kitchen, making it ready. She sat very still in her chair and heard the Sullivans get into the car and drive away, taking Bert and Sue to see their grandmama.

Goodbye, she thought sadly. I don't aim to get you all in trouble. But I've promised.

It seemed to her that daylight left early, that it was suddenly sucked up out of the world so the night would be longer—the long, long night and her there watching the dead corpse till morning. She would watch it all night and then it would be Sunday and she would have to go tell somebody. When she remembered that tomorrow would be Sunday, she got up from the chair and went to tear the crucifixion off her wall. She wouldn't have Him seeing. She folded the picture up small and put it underneath the bed pillow. Then she went back and sat down again and put the knife across her knees.

What else could I do? she thought miserably. Winnie-Faye warned me. Daddy warned me. If you're not married, it's as bad as murder anyway.

So she sat there sadly, thinking about how she would go to jail and never have a kitchen of her own with a new refrigerator; and sometimes she would test the blade to make certain it was sharp. After a while there was blood streaked here and there on her gown from the cuts she had given herself on the thumb, testing the thin sharp blade.

Finally she heard him.

She heard him walk into the yard and cross it and set his foot on the first step. She was sure she couldn't have heard that much from way upstairs, and yet she did hear it. She heard the grass-blades bending down when he walked, and the gravel stirring at the edge of the yard.

And then she heard him coming up the steps slowly, very slowly, as if he had all the time in the world. She counted them carefully. There were nine steps from the ground to her door, and when the door was finally opened she would be hidden behind it with her sweet, sharp knife. He would look for her and then he would step into the room, where she could see him by the window.

Clarissa heard him take the seventh and the eighth and then—

lingering, it seemed—the ninth step. She got up from the chair and stood there with the knife clutched in her right hand; and took a long breath and held it.

He opened the door and stood there so that through the crack she could see him in the light from the opposite window—tall, his legs spread, one hand still resting on the knob.

"Clarissa?" he called in a whisper. "Where are you, Clarissa?"

She had the knife all ready to step forward and strike; but she stopped to listen to the way her name sounded in his mouth, and then she let out a long breath in something like a sob. She put the knife down on the chair behind her and, stepping forward in the darkness, put out a hand and rested it flat against his chest. She put it flat where the blade should have been.

"Here I am," she said.

On the next day, which was Sunday, Clarissa went out to see her family as usual. She got off the bus at the highway and saw them leaning forward in the green chairs, watching her with their usual surprise.

"Clarissa, is that you?" her daddy called, before the bus had even gotten started again.

"Sure it's me," she said. "Who you think?"

"Listen to that!" cried Granddaddy. "Listen to that uppity female!"

"She's not uppity," said The Terrapin, defending her. "She's a credit to us. She's a credit to her people."

"Oh shush," said Clarissa irritably. "I don't want to be a credit. I just want to live good, that's all. Just for me myself." She touched her ear where the apple blossoms almost seemed to burn.

"Is everything all right?" her daddy asked. "You know. None of them men bothering you?"

She did not look at him. "Course not," she said.

"Your mama was a church-going woman," her daddy said. "She'd be glad you turned out so well."

"But it's not only for us Johnsons," said The Terrapin proudly.

"It's for everybody. The future belongs to them as can control it. As can control their freedom."

"You been to them meetings again," said Clarissa tiredly. She sat in one of the rockers and watched the cars go by.

"It's been a busy day," her daddy said happily. "Lots of traffic."

"That's good," said Clarissa.

She watched the cars coming around the bend, passing in the level place in front of the house, and going up the long hill and dropping over. There they went, she thought dully, over the hill and into the big hole with thousands and millions of other cars.

"Won't that a new Chevrolet?" said The Terrapin so suddenly that she jumped a little.

"Naw," said her daddy. "That's the Studebaker."

Granddaddy snorted. "Studebaker ain't never built no car like that."

"It's new, I tell you. New design this year."

"Shoot!" said Granddaddy. He leaned forward and spit angrily into the rosebush, which hardly quivered at all.

THE
DEAD MULE

As soon as he saw his wife leaning so casually against the wall just inside the front door, Buzzer began to look nervously left and right. Something was wrong. Her shadow on the screen was a warning.

He had not far to look.

At first it seemed no more than an incidental piece of brightness like sunlight against wet leaves, but when he looked more closely he saw it was a green car drawn off in the woods a hundred yards or so from his house.

A *green* car in them leaves, he thought. Well, ain't that sneaky!

His wife lifted her arm and waved, half toward him and half toward the back yard.

Buzzer understood. He thought of running, but where could he have run?

Besides, he had the feeling if he took to his heels Rita Faye might lift the shotgun from where it hung over the front door and shoot him down between the shoulder blades. He was always disappointing her. Lately she seemed right tired of that.

Better a live bootlegger than a dead fugitive, Buzzer thought. He liked that word. He had a clipping about the time he run off from the county prison farm and its title was: FUGITIVE AT LARGE.

He walked on toward the house but he didn't hurry. Some

(69)

rotten luck you had to learn to take, but no need to hurry to it.

"Aw, come on!" yelled Rita Faye impatiently.

He got to the steps and stood looking up at her and she stood looking down at him through the rusted screen.

After a minute she said with heavy disgust, "You was so smart." Who had time for that argument? "How many come?" he said.

She pushed back yellow hair. "Oh, you go first class, you do. The High Sheriff and his deputy both back there."

"What they find?"

"Nothing yet." At this Buzzer sat down weakly on the edge of the porch. "They will," she added.

"Shut up. I'm thinking," Buzzer said. "They been digging?"

"Right now they just poking. They gone through my flour bin and under the house and they run sticks through the hen nests." He started to ask something else but Rita Faye knew what it was and she just raised her voice. "I got that one poured out when I saw the car drive up. Kitchen smelled of it, but there was nothing but pure water running in the sink."

"Poured down the sink," said Buzzer in a hollow voice. He could have used a mouthful. But he was a practical man; he couldn't dwell on that. "Where are the kids?"

"The bus is late from school, and Kirb wouldn't tell anyhow." Rita Faye swung the screen out and came to sit by him, wiping her face with her dress tail. "Sure is hot."

"You think I better go down there?" He never looked at her.

"It wouldn't hurt," she said.

But Buzzer hated to go if it was going to mean arguing. It seemed if he could just sit still another minute and if Rita Faye would keep her mouth shut, he'd think of something to do.

He sat and looked at the dusty ground, spattered by crosses where the hens had walked.

No hope of Rita Faye keeping still. "You spot their car?"

He nodded.

"Cute the way it's green. I guess in wintertime they'll paint it sparrow color."

He had to think how he would handle the Sheriff's questions.

But it was Rita Faye's way to lay the problem out, clear and final, and then lay it out again. All she could do with a problem was talk it to death.

She laid it out. "What's it matter if they find it this trip or next? They'll watch till they do. You can't make your deliveries that way. You won't even be able to pour a glass in your own kitchen and get any comfort out of it. They'll be underfoot from now to next Easter, one way or the other."

Buzzer knew that, didn't he? Why did she think he was sitting here frowning into his own yard dirt?

"Sheriff Hobble don't give up. If it's not today, it'll be tomorrow —that's how he thinks." She shifted and put both feet a step down, flat on the dust. "And why shouldn't he think that? He don't get paid by the bottle like you do. He gets the same cash money in a month he catches ten as none. That man's got time."

Buzzer lifted his foot and stomped hers. "Just hush it, will you? I know all that!"

Rita Faye shrugged and leaned sideways on the porch post and he saw that her tow hair was lank and her mouth had got turned down the wrong way in the years since he had married her.

"Why ain't you a deputy with a steady paycheck then?" she said without heat. "You know so much."

Buzzer stood up. "I guess I'll go down there," he said.

But she stared away without facing him, letting her head ease off against the post. She was hot and dirty; if he took a finger and rubbed it now on her neck he knew how the skim would come off in tiny, moist rolls. Gray. Like the stuff under the beds in the house.

"I might as well," he said. He moved off a step but she didn't even turn her head to watch him.

"You don't think Hobble really believes I can make a living growing Mr. Wicker's tobacco?" He spat at the chicken marks.

Rita Faye said none of that was Hobble's business.

He walked back to give her an angry stare. "Well, whose business is it, I'd like to know! It ain't Mr. Wicker's business, that's for sure!"

She looked off past him into the sky. "Mr. Wicker don't have to have business. He's got money. You ever think of that?"

At that, Buzzer was so angry he walked quickly around the house and got in sight of the two men before he'd had time to set his face right.

He knew his mistake. Mr. Wicker could look mad if the law came on his land without papers, but Buzzer Martin better lift his mouth.

He lifted both corners and a friendly hand as well. "Evenin'," he said.

"Come over here," said the High Sheriff.

"Why, it's Sheriff Hobble!" said Buzzer. "Haven't seen you some time!" He had gotten close enough now to see the Sheriff's face and to know his own smile was too big; he toned it down.

"Where is it this time?" Hobble said flatly.

"Cross my heart there's not a drop on the place!" Now his face went worried and a little hurt. "You know me, Mr. Hobble. You know I been up for that. You know I give my word it was never no more again."

The High Sheriff broke in. "I know all that. I also know you're selling again. Now we can find it the hard way, Buzzer, if you make us. But you might as well say . . ."

"Nothing's to say!" swore Buzzer. "Nothing's to say, so help me, except tobacco in the field that's in need of water and . . ."

But he had made a mistake. The Sheriff's eyes narrowed.

"I ain't forgot the tobacco beds that time," he said in a hard voice, "and all them little plants so spindly trying to get down roots among the jars."

"But no more; no sir! Not another damn time," said Buzzer nervously, getting his words run together. And he fought to keep his eyes on Sheriff Hobble's face so he wouldn't look toward the place he'd dug that hole.

The Sheriff was losing patience. "I don't like lying 'cause it uses up my time," he snapped. He didn't sound like he was acquainted with Rita Faye's view that he had all the time in the world. "We got the whole story already, can't you see that? We've got it all and a man to testify."

Buzzer's mind flashed over his customers. He went over them picking like a bird and finally lit: that damned Peter Walley, or maybe the cab company—and them a week behind on paying. You couldn't trust nobody.

But now he was alert; now he knew what he was up against, and he settled down and cooled off and began to plan two sentences ahead.

"You think you got a testifier when all you got is a man who'd lie in court," he said blandly, "because he can't testify to what's not, and I'm not. I'm not making and I'm not selling. I told the judge myself that never . . ."

"Oh hell," said Hobble. "What's that Luther's found?"

Buzzer held his head as though boards were nailed at each side of the neck, walling in his face. *Don't turn now. Don't betray. Stand calm.* He made his two fists fall open to the palm. He put his left foot out an inch—lazy, unconcerned. *Be like a mule with the blinders at each eye; look straight at Hobble. Don't let a single look slide off like a pointing arrow.*

Like a mule, thought Buzzer. That was pretty funny, as it turned out. He started to grin.

"Luther can't find nothing when there's nothing to find."

The Sheriff looked disgusted. "Luther? Try the henhouse again."

Now Buzzer's grin spread. Pretty dumb the Sheriff must be, to think he'd go the same road twice. Nobody had clearly testified anything. The Sheriff was just hoping to luck onto something. Once there had been two floors in that henhouse and under the false one Luther had turned up twenty-four jars, but that was two years back.

I learned something from that, thought Buzzer, and that's more than you and Luther did.

Luther, his hat askew and his nose and chin turned upward, trying to rise above the chicken smell, came out of the henhouse. He slapped at his thighs and raised his shoes high. He would have floated above that odor if he could.

"Nothing," said Luther. He took his hat off and looked inside in a menacing way but there was nothing in there, either, and he replaced it carefully. Luther was a right prissy man, for a deputy.

Buzzer stood very quietly, looking into the space between the shoulders of the two men. He had heard the front door screen slam and he figured Rita Faye was halfway across the yard to them by now.

Thought I couldn't handle this by myself.

The muscle holding his smile leaped in one cheek but he held it steady and decided it was time to ease that left foot back to the other. Slowly he drew it in line, like a foot was the best thing he had to think about, looked at the shallow trail it left, and then looked up at the Sheriff again, grinning.

"Plenty hot," he said in his most appeasing tone. The trick now, he knew, was to keep the smile wide but free of triumph.

"Hotter than you know," sneered Luther, but he was trying too hard. None of my customers been talking out of turn to that man.

Rita Faye's drawling voice said, "Saw you in the henhouse, Mr. Luther. Want to buy a fryer?"

That worried Buzzer. Too calm she was, a little insolence in her tone, a piece of mockery no wider than a straight pin. He gave her an ugly look.

"Got plenty eggs right now—no charge for a bag of eggs!" he said cheerily, but it was already sliding in the wrong direction. Now the eggs seemed a bribe. Rita Faye had upset the whole balance.

The two lawmen said nothing.

"Them's my eggs and my profit you're so free about," snapped Rita Faye, "and they come twelve for fifty cents!"

Now that was better. The situation became like a rocking rowboat that quietens down under you just as you poise to dive. The quarrel between husband and wife had righted it. Buzzer beamed.

"They *is* her eggs," he admitted happily. He made an aimless shuffle toward the road. Now they could walk off talking together. It would be over.

"What's that yonder?" said the Sheriff. Oh, that voice was too quiet.

"That's where my mule is buried."

The Sheriff walked over. "Two, three days back?"

"Three days," said Buzzer.

Rita Faye asked did Luther want them eggs or not?

The Sheriff, who must have weighed two hundred, stepped onto the soft patch of earth by the fence. He walked the size of it: mule length, anybody could see that.

He said, "Luther, you poke in there."

"*Sheeeee!*" cried Rita Faye. "Don't stink things up!"

Be easy, Buzzer thought. Say little.

Luther looked mad at moving from hen smell to dead mule smell; and he shot Sheriff Hobble one look of appeal, but then he took up a pitchfork and jabbed without much enthusiasm into the soft dirt.

"Better get a shovel," the Sheriff said.

"I'm going inside if you gonna fetch up that stinking mule," said Rita Faye, and she rolled her eyes at Buzzer.

"I give you my *word,*" said Buzzer and, in fact, he could think of a whole string of words he'd like to give the Sheriff.

Luther asked about a shovel and Buzzer pointed to where a rusted spade leaned by the barn door. "I hated to lose that mule," he said. That was the truth. Buzzer and that old mule had a feeling for each other; Rita Faye had remarked as much a hundred times.

In getting the shovel, Luther had stepped inside where the mule collar hung on a wooden peg, forming a greenish zero, and when he came back he said hopefully to the Sheriff, "That mule's gone, sure enough. Tell it by the stall."

"Dig here," said Hobble.

"You don't hardly ever expect a mule to die," Buzzer was

saying. "Mules is right sensible. Don't eat too much, don't take too much water on a hot day. If a load's too heavy, they just lay down. This one just got old. I was right surprised."

Rita Faye said again she was going in the house but she stood on, watching Luther break ground.

"I was right fond of that mule," Buzzer said.

Nobody answered him a word and the dirt was flying.

"Ever chew that tobacco had a mule's pitcher on it?" said Buzzer desperately, and heard the desperation and cursed himself. It's still not all lost, he told himself.

"It don't seem right, to dig a corpse up again," whined Rita Faye. "Even a mule."

That woman just might lose the ballgame yet. "Rita Faye, you get inside and close that back window," he said to her. "There's going to be a stink."

She said to him in a level voice, "I hope not," but she turned and walked to the house. Any other time Buzzer would have turned to watch her go. The way she walked—that was the last thing about her that could still move him, the shifting under her skirt, a way she had of seeming to throw her left heel away with each step.

From behind, Rita Faye was still a woman worth having.

Luther said, "It's a dead mule, all right. Looky here."

Sheriff Hobble stepped forward to see. And Buzzer moved up, too. He thought of running but Hobble had a gun on his hip; he could shoot off a toe or chip an earlobe if he took a notion. *Well, hell,* thought Buzzer, but he moved nearer the hole and began to practice his surprise.

The digging had uncovered only one leg and the flank and belly of the dead mule. Luther stepped up and wiped his shoe soles in the wiry grass. "Jee-sus!" he said. "I never meant to wade in it."

"That's all?" said Sheriff Hobble.

"Smell it yourself," snapped Luther, and he prodded until the hoof stuck up over the edge.

I did like that mule, thought Buzzer with a pang. It did the best it could.

Luther said he was ready to give up. "Maybe there's no booze on the place like he says."

"Maybe so," said Sheriff Hobble. He was a big man and now he was sweating in a series of spreading stains—armpit, waistband, between the shoulder blades. He took out a handkerchief and wiped his face, lingering a little at his nose to filter the air.

Man, that is a stink! thought Buzzer. I hope them lids is on tight. He was beginning to feel better, now that the Sheriff and Luther had stepped back slightly from the edge of the hole.

"What's on your shoes?" asked the Sheriff, and Luther looked plain disgusted.

"What you think's on my shoes? Dead mule, that's what!" he roared.

Now the Sheriff moved closer and looked at the partial corpse again. "All in a pile, that soft stuff?"

Luther said it was *all* soft stuff after three days in this heat.

"Maybe," mused the Sheriff, "maybe entrails over there at one end of the hole, all by themselves?"

"What's that?" said Luther.

"Naw!" cried Buzzer. "It was old age, I told you, not any hurt he got; it was . . ."

"Here." The Sheriff held out his hand and Luther put the shovel handle into it. Slowly, as delicately as a surgeon, Hobble slid the shovel down out of sight and moved it a certain way. He said softly, "Now what you think that is?"

Luther stepped up to see. What could Buzzer do? He took a look himself.

Along some invisible slit low on the mule's belly lay the edge of the shovel blade; the Sheriff lifted up a flap of flesh and—within the cavity—light suddenly gleamed off glass.

"Well, I'll be damned!" Luther exploded. That made Buzzer mad because he had already planned to be damned, right off, and now Luther had stole his thunder.

"Now, ain't that something!" Buzzer said, but it was the wrong thing; it had a weak and nervous sound. "How'd that get there?"

"*Shoo-wee!*" sighed Luther. "Who'd drink that stuff after that!"

"Sheriff, it ain't mine! Like I said—I'm not making or selling. Some other fool done seen me dig that grave . . . somebody wanted to get me in trouble. . . . I got no dog, you know. People could dig out here all night and I wouldn't know!"

The Sheriff said, "Put on your gloves, Luther, and let's fetch it out."

Oh Lord, thought Buzzer, and it was made right—the corn sprouted before I made the mash. I took my time with this batch. He wondered if Rita Faye was watching all this out one of the house windows. Sure she was.

He said again, "Whatever's there ain't mine!" But nobody listened.

Now the jars were coming up out of the guts of that mule, and the Sheriff took them two-by-two from Luther's gloved hands and lined them up in a row like cops at a parade: twenty-two, twenty-four, twenty-six, thirty-eight, forty-two, fifty. Buzzer counted them coming up himself. He always liked to know his stock down to the last drop.

Fifty-six they lined up. Buzzer could've told them that was all, but he liked the thought of Luther messing up his gloves a little more.

"Fifty-six, I make it," Luther said. He climbed out beside the Sheriff, took off his gloves and looked at them once before he threw them over his shoulder into the grave.

"Half gallons, too," said Luther. "Maybe three hundred bucks."

Buzzer closed his eyes briefly.

"Let's take a little ride toward town," said the Sheriff, "and you might help Luther load it in the trunk when he brings the car 'round here."

Buzzer said nothing. Luther swung over the fence and cut across the pasture toward the woods where they'd left the car. I'd like to own a car sometime, thought Buzzer. I'd like to own a red car.

Luther had no more backed into the yard when Rita Faye flew out of the house like a setting hen coming off a nest. She had both arms spread wide and her hair was standing up in a dandelion fringe on her head.

"What you think you're doing!" she started to yell over and over before she got there, but the Sheriff had opened the trunk by then and Buzzer, silent, was helping lift the jars inside. *Shoo*—how they did smell. I hope Luther steals a snort. I hope it gives him some disease.

"You gonna leave that dead mule dug up that way?" screamed Rita Faye.

The jars kept going into the car; Buzzer lined them up neat and squared them off. Color looks fine, he thought automatically.

"It ain't my mule," the Sheriff was saying.

"You'd leave a woman to cover that up again, you fat old . . ."

"Want to ride down with him?" asked Luther in a cold voice from the car.

All Buzzer hoped was that Rita Faye wouldn't cry. With that grave stinking and his good liquor riding in the wrong car, if Rita Faye was to holler now, he thought he'd be sick on his stomach, right then and there; and he didn't want Luther to have the satisfaction. The jars were in and the trunk lid slammed.

"You get up front with Luther," Hobble said, and Buzzer went without a word and opened the front door of the car.

Luther must have been thinking hard all the time he went for that car, and now at last he'd come up with something to say. "White mule in a dead mule," he wheezed. "That's something, ain't it, Sheriff?"

The Sheriff thought it was something. The Sheriff liked his bright boy Luther. It would look good in the papers that way. "White mule in a dead mule!" he repeated, and shook like a wet mountain and wiped his face, and climbed in back and rolled up the window against the stink.

Buzzer looked at Rita Faye. "I'll see you after while," he said. She had her head sideways and wouldn't look.

He got into the car and closed the door. It was bad to leave like that—the liquor gone, the money gone for promised things, a good mule rotting out where everybody would know. He wanted to say something helpful to Rita Faye, something to show he knew how she felt.

Leaning out the car window he called, "We left the shevel by the fence."

Just then Luther scratched off, splaying sand in all directions, and the big rock she threw at Buzzer missed his window and landed with a crash on the top of the Sheriff's car.

All the way to town Buzzer could hear that rock moving and rolling in tune to the hills and curves in the road, and he carried the sound of its existence carefully in his skull, like a gift.

THE PROUD
AND
VIRTUOUS

She could see the row of them working, their backs turned sullenly to the sun, the arms rising and falling almost languidly in the August heat. Things glinted sometimes in their hands; picks or shovels or spattered buckets caught the sun and held it as brightly as little distant mirrors. Occasionally some of them shouted back and forth, for a head would come up, and down the road a second head to listen; and then the second man would do something by reply, nod or wipe his head with a bandanna or go for fresh tar. She couldn't hear them, of course; they were too far away for that. She could just move the edge of blue ruffled curtain in the living room and look down the long brown field to the highway where they had worked all that morning since the school bus had passed.

Their soundlessness made her think of ants moving; she knew they must live and communicate and move toward a purpose (completion of the highway), but they remained to her some distant, strange and very tiny species. Some kind of bug, she thought with distaste, and her white flesh crawled at the thought.

Mildred Stuart dropped the curtain and glanced toward the clock that had belonged to her grandmother. Half past ten and no one for lunch today but herself. The major work was done too—

dishes and bed making and sweeping and dusting. It was one of those days that left time for extra things: the back windows, or trying out a new recipe, or the bathroom fixtures. She supposed she really ought to do the bathroom fixtures.

She had started upstairs when the telephone rang and she recognized the anxious voice of her neighbor, Carrie Nash. Carrie was always anxious; she lived in a world where the catastrophe was always just about to happen—blizzard or accident or heart attack. Perhaps it was having eight children that made her feel that way, as if one were more divided up, susceptible.

"Are you all right, Millie?"

"Of course I'm all right!" She sat at the telephone table touching her crisp hair daintily, a little pleased with Carrie for calling. "You're a worry wart, for goodness' sake! You're worse than George." (Much worse, some honest corner of her mind put in. George didn't worry at all, except about the poor Oriental farming methods, which weren't any of his business really.)

"Well, I just wish George were home today, that's all. Where'd you say he'd gone?" Carrie Nash had already called twice that morning but she had a terrible memory for things. It was probably because her mind was always extended in front of her, groping for tragedy.

"Into town to price some stock," said Mildred patiently. "There's a sale on hogs at the market." As she said it she could picture George leaning halfway into the pen, his eyes wide with pleasure as the hogs came by. That was George all right; a good ham interested him far more than any human female curve. Her own, for instance.

"I sure would feel better if George was there with you," Carrie said. "And none of your kids getting home till the late bus. Looks like those men are going to be there most of the day."

"Carrie, they're *not* going to bother me." While she talked Mildred ran one palm around the other forearm, smoothing the pale hairs evenly, a habit she had acquired when she was a young girl. She had nice arms, slender and tapering, she thought, and the hairs like down on the breasts of birds. "They're way down at the highway, Carrie. None of them will be up here."

"Thieves and murderers and the good Lord knows what all," sighed Mrs. Nash. "It'll be a mercy if George doesn't come home and find you cold and dead on the floor!"

Mildred could not help but laugh at this, the picture of herself chilling delicately on the kitchen linoleum, her trim feet pointing mutely at the ceiling. It would serve him right, she thought. It would make him wonder what she had been like inside. Aloud she said, "You've no faith in human beings. There's some good in everybody, Carrie. You've got to depend on the goodness of people."

"Somebody's depended on it once too often with that crew or they wouldn't be where they are," snapped Carrie. "Any of them got a ball and chain? Or strip-ed suits?"

Feeling ridiculous, Mildred peeked beyond the blue curtain again but it was too far and the sun was too bright to be sure. She thought there was one striped suit among them but it was hard to tell in the glare.

"What would it matter if there was?" she said.

"Those are the bad ones. The lifers. You watch out none of them breaks loose down there, Millie. They don't have anything to lose, those lifers."

"I've got a gun," said Mildred. "Now quit worrying." She didn't really know where George kept the gun or how it worked but it sounded good. It sounded important, like the things women said in movies.

But after she had hung up the telephone she went to the front doorway and stood there, shading her eyes to see if any of them were wearing the striped suits like Carrie said. It seemed to her now there were at least four of them, and perhaps another, almost out of sight. When she went inside her eyes were full of sun so that there were yellow splotches all across the room. I wish Carrie Nash had left well enough alone, she thought irritably. I've been doing fine all morning.

Mildred Stuart always said nobody had ever done her a real harm in her life—she'd never been robbed, for instance, and the time she'd lost her glasses in the store a clerk had kept them for her. It was all in the attitude you took toward people; if you naturally expected a man to stab you in the back, why, the knife was as good as in your ribs, she always said. That's what she taught Janet and Peter too, though George said it wasn't fair to them.

"What kids ought to learn in this world is to purely mind their own business," George was always saying. That was one thing you had to say for George. Except for the Oriental farmers, he was the greatest Own Business Minder in the world.

But that was typical of the way George was in everything. She'd read a sentence in a history book once that described George perfectly. "After the crisis is over," it said, "the farmer or peasant is the first to revert to conservatism." That was the kind of sentence Mildred liked, the kind that rolled richly off the tongue and sounded important by itself; that was the way she wanted to talk, so people would notice. Sometimes movie heroines talked that way when they were involved in great international movements. There were some of those sentences in the Psalms and in Isaiah and in a little book called *Famous Speeches* she had bought for Margaret. The Gettysburg Address had them, and Winston Churchill and some of the radio talks of Franklin Roosevelt. She certainly did miss Franklin Roosevelt; the others sounded like mandolins beside him.

But all this wasn't getting the day's work done and Mildred put it out of her mind. It was just that she got bored sometimes.

Upstairs Mildred cleaned the bathroom fixtures with her usual grimaces of disgust, leaving the room whitely sterile. It smelled like an operating chamber. Sometimes she stopped and looked on tiptoe out the small high window. The men were still working on the road; it seemed they had not moved an inch. She wondered if now and then one of them glanced calculatingly up the hill to where her trim house sat, measured the distance and took into account the honeysuckle mat between and the remnant of old stone wall that might have served as cover. This thought tugged at her mind until she kept going back to stare out nervously, half expecting to see a striped suit sprinting up the hill, the bullets kicking puffs of dust about the running feet.

I could kill Carrie Nash, thought Mildred impatiently. She's made me nervous.

She kept the radio going while she ate lunch, although this was no comfort to her. She kept leaving the table to glance out a front window, half afraid the broadcast might have covered the excitement of an escape so that the renegade might be already standing in her living room.

Lunch was tasteless; the toasted sandwiches sandpapered her gums, the cheese seemed rubbery, the coffee lingered on her tongue with a peculiar bitterness. When the telephone rang she clattered her coffee cup into the saucer and caught at her throat. Then she realized it must be Carrie again and composed herself to speak coolly. I won't have you frightening me, Carrie, she would say. I simply won't have it.

But when she lifted and spoke into the mouthpiece it was George's voice on the other end.

"Mildred? Is that you, Mildred?" George always opened his conversations this way, irritating her beyond endurance and tempting her to say no, it was Lana Turner or Amelia Earhart or Helen of Troy.

"Yes," she snapped impatiently. "It's me, George." Sometimes she had the feeling that if she should squat in the hall of an evening George would come through and drop his coat upon her without noticing. This thought made her especially angry with him and she sat at the phone with her face set.

"Look, I thought I'd get home early in the afternoon but Pat Walkins wants me to go by the county agent's office. They're giving away some experimental wheat to see if this section can make a crop."

Mildred experienced complete and overwhelming boredom, the way she nearly always did at George's progressive farming. "Oh," she said, almost contemptuously. "New wheat."

"You need anything from town?"

An armed guard, she thought irritably. The state militia. But aloud she said without much interest, "A box of aspirin. Oh, and buy me a magazine, will you?"

There was a silence that was calculated to give her time to take back this unreasonable request. George hated to buy magazines; drugstores were so cluttered, he said, that you were always expecting to knock things over. George was a fairly awkward man, with hands and feet that always seemed to be going out in all directions, and he generally did manage to upset something, looking woebegone about the whole business.

Finally, seeing she would not give in, he grunted, "What kind of magazine?"

She felt a glow of triumph. "Oh, movies I guess. Or one of the fashion magazines."

George did not exactly snort but Mildred was sure if he had not been at a public telephone he would surely have snorted. He was an expert at this noise; it always sounded like a mule drinking, having suddenly got water up his nostrils. It was, thought Mildred now, an exceedingly irritating sound and she waited for him to make it. As it was, she heard a faint and unmistakable sniffle.

"On second thought, bring both magazines," she said vengefully, and was about to hang up when she remembered the other thing. "They've got a chain gang working down on the road today," she said.

"That so? Needs it bad on that curve. Putting on shoulders, I expect."

"I expect so," said Mildred, and waited.

"Well, anything else?"

She could have throttled him with the telephone wire. "Nothing," she said dryly. "Not a thing, George. Enjoy your wheat seed." It sounded rather as if she were speaking to an out-of-sorts canary.

When they had hung up, Mildred sat for a few minutes eying the phone and reflecting on Carrie's suggestion that George might come home to find her cold and dead on the kitchen linoleum. He might, too, she thought with some satisfaction. How like him not to consider it, never to worry about her, always to take her for granted! She felt like a competent electrical system that warmed his bathwater, toasted his bread, kept his beer cold. He might open the fuse box if anything ceased to work, but normally he would bathe and munch toast and slurp beer and never notice it.

When she got back to the kitchen the coffee had gotten cold and she saw there were bread crumbs scattered all about her chair. I'll let it alone, she thought tiredly, until suppertime. The kids will be back here after school anyway.

It was the picture of Janet and Peter tracking in dust and banging the breadbox and rattling through the refrigerator that suggested to her the magnanimous gesture. The minute she thought of it Mildred was amazed it had taken her so long. It was the kind of thing Carrie Nash would say was typical of her ("Absolutely typical, my dear")—the complete vindication of her whole philosophy that no one would harm a person who had trusted him. (Here she recalled angrily that George was forever comparing this attitude to the old theory of staring a wild animal in the eye to avoid being bitten; and how this was probably all right if the animal had read the same book you had. She could remember George comparing the two completely unrelated things, just as he had that horrible afternoon to the vacuum cleaner salesman. And the salesman such a gentleman, too, and so complimentary— something George would never think of being. . . .)

Mildred broke off her thoughts and went back to the original inspiration. She would walk down to the highway herself (it was a public highway; there was nothing wrong in that) and she would nod and smile distantly the way she always did to working people, grocery boys and things. She might even, for good measure, seek out with her eyes the striped-suit men, looking at them compassionately and with understanding. It's all right, her eyes would tell them. I'm not afraid, you see.

She could almost picture the scene in the cell block (that was what they called them, wasn't it, cell blocks?) late that evening, the men nodding thoughtfully to one another and talking about the rather attractive mature woman who had passed them on the highway. "A real lady, she was," some of them would say respectfully, by their very tone making of her a symbol, a symbol of mercy and decency—all the values of a world they had by some lone act renounced. Perhaps then one of the men would begin to play some haunting tune on his harmonica and the prisoners would fall silent in their cells, lost in the thoughts that the unknown woman had called forth in them all. And there would be perhaps one sensitive-eyed young man who looked like Montgomery Clift; he would think of her long after that day had passed, he would be released, "go straight," build a whole new life around that momentary inspiration she had given him on a summer's day. When he was old he would say nostalgically to his children: "Once there was a lovely lady who believed in me . . ." and then he would let the sentence trail off, full of mystery and time and the faintest of perfumes. . . .

Mildred woke from her reverie with abruptness as she thought of still a further act of kindness she might do, something more she could give these men. She would speak to the foreman; she would tell him what a hot day it was; she would suggest that later in the afternoon he bring the men to her back porch for cold water. No, not just that, real ice water (she thought happily), with real ice floating in the tall glasses and tinkling from side to side in their grimy, respectful hands. How they would look at her then! As if she were a ministering angel from some better world.

She was so excited that her hands were trembling while she dressed—the crisp green skirt, the fresh blouse, a string of pearls clasped chastely at the neck. As an afterthought she added a white rose to her hair. Too frivolous, she wondered? But then a white rose was never actually frivolous; that was for scarlet and fuchsia flowers. A white rose was like the unattainable.

When she was through Mildred examined herself carefully in the mirror. A *young* thirty, she thought, hardly looking like the mother of two school-age children, the wife of a "college-trained" farmer. Indeed, she had once been told she had a mouth like Gene Tierney; she moved it back and forth in smiles and sneers into the glass. Again she touched with her fingertips the one white rose; yes, that was just right, that was absolutely the perfect touch.

Mildred had forgotten how hot it was outside until she stepped from the front door and the sun struck her whole body with the force of a physical blow. The faint touch of perspiration starting underneath the arms irritated her as though it were an insult; its presence was incongruous with the cool clothes, the flower in her hair. There was a wind blowing but it was as hot as sunlight; it was like the air that billows out of floor registers in the wintertime. She started from the house, feeling the wind and the crunch of dry grass underfoot and the pelting sunlight all as one sensation, some personal thing that was being done to her directly.

As she came down the hill and drew closer to where the men were working they began to watch her furtively, not lifting their heads. A thought struck her suddenly that was far more earthy than either the lady or the ministering angel: that perhaps they had not seen a woman in a long time, some of them for years. She became acutely conscious of the hot wind that was whipping her skirt between her legs, outlining her thighs sharply; she realized that the sun was behind her and everything must be transparent (the lacy nylon slip and the thin brassière and pants) so that all of them could see her—the swell of stomach and the curve of breast and the shadowy suggestion of nipple, navel, triangle.

Mildred almost turned and ran when a man detached himself from the group and stepped out toward her, until she saw the gun propped carelessly across his arm.

"Hello, ma'am," he said. He did not seem pleased to see her. It was all wasted on him, she thought, even the flower.

"Hello," she said pleasantly. "It's awfully hot down here."

The man didn't offer any answer to this, as if such an obvious remark was beneath his comment, and Mildred began to feel chastened. He thinks I have no business here, she thought.

After a pause she said rather coldly: "Are you in charge?"

"Yessum, I'm the guard." He smelled of beer and she reflected that he was just the kind of man to have a thermos of cold beer while the prisoners worked thirstily in the hot sun. All the time she stood there with him she was aware of their eyes stealthily upon her and almost involuntarily she threw back her head so that the wind could show her dark hair, the contrast of the rose; she tilted her chin so they could see the string of pearls and the Gene Tierney mouth. Then she did an amazing thing. She did it very quickly as if that would keep anyone from noticing it was deliberate, even herself; she spread her feet so that the skirt clung to her legs and rushed in billows in between her thighs. I won't be prudish, some corner of her mind said to some other corner. It's really an act of compassion.

To the guard, without any change in her tone, Mildred said: "I wanted to tell you to bring the men up to the house late in the afternoon. I'll have ice water on the back porch." She decided to make some concession to the man's vanity; people in his position were usually strong on vanity. "And a piece of cake for you," she added, glancing up at him.

She observed that the man was fat and gross; there was stubble all across his face and streaks of light and dark where sweat ran down and had been wiped. There was something faintly obscene about him, as if he had absorbed all the contamination from his charges so that it clung to him in dirt and fat and whiskers. Mildred thought for one minute the lips slid back on the soiled teeth in something that was very like a knowing grin, but it was gone too fast. She could not tell. I do not like this man, she thought sharply. I do not like anything about him.

Almost jovially (with a tone of familiarity?) he said to her, "Yes, ma'am," and nodded his head. "Yessum, we'll be pleased to come. It's mighty hot." He ran his eyes along her hip and into the curve of waist insolently, and her face hardened. "Mighty generous of you," he added slyly.

Mildred nodded coolly to him and moved back up the hill, feeling the eyes as hot upon her as the ends of cigarettes. There had been two, she thought with a delicious shiver; there had been two striped suits among them. The guard had stepped over to the men; she heard the whispering and talk; somebody snickered, like a little boy. It seemed to her she must make a handsome picture as she moved away—the sun falling brightly about her head, pinpointing the white-and-greenness of her for one instant on the long brown hill. She forced herself to walk slowly so all of them could see that she was not afraid.

Back in the comparative coolness of the house Mildred swept the kitchen floor like a careful hostess in anticipation of callers, checked the ice cubes and added some jars of water to the refrigerator shelves. The thought of what she had done filled her with youthful excitement, so that she hummed snatches of old songs she had not thought of in years. For a minute she stopped by the telephone, debating whether to call Carrie about it; then she realized how much better it would sound when they had come and gone and all the dirty glassware sat around the kitchen. It would have to be boiled, she supposed, all of it boiled after they had handled and drunk from it. Carrie would say how typical it was that Mildred should have done such a thing. "I should never have had the courage, you may be sure of that," Carrie would tell her admiringly.

Mildred felt quite exhilarated by the whole afternoon. Looking down the long hill now was like watching a group of acquaintances whom she was soon to know better. This sense of familiarity sent her back upstairs to see herself in the long, cool mirror; the rose had wilted and she cast it down, making a disappointed face. Perhaps it was better not to wear it for the second time. Perhaps it was better to leave that bare wisp of memory so they could argue about it later: "She had a flower in her hair, I'm sure of that."

"A flower, sure, a white one. I think it must have been a lily."

It seemed to Mildred that the waiting afternoon dragged by. She walked through the house nervously, poking at the unfrozen ice with an impatient finger, opening and closing the cabinet door where the glasses were. The jam-jar glasses would do, she thought, and the odd ones from a broken dime store set, and after that the ones someone had given her that had the rather hideous painted vines. They would none of them notice the glasses anyway; they would all want to remember how she herself had looked.

By three o'clock she was nervous. Perhaps after all this had been a very foolish thing; perhaps once they got near the house they would all unite, grab her as hostage, take her in a group to the woods back of the house and there shred her of her clothes, savagely, like men who have nothing to lose any more, like starved men taking the skin from oranges. Mildred cringed at the thought of herself in their midst, naked and afraid, the brutal hands that would touch her, twist her, bend her back. Her shoulders jerked as she ran to pull the curtains and look at the men working harmlessly in the sun, their minds busy with the Lord knew what unspeakable plans! And where was the gun; what had George done with the foolish gun?

Mildred felt quite faint with her terror. What had she done after all? It had been an insane gesture, a moment of madness that had come upon her when she stepped into the sun. For a minute she was almost convinced that the thought had never entered her head until she stepped into the yard and had some sort of blind attack that left her senseless in the heat.

Once she began to be afraid, the hours flew; the hands of the clock seemed to circle wildly before her eyes and the echo of one quarter hour striking would hardly die away before the next was starting. Like a death bell tolling, she thought nervously. Like the death bell in "Barbara Allen."

At five o'clock the men began to move and collect their tools. Mildred had been clenching her fists all during that last half hour, half believing the school bus would draw up in front of the house before they came and Peter and Janet would come clattering in ahead of them. She sat thinking all this and yet a little ashamed of her willingness to involve the children in her danger. I could still call Carrie, she thought frantically, but she made no move toward the phone.

When the men began finally to shuffle into an awkward line and the mustard-brown truck edged toward them down the highway (as if it had been waiting all this time drawn off the road somewhere), she gave up hoping for the school bus or for Carrie and went stiffly to the kitchen, where she stood against the refrigerator as if for a firing squad. They would be here in a minute, she thought; it would not take long, loading the truck and driving it up the narrow road and around the back yard to the porch, dropping the mesh door for the men to climb out. She pictured them riding up the hill, sitting quietly along the narrow benches like the carefully arranged dead, not saying anything or giving anything away, but locking eyes now and then, knowingly.

Mildred squared her shoulders, placed her palms against the coolness of the refrigerator. In a few minutes she would hear the wheezing of the motor as it brought them (the men in the striped suits) nearer to the house, nearer to where she waited. She closed her eyes in resignation, flattening her back to the door as though it were her marble slab.

She stood that way, waxen as a painted saint, for a few more minutes and then her eyes flew open and she was sharply aware of the silence about her. Even when she strained both her ears she could hear nothing but the buzzing of bees against the mat of honeysuckle in the yard and the closer hum of electric current at her back. She could not hear the truck coming at all, not even when she took a step forward and cocked her head.

In another minute she had walked to the back screen and from thence to a side window, and after that she ran through the house to the living room and flung the front door wide.

They were gone. The long brown hill stretched ahead of her to the deserted highway; there was not even a puff of dust to show where they had been or where the truck had passed. Unbelievingly she looked up the little road to her house, searched the trees for the outline of a sinister parked vehicle, looked for the blobs of stealthy men that might be anywhere, watching her.

But they were truly gone, the striped suits and the furtive glances and even the unshaven foreman—gone off in the truck without a word to her. She waited still another minute in case they had driven down the road for gasoline or turned the truck around, but when three shiny cars came round the curve and flickered brightly out of sight, she knew none of them were coming. They had all climbed into the truck in an orderly line and driven off and none of them were coming.

When she went back into the house Mildred slammed the door viciously behind her and stood motionless for an instant between the door and the faintly blowing curtains. She turned then on her heel and opened the door and slammed it a second time, louder than the first, so that the delicate china ash trays quivered on the coffee table and a magazine slithered to the rug. She said aloud: "The scum. The filthy scum."

After a while she worked purposefully through the house and back to the kitchen again, talking to herself. What could you expect from people like that? If they were decent they wouldn't be where they were, would they? She thought for one wild moment she might burst into outraged tears, like a teen-ager cheated out of a party.

But by the time Janet and Peter came in from school she was much calmer. She didn't say anything about it to the children. As for them, they were too busy eating peanut-butter cake to see the ice cubes melting in the sink.

ALL THAT
GLISTERS
ISN'T GOLD

When I was a little girl, before the term "babysitter" had been invented, I used to stay with Miss Carrie whenever my parents were going places. Now that I think about it, I wonder where they went and what they did—but I never wondered then. Certain days I would be taken to Miss Carrie's house on Ingram Street. About the time all the possibilities of her house, yard, and possessions had been exhausted, my mother would arrive to take me home.

There was an odor in Miss Carrie's house, hard to identify. If you put your face close to a plate of cold leftover biscuits and breathed in deeply . . . Not exactly that odor, but it would be close enough. When I came home I would stand in the hall and try to discover the smell of my own house, but I never could.

With Miss Carrie lived her twenty-three-year-old nephew Granville, whom she had reared like a son for family reasons. Miss Carrie worried about Granville, who had gone off to the university in Chapel Hill and learned to be an atheist. She worried out loud and in his presence. I worried silently, because I loved Granville and I wasn't sure love was permitted atheists.

All the time Granville kept arguing religion with my mother and his Aunt Carrie. Anybody could tell by their voices his arguments were better than theirs.

My mother might say, her tone defensive, "You been to college and can *talk* good, but the Lord looketh on the inner man!"

The talk would go on and on: Granville speaking and explaining and making his points, and my mother quoting. And Granville asking long, serious, involved questions; and my mother reciting.

If Granville was uptown in his new insurance office, my mother would comfort Miss Carrie and give her advice. "Don't you argue with Granville your own self. You let the Lord do that. That's why we've got Scripture."

I lay on my stomach under the bed. Even the dust on the linoleum was cold.

"I want you to know, even a little child can ask some hard questions!" my mother sighed. I smiled proudly and let my finger travel the long closing spiral of the bedspring overhead.

It was not necessary that I listen to Mother's side of these planning sessions with Miss Carrie. Long since I'd heard all these things. By now I could say great chunks of catechism and memory work, could duplicate my mother's faith in the mirror of repetition. I had been taught all the references available to doubters. I knew the way to open a good Christian discussion with any atheist was to announce, "In the beginning was the Word, and the Word was with God, and the Word . . ." Some days I hoped this made more sense to atheists than it did to me.

So it was not necessary that I listen to the two women as they ran through their review, in preparation for Granville's test. Those words lay in me so precise and long familiar I never thought of them any more than I noticed my fingernails. I found a hairpin under the bed and began to scrape old dirt from between the boards in the corner.

I knew everything my mother and Miss Carrie would say; but where did Granville learn *his* words? In what class had those strange verses been taught? Sharp words, hostile ones, words that built up some sort of idea tower and then toppled it down like

Babel, keen words—yet for all their edge they fell from him lightly, as if it were not hard work to blaspheme.

Each of his words was like a splinter and each slid invisibly inside me. There was a sore spot wherever one had penetrated; soon there were bruises all over my religion it was not safe to touch. I preferred the soreness from those splinters to the painful operation of having them removed.

My mother sometimes complained that if Granville was home when I spent the day at Miss Carrie's I later had a restless night and tended to fever; but I think she only said this so she could add, obliquely, "By their fruits ye shall know them." And nudge my daddy, who was Granville's friend.

Whenever my mother brought me to Miss Carrie's we usually found her sitting in an armless rocker on her front porch, behind a jungle of fern and geranium plants. Neither my parents nor Granville nor Miss Carrie owned an automobile, so it always seemed to be summer when we set out on foot for the three blocks to her house on Ingram Street. Miss Carrie owned seventeen fat clay pots of geraniums and eight more of fern which she kept on her porch from April to October. Every bright day these were moved off their regular shelves onto the steps and along the front railing to catch the sunlight, and twice a day each was watered out of an antique blue cream pitcher which held just the right amount. Twenty-five trips old Miss Carrie made from her kitchen night and morning, rather than bring out one big bucket to dip from. It made her appreciate things, she said.

Miss Carrie would part the fern fronds as we came up her walk and say with surprise, "Now look who's here!" even though everything had been prearranged.

Courtesy required that my mother sit on the porch awhile with Miss Carrie. She figured this into her schedule before we set out from home—how long to walk, how long to sit and talk. A hundred times now she repeated to me the rules of good behavior she had already told me on the way, while exchanging news with Miss Carrie and admiring the ferns. I rolled around on the front yard's mounds of summer grass with its texture of pine needles, never mowed, which simply grew longer and tougher and leaned over and covered the ground in lumps. Sometimes Miss Carrie would lead her old cow up from the barn and stake her in the front yard. You could hear front doors slamming up and down the whole block of Ingram Street.

At last Mother would leave and I would move to the porch steps and hand Miss Carrie her spit can each time the snuff juice swelled too far, and pretend to listen while she complained about the neighbors behind those closed front doors. Miss Carrie did not get along with any of her neighbors. To hear her tell it, it was rotten luck the only nice people in town lived along different streets. All this was ritual and never varied.

Finally she'd say, "Want something to eat?" She emptied her mouth into the can, spilling some down the red tomato label. And we would go inside.

First I took a deep breath of that biscuit odor, then peeked left into the front room, where I was never allowed to play. That room was dark—dust motes ascended and descended before its only window—and on the floor was a mustard-colored fabric rug instead of the usual linoleum. There was one worn sofa which my daddy said had been manufactured without any springs in the seat.

In one far corner stood a huge roll-top desk, always closed and locked. My daddy said Yes, that wooden part would really roll up out of sight, but I didn't see how there was room. A floor lamp with a fringed shade was placed near the desk, and in the other far corner leaned a single crutch—just the lone crutch. Every time I passed the door into the front room, I watched for it. ("Granville borrowed that once, I think," Miss Carrie once answered me. What kind of sense did that make?)

Last of all, beside the hard sofa there was some stringed instrument. I think it must have been a mandolin; and yet how in the world could it have been a mandolin! Like everything else in the room, whatever-that-was could never be touched. I always had to see it from the hall. I never heard it make a tune.

Past that door and down the hall we went into the back room where all the living and eating were done. Here Miss Carrie and I ate bread and milk off an enormous oval table, saying nothing. Then I would be sent outdoors to play.

What Miss Carrie called "play" was work for me, since each time I came I cleaned out the lily pond beside her house. Probably she never knew I cleaned it. The routine was a game and a self-imposed duty. I itched to get the bread and milk swallowed and run out to the pond.

It was really no pond, only a big barrel buried in the ground with rocks heaped around its rim. The water which filled it to the edge was rank and stagnant and crowded with rotting lily pads. Around the edge, like a layer of paint, was a green scum which sometimes bubbled.

The pond had been lost until the first time I came to visit Miss Carrie. It had entirely vanished under a matting of vines and weeds and old lilies. I would never have guessed a pool was there had she not shown me the place. "Don't fall in there," she called in her cracked voice. I poked through the leafy net and my fingers fell into the shock of cold water.

"Used to fish," said Miss Carrie. "Kept my minnows there."

I knew it was impossible she had ever been young enough to *fish!* But, after the first discovery, the deserted pond was mine. Between visits it would often grow shut again, and I would have to feel among ivy and honeysuckle for the stones and the sharp edge of the buried barrel. The hottest summer sun failed to reach this place. Privet hedge on one side had grown thick and tall as the eaves of the house. There were trees and shrubs-which-had-turned-to-trees crowded on the other side.

On nearly every visit I had to twist off vines or bite them free with my teeth until I could locate the top of the pond, then pull up those lilies turning brown or which I thought had lived long enough. Very rarely one of them would bloom and float on the dark water like a boat which had been carved out of a white star. This one and surviving lilies for which I still had blooming hopes would be held back while with the edge of one hand I skimmed off the green scum and wiped it onto the grass. I can close my eyes now and be there again—leaves making a dapple of black shade and gray shade across my wrists. My fingers remember how the stem of the lily gives and pops off underwater; it comes up slow and brown and slimy. I can still feel the ridge that top stave of the sunken barrel left on one palm and the patch of slicky scum on the other. All that—and yet I cannot remember hearing the song of a single bird.

Not until the day waned and it grew too dark to see was I called indoors and fed and, if my parents were expected late, put straightaway to bed on a fat feather mattress in Miss Carrie's room.

Sleep was not possible in that room, because of the wall curtains which lined it, and menaced and moved on all sides. It was like being Jack in Beanstalk Land, hidden in the folds of the giant's kimono.

Suspended from the top molding a foot below the ceiling, there was a high wooden shelf around all four walls, even across the windows. On the edge of that shelf old bedspreads of varying colors and patterns had been tacked like tent hangings. These reached from the molding to the floor. Miss Carrie's clothes, and Heaven knows *what* else, were stored behind these curtains, which billowed and swung so you could never predict where the next suspicious ripple would occur, or what unseen Thing set all that cloth in motion.

And on top of that high shelf just under the ceiling stood a thousand boxes—hat boxes, greeting-card boxes, corrugated boxes, suitcases, and one fine row of baskets. Could they have been sewing baskets? There were perhaps thirty of these in all shapes and colors and, like the mandolin, they were never to be touched. I wanted to feel their surfaces, terribly, but there was no way to reach that high shelf even with a broom handle. Miss Carrie had grown too old to go up the ladder and sometimes Granville would help her get something down, she said. Some baskets were woven in a round shape; one was an octagon with an amber handle; and the one I especially remember—brown and yellow— was formed in the shape of a castle-house, and little roofed towers lifted up on compartments while one entire golden wing was hinged to open out in another direction. I lay there wondering what was inside that row of baskets.

Struck wide-eyed and sleepless within four walls which breathed in the slightest air, sunk helplessly in the quicksand of that unfamiliar featherbed, I would lie tensely in the growing dark. Under my stare the baskets grew dimmer and dimmer and less believable. Sometimes they began to float before my mother's voice was heard in that house.

At the sound of her words and Miss Carrie answering, I always dropped instantly into relieved sleep. When next I came groggily awake Miss Carrie would be saying how good I had been and Mother, smiling, would whisper softly above the pillow that the sleep of the innocent was a wonderful thing.

Ingram Street was four city blocks of neat brick homes, except for Miss Carrie's. Her house was old-fashioned, had once been painted yellow, and was peeling. In front of the brick houses grew thin borders of thrift and candytuft and bulbs and spreading juniper. At Miss Carrie's the privet was shading her neighbors' flowers, and she tied a cow in the yard to crop the grass. The neighbors owned Scottie terriers and Siamese cats. Miss Carrie kept scrawny chickens who didn't mind plopping manure on sidewalks, or flapping to the edge of garbage cans to see what inside was still edible. Walking the three blocks to Miss Carrie's was like a stroll through the twentieth century; then, like a hole in time, you stepped down fifty years right at Miss Carrie's yard, and at the next house you could step back up into urban life. Daddy said half the city regulations on cows and indoor plumbing were finally started by Miss Carrie's neighbors, which may explain why she disliked them so much.

Next to her neighbor's brick garage was her rickety woodshed where pine slabs were stored for the kitchen stove. Another small building held kindling and corncobs, and beyond them both was her outhouse.

It was hard on Granville to live with an old aunt who still used an outdoor toilet. The summer between his junior and senior college years, he worked in the cotton gin to pay for plumbing, only to have Miss Carrie use that money for his tuition in the fall. He never brought any of his university friends home with him, or later his business friends, fearing they might need to go to the bathroom while they were there. ("So let them go!" cried Miss Carrie. "Damned if I will," said Granville.) Worse, he would never bring home prospective sweethearts to be inspected for the same reason. ("Your schooling has ruint you in more ways than one!" she complained. "What's *your* excuse?" he parried.)

The only time I ever heard Granville offer an argument that didn't fit the case had something to do with the outhouse. They had been fighting over flesh and spirit. He told her about brains and neurons and how Pavlov trained dogs. She started out with the soul, and said from the book of Job, "There is a spirit in man." At this he gave a sudden yell that if Aunt Carrie *really* believed man had a soul she would put a bathroom in that house. The whole thing upset Miss Carrie "pretty bad," she told my mother. It took them an hour to talk it over.

Besides the outhouse and those other buildings there were: fences, barn and barnyard, vegetable garden, stable, watering trough, twelve hens, an unpopular stray cat who bit the Siamese and—from time to time—kittens with odd colors in their fur. Miss Carrie's house was not unlike my buried pond; if you didn't know what was there you might trip at the edge of her yard and fall into an unexpected rural world.

It was the wrong world for Granville, who had been in a library he said was the size of the town hotel. But it was right for

Miss Carrie. Even the skinny chickens and the cat with one tattered ear seemed tailored to match her bent form and her snuff-smeared chin.

For Miss Carrie was ugly. I wasn't allowed to say this, but any eyeball could tell it. Her hair, which had once been red, was now red and brown and gray mixed, wadded behind in a stingy knot that wouldn't hold it all. Always her neck was full of the mottled stuff.

In her youth, too, Miss Carrie had been freckled. Now her face had fallen in wrinkles so that freckles and liver spots were trapped inside the folds. A shift of her face and some new blemish sprang suddenly into view while another slipped out of sight.

She was a small woman, not much bigger than I, and rheumatism had twisted her a little to one side. Grim glasses with steel edges rested on the tip of her nose, where they wouldn't inconvenience her vision. The color of her eyes was the color of worn mahogany; sometimes I thought the wet snuff had permeated them. And her walk was rapid, half scrabbling to incorporate that lopsided lurch into her gait. Miss Carrie was ugly, and the first time I saw her I maybe was afraid. I can't remember the first time.

Yet I loved Miss Carrie. She refused to play games. She would not converse except on matters which interested her and bewildered me. She seldom gave presents, and then they were the sort of thing a child dislikes—one breadplate ringed around in gold script, "Give us this day our daily bread," which I was to save against the day of my marriage. She did not even believe that I would grow up to be an artist and never marry. When I spun out my future in a shining web her thoughts were on milking time.

What did I love in her then?

Her love for me.

Because I *pleased* her—though she never said so. She did not hear a single important word I spoke, but she did listen to the general sound of me. Discolored by snuff and spit, her grin was approving. She allowed me to water her potted plants with that cream pitcher which was a hundred years old; nobody had ever trusted me that much before, and not a whole lot have since.

I never thought twice about her loving me, about deserving it or returning it or being especially obedient because of it. Love was simply mixed into those days the way that biscuit odor lay in the rooms of the house. You forgot to notice. Nostril and heart, having once put the thing on record, moved on to something else.

Some days I was with Miss Carrie for milking time, and through the barnyard we went together, I a stealthy mimic coming behind her, playing at being old, playing at being ugly—neither of which I ever thought possible for me to be.

Inside the stall, Miss Carrie would halfway crumple under the cow. It was the only way she could manage, folding down first and easing up again to the level of the stool. Her dress tail dragged in manure. It was embarrassing. I didn't feel like imitating that.

In the house again with a pail of warm milk, we waited for Granville. Since he had earned his degree from Chapel Hill and nailed it over that roll-top desk in the front room, he ran an insurance office and turned his money over to Miss Carrie, who kept feeding it to banks.

("People sell insurance that never go to college," my mother said. "I can't see it helped him much."

"He ain't working in a cotton mill like me," growled my daddy.)

"Aunt Carrie?"

We heard the front door bang and his steps, as even as a march, came down the hall.

"Back porch!" she'd scream. Even when Miss Carrie smiled her voice was sharp and loud and kept a whine in it. Thinking back, I suppose she talked through her nose. All I heard then was the ugliness, another example of how I would never sound.

Granville patted her on the back—I never saw them kiss—and crowed something crazy at me and lifted me onto his shoulders where I could enjoy his beautiful hair. Granville's black hair was curly, almost kinky. Thrust one finger into it and a strand twined up like living ivy.

("Makes you wonder about that family tree," my mother said. "His papa *did* leave her, and they gave Miss Carrie the boy."

"I reckon you think that would explain everything," answered my daddy.)

Granville chuckled when I pushed all my fingers into his hair. My hands were tied to his scalp with wire. "Punkin, what you been into today?" Granville took nibbles from my kneecaps. I clamped them tight to choke him and he bent forward as if to throw me over.

"Don't hurt her!" said Miss Carrie. "Granville, I'm leaving cold supper in the safe for you two so I can get to prayer meeting. Her mama's coming about seven-thirty."

My knees could feel vibrations in his throat. Granville was grinding his teeth. It angered him that Miss Carrie would struggle like a grasshopper the five blocks to the church, people out in the cool of the evening watching her pass, feeling sorry for her. Granville thought she blamed him for the lack of a car the way he blamed her for the outhouse.

"You could miss prayer meeting one Wednesday night," he complained. "Something good on the radio tonight."

She put her apron away and went to her bedroom, to get something from behind those throbbing walls or out of the castle basket.

We were eating on the oilcloth in the kitchen when Miss Carrie came out, unchanged except for a black straw hat with spindly bunches of lilac around the crown, her dress tail still damp where she had scrubbed briefly at stains from the barn. Maybe she had rinsed her mouth of snuff. No more.

She said politely, "Now you come back, honey. Tell your mama I enjoyed having you." She said, "Guess you don't want to come along, Granville?"

Then we could hear the sound of her sensible shoes, hitting out of rhythm, *hard*-soft, *hard*-soft, down the hall, past that doorway showing the crutch and the mandolin, past the geraniums and ferns. Gone.

Granville pushed food into an angry face. I intended to be tactful and not talk but there was so much to tell him—a movie where hands came out of a bedroom wall where a beautiful girl was sleeping, dirt daubers under the front steps; and this scratch, right here on the arm—would I get lockjaw?

Interesting, he said. Fine, he said. No.

Absently he mangled the last biscuit in his fingers. Then he looked down at the plate of cold crumbs and said one of those swear words they had taught him at Chapel Hill.

I was glad when Mama came.

My daddy liked Granville. He would not side with Granville against my mother and Miss Carrie, but sometimes he would wink or hold his thumb up or down in the air beyond their view. Five years back he had spent two days at the university as Granville's guest. My daddy had started working in the textile mill before he ever finished high school; he couldn't get over that place in Chapel Hill—all that land and those big buildings. And not a factory, not a place where you could hold some finished product in your hand. There was no way to tell whether a college was failing or succeeding, my daddy said. It must be happening around you on all sides, success or failure; but it would be years before anybody knew which.

I can imagine his telling this to Granville and Granville saying, "You mean the utilitarian aspects are long range," and Daddy scowling, "That's what I said, ain't it?"

From that one visit to the state university, Daddy brought home a stack of small picture cards of campus scenes, each not much bigger than a postage stamp, and stacked in a tiny wooden box. Later he gave the set to me. On rainy days we shuffled through the library, the administration building, the old well, the stadium, the science lab. He showed which buildings he had gone inside with Granville.

"Someday you might go to college," he'd say wistfully. "When my ship comes in."

During the August I was eight years old Mama spent a day with her sick sister, so my daddy walked with me to Miss Carrie's, where I was to stay till his shift was over at the mill. I didn't much want to go.

"You're mighty quiet."

I said I was counting how many steps it took to get from our house to Miss Carrie's. That was true, but mostly I didn't want my feet to take those steps at all. I wanted Miss Carrie and Granville to be right about everything from prayer meeting on up and down. If they couldn't both be right, I'd rather stay home than sit by that pond and wonder which was more right than the other.

Daddy looked at me hard but he didn't speak again till we were nearly there. "Watch for a surprise today," he said. He sounded nervous.

"Something from Mama?"

He was hasty in eliminating hope of any gift when she came home from her sister's. "Nothing like that. Something new at Miss Carrie's. Something you won't expect to see."

I couldn't imagine. Miss Carrie never bought anything. Even the hat with the lilacs was an old one of my mother's. Granville had built the radio out of three used sets he got for nothing.

I thought Miss Carrie might have proved she owned a soul by installing the indoor plumbing at last. Since I preferred the outhouse and the thrill of wondering if the granddaddy longlegs would make his stilting march across my bare toes, I didn't much favor that bathroom. But I did want the arguments to end. If Miss Carrie had put in a toilet, I would have to start brushing my teeth at her house.

Miss Carrie was waiting, as usual, on her porch, fanning with the *Sunday School Journal*. As Mama's substitute, my daddy went through a feeble form of the talk ritual. I had my glass of milk with cornbread crumbled into it. Then I went outdoors, enjoying the mock resignation of the task of cleaning the pond again.

I stopped so suddenly one foot hung in the air and I nearly fell. This time the undergrowth had been chopped back and there were branches and lengths of vine turning brown in piles around the yard. Dead leaves had been raked away. The water in the pond had been opened up to the sky like a mouth, and although it was still dirty a nearby hose hinted that fresh water had been added— an improvement I had never thought of making and now resented.

I began to quiver from rage. Which of them . . . which of them had dared . . . Was it Granville or Miss Carrie who, after years of neglect, now came tramping into my place and stole my work and—by making it neat at last—killed all the joy forever?

I grabbed a rock to throw and shatter what they had done, and then something flashed. A mirror moved inside the pond, or else light was shining all the way up from China through a chink in that inverted floor. I lowered the rock and got on all fours. My nose nearly touched the water. Suddenly the surface folded up once on itself and a bubble came to the top and paused and broke; and I saw the goldfish.

He was black and orange, a parody of a tiger. He flicked away under a lily pad and waited, then darted across to another.

I saw then a box left conveniently near the pond full of crumbs and oatmeal, and I scattered these with a gesture of spread fingers, the way God must have thrown forth a solar system onto the night.

The long August afternoon I hovered over the pond till my knees ached, watching that elusive fish, sometimes losing him in shadow and having him found again by a glint of sunlight. He would arch upward to gobble and dive again, swimming at the food in a pattern of arrowheads. Large bread chunks he dragged underneath to separate; others he gulped whole. He seemed to vanish and reappear, like a light going on, going off: Here, gone. There, gone.

Once and for all I wanted to prove whether eyes located on each side of the tiny head could really see me dead ahead, and I kept wagging my body trying to stand in the very center. Each time I froze in the proper place he disappeared and took the perspective with him. Once he brushed ever so lightly against my dangling thumb and I drew it out in wonder and held it, wet and still tingling, in the warm place underneath my chin.

The times I could see him I gave myself over to the delight of seeing him, but when he dived into the dark I worried. Whose handiwork was the goldfish? I tried to touch his fin and he thrust himself to the depths. Who had surprised me with this splendid lighted thing?

It was Granville, of course. It was typical of Granville, his pockets heavy with chewing gum, his head of hair growing into a private game. Once he had taken me to the circus and paid for everything. It had to be Granville who had cleaned the pond and hid the golden fish for me.

The fish shot to the top and rode across it almost like a boat, slicing the water with a transparent tail. I reached for him and he swam to China.

No, no, it had to be Miss Carrie who had fixed the pond. She was the one who knew about it, had once kept minnows there. She had described the dangers of drowning, while Granville had never said a word. And wasn't it Miss Carrie who liked animals— her cow, those chickens, the scarred cat?

Now that I thought about it, she had even hinted. With my own ears, just as we came up the walk that day, I had heard her tell Daddy she was fanning with the *Sunday School Journal,* having just read the lesson on "fishers of men." There! Wasn't that a clue? Wasn't she telling me then?

No, it had to be Granville. He loved surprises. At the circus he once bought six boxes of Cracker Jack just to get the little toys. So it had to be Granville, even if he didn't own a car to drive Miss Carrie to prayer meeting. Yet wasn't it bound to be Miss Carrie who had given this gleaming fish, even if she wouldn't put a bathroom in the house?

I knew it was one of them but not both who had put this brightness in my pool. And I couldn't choose. I wanted it to be both. If Granville had only cleared the underbrush . . . if Miss Carrie had only slipped the fish into the water . . .

I did not believe it had been both of them together, yet it had to be nothing less.

Not until they called me twice would I go indoors. I said nothing about that fish wearing its colors of Halloween. Eating in silence I would not mention the underbrush cleared or the water made pure in my pool, or the long afternoon I had spent trying to catch on my fingers that flying piece of light beneath the surface.

Behind the tumbler of milk I watched them. I waited for one to say, "How did you like my fish?" I waited for one to confess and one to be silent.

Both Granville and Miss Carrie looked tickled and secretive. The one who had given the fish had clearly told the other; but which was which? *Oh, let it be both!* I thought, but I knew it was not.

We finished the apple dumpling. Miss Carrie cleared the table. She and Granville had begun to look bewildered, worried, at last a little hurt. Eyebrows were raised over my head and shoulders were shrugged. Still I would say nothing. I kept the fish inside me where it burned and shone, but I never looked directly into the face of Granville or Miss Carrie for fear of dividing them one from the other, forever.

At last my daddy came to take me home. He could tell something was wrong.

Usually I liked to walk home after dark and see how things changed when the light went out of the world, but tonight I hurried. He asked, "What was the surprise?"

I answered that they—yes, I said *they*—had cleaned out the pond. That's all I told him. Once he glanced back toward the lighted windows. Were the lights shining in Miss Carrie's room or in Granville's? I wouldn't turn my head. We walked home without much conversation.

When next I went to Miss Carrie's I couldn't find the goldfish anywhere, and although the vines were growing back over the water none of my fingers cared any more. I didn't even play there, and I didn't ask a word about the fish. I guess it died.

CAREFUL,
SHARP EGGS
UNDERFOOT

The long strip of white fabric, like a giant's bandage, was stretched high across the town square. It moved slightly, not from any breeze but because it rode on layers of heat waves rising off the cracked asphalt street.

Every time he drove his car under that banner, Wink Thomas swore he would not read it again, but each time his mind recaptured the words no matter where he sent his eye to look. In crooked red capitals the sign said, AIN'T NOBODY HERE BUT US CHICKENS.

Thomas groaned at it anew, stamped the accelerator and shot beneath the banner and into his usual Main Street parking place. Daily he fitted his car into an invisible rectangle at the right curb, where all painted guide lines had long since worn away, and he prided himself on parking precisely in the same spot every morning. If the area was measured, Wink Thomas thought, it wouldn't vary two inches from day to day.

Locking the car, he walked past the grimy plate-glass windows of what had once been Main Street Grocery & Notions, and was now his law office. His image there was powdered with dust and he stopped to frown at the dim reflection of his face—eyes, a mouth; the rest was blurred. Below that his body fell, almost crashed, down the curve where a once husky chest was suspended below his belt. He looked his fifty-eight years, and the summer heat had already wilted his suit and wet his thin hair.

He wiped the dust from black lettering on the glass door. This he did read, looking for flaws. WRISTON PEALE THOMAS, JR. ATTORNEY AT LAW. PRESIDENT, PARSONVILLE CHAMBER OF COMMERCE. STATE SENATOR, 1938–40. NOTARY PUBLIC.

He shook his head. No, he still couldn't see what his daughter found wrong in all that information on his door. "Some people wouldn't *know*," he argued aloud now, and went in and spoke "Good Morning" to Miss Ida Kay King at the front desk.

"Another scorcher," Miss King said without looking up from her novel.

Wink agreed that this summer was hotter than last, quoted the weather predictions from the car radio, and complained about the humidity. She was no longer listening. With a forefinger enclosed in a coating of lotion and tipped with pink polish, she turned another page. For the hundredth time, he almost asked her to leave those library books at home. For the hundred-and-first time he decided against it, opened the gate in the low railing behind her desk and sat down at his own.

Wink Thomas didn't know why he persisted in calling that thing a railing, as if it were cousin to those polished ones dividing federal courtrooms. Everybody in town knew it was only the porch banister off the decaying old Richards house, and half the male population of Parsonville could still find the initials they had carved on it as boys. He used it now as a shelf for sorting half a dozen letters.

Miss Ida Kay King said, "It's Egg Day tomorrow."

"I know it. I know it." He hated Egg Day. "Phone calls this morning?"

"None," she said crisply. She was a woman of few words, chiefly because her new dentures hurt and she preferred to let her tongue lie slack between cheeks slightly puffed out like a couple of air cushions.

There were seldom many telephone calls, except that time last summer when the banner above the square had read discreetly, PARSONVILLE EGG FESTIVAL. All that week the sign had stirred citizens to call him and argue the old question about the town's name. Some said it was really Parsonsville, after old Nello Parsons who had built its first house and let his chickens roost in the chinaberry trees; but others claimed there never had been an extra *s* and the banner was correct as it stood. Or as it floated.

The jangling telephone and the mixed history and argument had so worn him out that this year, when the midsummer week came for honoring the town's only industry—poultry raising—with picnics and events, Wink had appointed a committee to hang a new banner over Main Street.

Well, he had only gotten what he deserved, trusting the job to somebody else. He understood that, in private, they had even called themselves the Cluck Committee. No wonder the current banner became a joke. Was it the county farm agent, who, at thirty-six, still wore his hair in a crew cut, who had swayed the others to this silliness? And helped them hang it, at night, in a mood he could only describe as anger?

All Thomas prayed now was that nobody he had ever known in the North Carolina Senate would pick this week to drive through Parsonville, at least not before Saturday, when he could take the thing down and burn it.

Thomas hung his coat across his chair. "Did you hear me say it was going to be a hundred degrees today?"

"Yes," said Miss Ida Kay King. She refilled her mouth with air, trying to give her gums the illusion false teeth were merely floating lightly in her mouth. Besides, she hated to interrupt her book about plantations, lusty octoroons, and dueling pistols fired through curtains of Spanish moss.

He threw away a notice about the County Democratic Rally and Barbecue in Roxton. It angered him to go for any reason to Roxton, with its lace factory and trucking concern. Roxton was a regular stop for all the trains on the north-south line. The county fair was always held in Roxton, which had good schools and the

only hospital for miles. He thought of the county as of a young
tree: Roxton was the leader, the main stem, while Parsonville
shriveled for lack of nourishment. And, in time, they will prune
us. The state and the nation will chop us off for compost, he
thought. He made a note of that in case he should be asked to
speak at the service Sunday, honoring the city's founders and early
settlers.

That made him think of tomorrow's duties. "Have the eggs
come?"

She pointed. On his side of the railing was a small wooden keg
brimming with eggs in all shades of cream and tan. Small eggs,
of course. No need to waste what might be good for market.

"Teed Kiser brought 'em in early this morning," said Miss
King. Regretfully she closed the book on her thumb and fixed her
mind on musk and verbena. That's how book people smelled on an
August day, back in the *real* South. Musk and verbena. She came
back to Parsonville with a jolt and found her armpits damp and the
glare off Main Street painful against her bifocal glasses. "Half of
the barrel," she said, "must be nest eggs for Teed's setting hens.
Be sure not to drop one with an *x* marked on it."

He could see a few penciled crosses from where he sat. "I've
never dropped one."

"Some of those eggs must be older than I am."

I doubt that, he thought but did not say. Miss Ida Kay King
had been his father's secretary and the veins ran in her skin like
swollen rivers down the globe. Her face was the color of gray
granite and like granite it had merely eroded with time. There was
no break in her anywhere; she was compacted by her age. On
that stony surface rode layers of powder, rouge, lotion, cream; and
they counted for no more than a dust mote on the side of a mountain. And at its peak, rising cone-shaped on her skull, round piles
of gray hair grew in clusters like lichen on a stone.

Thomas took off his tie and let it droop across one shoulder.
"Collection letters?"

"Sent them out Monday." She opened her book again, waited,

and then returned to a land of gallantry and high-spirited horses. Irritably he tagged her "Miss Scarlett O'Hara of 1889."

But he was silent, suddenly depressed that the letters had been mailed and now the day, and even the week, arched round him like a shell with its contents already blown out through the other side. Collection letters on behalf of furniture stores in Charlotte and Greensboro *were* his week's work, although he knew how few Parsonville people really understood their references to payments and signed contracts. He felt about debt the way he felt about capital punishment: the jury who said "Guilty" ought to pull the cyanide switch, and the manager who bragged on his sofa ought to go collect for it, and look into that pitiful living room where the foam rubber stood, well tended, under the tinsel sign, GOD BLESS OUR HOME.

After Egg Day ceremony tomorrow, a few chicken farmers might amble into his law office, and take up an hour apiece talking about how the government kept dumping eggs into the Potomac until all the fish between Washington and the sea grew fat— indirectly off the expensive feed thrown down right here in Parsonville before these very hens.

At the end of that ritual there would be a dollar bill or two, stacks of damp quarters, a tiny trickle of soiled money like the drop of water the wicked rich man begged Lazarus to bring to Hell and lay upon his burning tongue. Those bits of money would never quench so much consuming debt, and there would be stronger demand letters and repossessions. Thus, with a rare title to search or a will to write, another whole year would slide by, and there would be a new banner sewed from bed sheets and lettered with house paint, hung quivering in the heat of next August.

He talked now in a search for friction, anything to impede how slippery time was.

"Didn't see you last night at the sack race, Miss Ida Kay."

"Too hot."

It had been hot, and he still felt heavy from the picnic afterward: rows of cakes yellow and sad under seas of seven-minute icing, lukewarm custards, deviled eggs, chicken salad, broth and dumplings, egg-salad sandwiches, fried chicken, puddings under towers of scorched meringue, gumbo and giblet gravy, pot pie and chicken croquettes; and, at the end of the eating, bushel baskets full of drumsticks for the dogs to crunch and get hung halfway in their throats.

Hens and eggs—he was sick of them. He would have liked to march back through history and locate the first man who ever said, "Make the most of what you have," and beat him to death.

His daughter Sherrilee came into the office, squeezed a smile from Miss King, and swung across the banister to him in a pink whirl of skirt and lace petticoat.

"Place looks like a ghost town," she said. "And your office isn't much better."

His daughter's body seemed to move to a music he could not hear. He watched her turn gracefully and sit on the edge of his desk. "Hello, Ducky."

Her voice was irritable. "Don't call me that!"

Sometimes he felt they were changing her over at that Greensboro Woman's College, pulling her loose from him, while he paid with tuition and taxes for their end of the tug-of-war. He felt like writing somebody a letter about it.

"It's a good nickname for you," was all he said. "As good as the day it was given."

"Yes, yes."

He saw she was annoyed. To Miss Ida Kay he called, "I ever tell you how I gave Sherrilee that name?"

Patiently she closed her book and waited behind glazed eyes. Sherrilee (*that* name had been her mother's idea) snapped, "A hundred times!"

He went on with it anyway. "The day I first heard Marva and I were going to have a baby, I'd been duck hunting down east. . . ."

("A thousand times, maybe," Sherrilee said toward Miss Ida Kay.)

"With Harvey Leamon—you remember him? Had a feed store down the street. Fell over with a heart attack taking up church collection. And Pete Willett went, you know? It was 1942 and he was home on furlough. Died later in the war."

"Daddy!" she groaned. She walked over to a chair and sat in it. He half thought her bones were made of perfume.

"Anyway, I came in that night and Marva had been to the doctor. My head was full of those wild ducks. Like women, they moved all of a piece."

Seeing they looked puzzled, he spread his hands into false wings to demonstrate. "Ducks don't exactly *turn* in flight. . . . I thought then it was more that they had swayed a little and leaned into a new course. It seemed to me they fly in air the way fish swim in water. Ever been duck hunting, Miss Ida Kay?"

"Never." She was still watching him politely but her hands of their own will had already opened the novel to the proper page.

"It was just how they moved," he finished lamely. "I remembered it when Sherrilee was born. Such a pretty baby. I called her Ducky from the start." He did not add that he had thought Sherrilee a terrible name, and by the time she had her first birthday he was already sick of spelling it for people.

"All that," said Sherrilee, "was before I was born."

"It's still nice to know these things."

She seemed to be angry. "Do you know I've never seen you go duck hunting once, not in my whole life?"

He shifted on his chair. "Time, you know. Family. The office . . ." His voice got smaller and smaller. "But I really did like it. It used to mean a lot to me."

He saw that Miss Ida Kay, without comment, had begun to read again.

"I came in," said his daughter firmly, "to talk about Scandinavia."

"What about her?"

Scandinavia had been their cook since he and Marva were married, had nursed Marva through cancer, operations, death.

Then she stayed on to run his house and rear his daughter; at present she was supervising the long, slow death of Wriston Thomas, Sr., his father, of strokes and old age. Scandinavia seemed to him like a large, dark lodestone, drawing pain and trouble into herself, sponging up his own fatigue, absorbing his father's senile temper. He relied on her as sailors might rely on the North Star.

But now even that seemed under threat, with Sherrilee home for the summer and forever talking minorities, underprivileged homes, and Southern mores.

"Scandinavia," she declared now, "should send her son to college."

"Apart from the cost, Kestler wouldn't know what to do with college."

"There you go!"

"I mean it, Ducky." (She said, "Don't call me that!") "Scandinavia is a fine woman and a smart one, but Kestler hardly knows dark from daylight."

"What do you expect in this environment? Don't you ever take environment into consideration?"

Thomas closed his eyes. She could ask him that while he spent his life watching Parsonville disappear beneath the Industrial Revolution like a ship falling under the sea! Every year the grass slipped in on another street, but he and Kestler Burns would die here because neither one of them . . .

He said, "Have you talked to Kestler?"

"In a general way. About incentives. Self-improvement."

"Uh huh." How long would it be, he wondered, before she joined the other college youngsters, all colors, and marched in the Greensboro streets under a placard about equal rights? Marva would spin in her grave like a pinwheel.

"I still say Kestler couldn't pass fifth grade. I only let him vote because of his mother."

"If Kestler is undereducated, whose fault is that?"

Undereducated! He said, "I don't know," and looked into her cool face, pink lipstick on an indignant mouth. She had thrown her left arm westward, like a wing lying on the wind. "Is it mine?"

"Oh, Daddy!" She began to pace between his desk and the small barrel of eggs at the railing. He guessed summer in Parsonville must be pretty dull, a record heat wave surrounding the house in which her grandfather was dying. He couldn't afford Wrightsville Beach, or her own car. Perhaps in the future she would understand, when she found herself paying the bills for another generation's ruined arteries. He had an awful feeling she would never pay for his; he would have to go off and have his death alone, under sanitary conditions. She and Geriatrics would tell him how really humane this was and he could only nod—as he discovered he was nodding now, although for the life of him he did not know to what.

"I give up. I'm going to get some ice cream," said Sherrilee. She stood pressing one finger to her cheek where she feared that once adorable dimple might soon wrinkle her before her time.

He was relieved. "Go ahead. It's mad dog weather." Too hot to talk of such things. Too cold in the winter. In the spring, wet.

Miss Ida Kay King, who liked her heroines safely closed in books, watched the girl swing across Main Street with a long stride. At thirteen, those legs had seemed to be hinged at the neck. Now there was this grace . . . In the sun, Sherrilee's hair, which had Marva's same auburn lights, burned like a torch. He thought of marathons and torches.

"She's very pretty," said Miss Ida Kay King, making it sound like a disease.

Egg Day dawned for the fourth year hot and cloudless, and the air felt hard.

From his bedroom window, Wink Thomas looked out into the morning. The good weather depressed him. Other towns rated an occasional tornado and federal aid but Parsonville—nothing.

When he, single-handed, had founded the Parsonville Egg Festival four years before, it seemed a possible answer to the poverty of the area and the monotony of the summers. He had imagined it would draw tourists, county officials, perhaps the State Secretary of Agriculture to have his picture taken while plucking chickens. There might have been a handicraft business painting eggs for the Easter trade. News dispatches could have been written with leads like "All the good eggs in Parsonville gathered today for . . ." or even "Egged on by fair weather . . ." *Life* magazine might have done a picture story tracing the egg's role in human civilization. He had pictured chickenfeed companies that would sponsor baseball teams, a firm to package and deodorize hen manure for flower gardeners, ceramic bantams on ashtrays which claimed Parsonville as the Egg Center of North Carolina, Mother Nello Parsons' Fresh Egg Mayonnaise. . . .

Well, it was a farce; he had counted all those chickens long before they hatched. Even the weekly newspaper in Roxton no longer sent its old maid reporter. Only the old ladies and old gentlemen and Negroes of Parsonville came to the annual events. They came because the summer was very hot and very long, and it was better to eat chickens or talk chickens than feel so trapped in feeding the unbearable rhythm of their hunger, or sorting eggs against a candle's worth of light.

Wink Thomas went downstairs and into the dining room. He still called it that, although the table and sideboard had been stored upstairs for six years, and his father's hospital bed was stark and incongruous under the small chandelier.

"Who's that?" called his father, rising on an elbow. His flesh was like papier-mâché. "Who's coming in?"

"It's Wink. Did you sleep?"

"Never. I never sleep. There's a dog barks all night."

The only dog in any of the yards on Chestnut Street was Mr. Bison's old cocker, and it barely had strength enough to snore. The only sounds in the summer night were the songs of mockingbirds, and their sweetness was sufficient to pierce window glass, but he never mentioned that.

"Has Sherrilee come down?"

"Who?"

"Your granddaughter, Sherrilee."

"So much traffic in and out this house I can't keep track of it all." Abruptly the old man hacked, emptied his throat into the palm of his hand and held it out. "Looky there," he breathed, his voice respectful. "Solid blood. That's what happens. That's why I don't get well. During the night I bleed away all my strength."

There was nothing but spit, slightly yellow, in his hand. Wink nodded and patted his father's thin shoulder, which felt like a coat hanger. "You're going to be fine," he said, and pushed past the swinging door through the butler's pantry to the kitchen, where he drank half a pint of tomato juice—hideously red—and almost choked.

In the kitchen Scandinavia stood feeding clothes through the wringer. He hoped she would not begin again about spin washers and electric dryers. They said "Good Morning" and, as usual, he turned down her offer to cook him breakfast. He never ate an egg if he could help it.

"Sherrilee has been telling me about your boy. How old is Kestler now? Eighteen?"

Scandinavia looked withdrawn and sullen. She looked as if it gave her satisfaction to be crushing his wet shirts between rollers. "He done it," she said.

It was not possible. "Kestler? What?"

She dropped a balled garment into the basket with a thud. He thought of guillotines. "Heard all Miss Sherrilee's talk about bettering himself. First thing at sunrise today he hitched straight over to Raleigh to join the Army."

He sat hastily at the table. "Does Sherrilee know?"

"Now who'll cut my stove wood?" A sheet came forth like a flattened white worm and fell, squirming, into the basket. "Left me here," she grumbled. "Left your shrubbery to grow and nobody to do them windows at your office. Left Mr. Teed Kiser with nobody to cut his yard or clean his chickenhouse. Left us all."

"The Army." Acting mentally as Parsonville's one-man Chamber of Commerce, he lowered the census by one. Left us here, he echoed. Sherrilee soon. First college and then . . .

"I can't crawl up there and shingle my roof," said Scandinavia. She was less sad than angry. "I can't shoot no squirrels for stew. I need help turning Mr. Thomas in that high bed."

Left us here. Thoughts flared in his mind: *If Daddy would die . . . if I were a better lawyer . . . if all my old contacts in politics weren't either dead or too prosperous . . .* One by one he snuffed them all and a feeling of great sympathy for Scandinavia swept over him.

"Well," he said crossly, "the Army won't keep him forever."

There was a companionable silence. She turned off the wringers, set the basket on the back porch. "Egg Day, ain't it?"

Wink nodded. He put the rest of the juice into the refrigerator and stood gratefully for an instant in its cool air before he closed the door.

"Think I can leave Mr. Thomas long enough to step uptown for it?"

"He'll be fine. He'll probably sleep."

"Good weather for Egg Day. Hot."

He sipped some coffee and began to sweat. For all he knew, Kestler Burns was now riding to Fort Jackson on an air-conditioned bus. The coffee was bitter.

Scandinavia said, "Is they a pee-rade this year?"

He shook his head. Only the first year had there been the straggling young marchers, their brass horns filled with noise and sunlight. Now the small high school population of Parsonville had been added to Roxton High, and the few youngsters who rode to it each day on the orange bus were not students of drum or trumpet. Indeed, already they belonged to Roxton—to its formica-lined drugstores, its motion-picture house and public swimming pool. They would not be home on any August afternoon to watch a bald man fry eggs on the sidewalk.

"No parade, but the sewing circle will sell lemonade," he offered. "You buy a glass for a quarter and they embroider your name on the church memorial quilt."

"Not my name they don't," laughed Scandinavia, who viewed

Jim Crow as a complicated joke on white people. She enjoyed watching them try to keep it all straight—yes to this, but no to this other. Her money, she knew, would buy lemonade in a good goblet, which would then be set aside for an extra-careful washing. It would be served her by smiling ladies who would remember to ask how Kestler was and if her bad back was better this dry weather; but no "Scandinavia Burns" would ever be silk-embroidered on the Methodist Church quilt. She was glad she didn't have the responsibility of drawing that line between what was allowed and what forbidden.

Wink put a quarter onto the kitchen table. "You have a glass anyway," he said. "Made in the shade and stirred with a spade. Best ol' lemonade ever made."

"I see you're the announcer as usual."

"As usual," he muttered.

On the way out he said goodbye to his father, who, after a silence, called, "Goodbye, Orlando."

That made him stop. Wink's brother Orlando had been dead for forty years, had died before he was ten, and was thus hung forever in a time still safe for believing princes sought and won their fortunes, fish offered three wishes, and magical hens might lay a golden . . .

"It was a goose," he said aloud. "It was a goddamn goose!"

"Goodbye, Goose," called his father, trying to be agreeable.

The people of Parsonville gathered in the town square, clustered in the street under that silly banner which seemed to be describing them all. The street was as safe as sidewalks because most traffic stayed on the bypass and never drove through the small town at all. The lemonade stand had been built of packing boxes and stood on the Main Street corner near his parking place.

When Wink came squinting into the sun from his office, he thought the small crowd looked funereal, and the street lacked only a gallows to complete the scene. He was still irritated with Sherrilee's good intentions, Kestler's flight, library books in his office.

His father had set him thinking about Orlando—Orlando, the clever brother, the quick lad in school, the boy with straight teeth who won all the races and could swim upstream. If Orlando had lived, he would not now be here in Parsonville on a hot afternoon breaking eggs. Wink Thomas knew that much.

Men and women who waved to him were all his age and older except for Sherrilee, who had put on a flowing wide dress and white high heels and earrings that glittered. Teed Kiser came from the group and took the small barrel of eggs. Both men spoke politely to the lemonade ladies with their pasteboard fans which said SHOP IN ROXTON. Miss Suffolk, who could make hand stitches as tiny as any sewing machine, remarked that this year's banner was real original.

Wink said, "Teed, is that thunder?"

"I don't hear nothing."

He knew as soon as he came to the center of the intersection of Main and Carter that Kestler Burns had run off to the U.S. Army without painting the customary oval outline of a giant egg on the asphalt. Someone from the lemonade stand had already noticed this lack and brought a bag of sugar to trickle a wavy, uncertain circle in place of it. The crowd was watching Wink nervously to see how he would take it.

"All we could think of," somebody said.

"Best we could do."

"Knew it would be an aggravation."

Wink saw then, for the first time, that just as he went through this silly business once a year for their sakes and to break the boredom, so they only came for his; and he scrubbed at the sun glare in his eyes.

"Hot as Hell," he managed. "It's a fine egg." It seemed to him Sherrilee ought to learn something from all this, but she had already gone over to the lemonade stand and begun spelling her name carefully for the chairman of the Embroidery Committee. "Mightly resourceful," Wink added and then, with haste, "Smart. Real smart."

Faces beamed and for an instant the crowd seemed to fuse, at the points of nudging elbows, into a unit.

But then somebody was heard to say, "Always something goes wrong!" and he saw flickers of anger. At the speaker? The egg? The heavy spilling of sun about their heads?

"Ain't one thing, it's another," said somebody else.

Teed Kiser whispered to him, "I do hear thunder, sure enough!" He put the barrel of eggs alongside the sugar outline on the street.

Wink went on sweating, although by now he could see a sudden cloud south, blotting up some of the blazing light. "I didn't hear it that time."

"You better hurry." Kiser raised both hands to quiet the talk, then gave him a nod.

"Friends," Wink began. Suddenly his voice, as if it were brittle and hollow, caved in. He wondered if that embarrassed Sherrilee.

He was handed lemonade and heard his name called toward the booth to add to the Methodist quilt.

He tried again.

"Friends, this week the city of Parsonville has been engaged in a celebration."

Their faces were sober.

"Once a year we meet together to . . . to count our blessings. You've all heard, ha-ha, of walking on eggs; well, all of us walk on them here, because our community was founded on eggs. Eggs and hens, of course."

Now, belatedly, they smiled. Over their heads the sun faded. He could hear the thunder sliding across the sky. He spoke louder.

"Nello Parsons was the first man to make a good living here off chickens. You all remember that in 1937 every ribbon at the state fair in Raleigh went to Parsonville eggs and Parsonville chickens. Because we've got standards here. We've got standards."

He wiped his forehead on a handkerchief. At the edge of the crowd Scandinavia leaned forward to make sure it was a clean one, worn thin by steady bleaching, so he would not disgrace her. One bird passed overhead, outflying the storm.

"So every year," he continued, "the first week in August, we take this way of thanking our lucky stars that Nello Parsons had foresight. That Nello Parsons had standards."

He whispered to Teed Kiser, "Is the road cooling too fast? Will they still fry?"

"They always have," said Kiser. But he shifted from one foot to another and frowned upward.

"You all know," said Wink to the crowd, "that on Monday we met and cleaned up the cemetery, put flowers on the Parsons plot, and heard a fine poem about Easter and rebirth composed by Miss Tildy Perkins. . . ."

(Miss Perkins, who was deaf, had asked to have her left foot stepped on when she was named so she might smile; now three shoes ground onto hers and she cried out instead. The people around her stirred uneasily.)

Wink pressed on. "Tuesday evening we heard some fine quartet singing, enjoyed an egg hunt, and a bountiful picnic supper out at the old school grounds. And last night the competitions for heaviest hen, egg with most weight and biggest circumference, and our other contests. I might add that Mrs. Lockley, who fell from the judges' platform, is resting comfortably in Roxton hospital and the fracture was not a bad one."

Somebody applauded.

"Today, we fry the traditional eggs on the pavement. People are always saying it's so hot you could fry eggs on the sidewalk, but we do it every year right out in the street, and Mother Nature acts as our cook."

Sherrilee, he saw, had stopped listening to his speech and was gazing way down the road as if she saw something he could not see, something that moved.

"We break our eggs," he said loudly, "and drop them around the outline of a larger egg, remembering as we do that the egg is the seat of life, that life begins in the egg and feeds on the egg."

With a fine, high-wristed gesture he reached behind him, cracked the first egg on the barrel's metal rim, and dropped the contents neatly onto the wavery sugar outline at his feet.

Even as it fell he knew his error. Two flies glutting on sugar were drowned in the egg's liquid, but the sudden smell sprang forth until they all were choking in it.

"Teed Kiser!" he cried in an angry voice, then gagged on the rotten, sulphur smell.

They were drawing quickly back, noses clipped shut between fingers. Sherrilee had begun to trot gracefully in her white pumps toward his office door and Scandinavia, laughing, poured out her lemonade onto the curb.

"Shame on you, Teed Kiser!" somebody yelled.

"Old cheapskate!" called another.

And, "Fed your hen buckshot before the weighing!" accused a third, and one of them rushed forward and grabbed an egg—not rotten—and smashed it atop the old man's head. At this Kiser, insulted, let fly with a whole handful, one of which fell unbroken into the lemonade pitcher and sank in slow motion onto a bed of sugar grains. Another flew from his hand to splatter on the blouse of Miss Tildy Perkins, the Easter poet, so that it seemed her shriveled breast had suddenly gushed forth; and she flailed out with her parasol at Mr. Wilson, who had stepped on her foot during the speech, and opened a long cut above his wrinkled ear.

Then all of them swarmed forward to the egg barrel, like Jews stoning Stephen, and screamed as they threw at each other. Strange white-and-yellow blossoms plopped into being on backs and stomachs; Mr. Bison's eyeglasses were covered and he walked blindly into Aunt Christy's wheelchair and she beat him with her crocheted pocketbook. Mrs. Kiser, rushing to her husband's aid, slipped in a puddle of egg white and fell heavily onto the street and got her hair frosted with dust and sugar crystals.

A little man struck Scandinavia in the neck with another rotten egg, yelling her nigger son had enrolled at the University of North Carolina, and she lumbered off toward home like a brown bear, her hands splayed up as if she were surrendering under fire.

In the general rush the whole lemonade stand was overturned; Mrs. Wicker was pinned beneath it with her sewing needle jammed up under her thumbnail; and the last remaining piece of Mrs. Atkins's crystal—her prized pitcher—broke on the curb into bits no bigger than breadcrumbs.

Then, like the roar of Jehovah's rage over the recalcitrant Israelites, a clap of thunder broke in the town square and froze them into sudden statues. They were transfixed with their raised fists and mouths open upon insults; and one egg which was already in the air seemed almost to float above their stillness before it hit the trembling banner and came down and broke like an echo. They looked upon each other, unbelieving, terrified. A river of light ran down the sky and thunder broke over them again. Then the first hard raindrops were thrown down around their heads and they scattered, running, down the four streets, and Aunt Christy's wheelchair rocked crazily as it rolled away downhill behind them.

It was a downpour, ruining the little drawstring bags and melting the words on those paper fans the ladies had dropped in their headlong flight, diluting both the ruined and good eggs which lay where they had shattered, breaking up the sugared oval outline and washing it away into the gutter. The banner, heavy with rainwater, sagged down toward the street and Wink Thomas slapped up at it as he began running too, his heart trying to thrust out between the rib bars and burst forth through his coat. He slipped and slid on a street slick with raw eggs, and bits of shell crunched with a terrible sound under his running feet. And, although he had not run all the way to Chestnut Street since boyhood races with his brother, he ran the distance now—heavy-footed, jarring the earth, putting new cracks into all the sidewalks. Without even slowing down he worked out of his wet coat and slung it into Mr. Bison's forsythia bush as he passed.

Sherrilee had ridden with Miss Ida Kay King and was already home when, heaving from his effort, he burst into the house. She came forward and started to touch him, but drew back from the wet clothes, sulphur, sweat. He staggered past her, huffing, and she followed him into the living room.

"Who's that?" called old Mr. Thomas before she could say a word. "Who's coming in?"

He tried to get his breath. In a minute he managed to croak, "Ducky, I threw them too! I did. I did."

"What got into everybody?" was all she said. And, as an after-thought, "Are you hurt?"

"I threw the most of all," he panted.

"I never saw anything like it," she said.

He did not have enough extra breath to explain. From under his chandelier his father bawled, "Who's out there?"

"Miss Perkins laid on her umbrella like a broadsword," said Sherrilee. He was able to smile.

"And Scandinavia got covered. If you'd had the reporters you always wanted, you'd have hit every newspaper in the country. Typical race riot in small Southern town."

He laughed, fell weakly into a chair and laughed some more until his lungs were as empty as envelopes; and when he sucked in the next breath it stretched them painfully, and rushed forth as a groan, a wail. He huddled into a ball in the old rosewood chair, shaking with a chill and crying like a baby.

"Daddy?" With a smooth movement she put her hand halfway in the air between them. "What is it, Daddy?"

Out of what once had been the dining room the old man began to whimper and to beg, "Don't cry, Orlando. It can't be that bad. Whatever it is, Orlando, don't cry."

But he did.

THE

ASTRONOMER

It was his last day.

Mr. Beam gave close attention to his two soapy hands, clutching and loosing in the lavatory. He wanted the fingers washed as clean as Pilate's for the moment they would receive his last envelope at the pay window. Besides, he did not care to glance into the cloudy mirror and meet his own eyes. They might be fierce. Or, worse yet, they might not be fierce at all. The paper towel was brown and tough. He folded one edge to a triangle, scraped dirt from under his fingernails.

The door to the washroom opened, letting in hot air and a great roar of machinery.

"Your last day, ain't it?" somebody said.

"Yes." He wiped his palms.

"Wish it was mine." The man pulled a paperback book from his pocket before he sat on one of the cubicle toilets, coveralls hanging loose onto the tile. He began to read, moving his lips carefully.

Mr. Beam took a second towel and dried his hands again as if he might polish them to a high luster. "Somebody's already checking how long you're taking in the toilet."

The man turned a page.

"What a stink!" grunted Mr. Beam.

"It's your last day. Give you something to remember." The man sighed happily and thumped his book. "They're on this planet, see?

And this girl, she's some kind of doctor, gets locked in the space-ship with this creepy thing they found; only it's built like a man. Green fur and all, but built just like a man where it counts, and the earthmen can't get through the outer lock. And this girl is screaming and moaning."

"You'll be moaning when they dock your pay." Mr. Beam had already changed to trousers and a white shirt. Now he folded his coveralls into a neat packet and pinned his factory name tag to the collar.

"It's called *Bride of the Green Planet.*"

Mr. Beam checked his pocket watch. "Maybe you got all day, but not me." He picked up the clothes and, at last, permitted himself to study his image in the mirror. Not bad, he thought. The wet comb had made his gray hair lie flat but his mustache stuck out in all directions. Looked like something he'd made from a chunk of squirrel tail, with two smaller whacks glued over his eyes.

"What you going to do with all that free time?"

"Nothing," said Mr. Beam. "Keep it free." He picked up his coveralls and opened the door.

"Hey," called the man on the toilet, "what about the watch they give you? I see you already got one."

Mr. Beam walked rapidly down one of the dusty aisles, pre-tending he had not heard. He slid his eyes to one side. Blur of machinery. To walk through Corey Knitting Mills always re-minded him of a fast car ride in the country, with farms and forests melting and running together in a mottled ribbon along the highway. If the spinning frames could only see, then he—Horton Beam—might look to them like a wax man inside a fur-nace.

He opened the heavy door, stepped onto an overpass bridge which spanned an alley. The air was sweet with honeysuckle. He entered the second building and started down the concrete stairs.

Place is built like a prison, he thought. They ought to hand me twenty dollars and a suit of clothes.

The girl at the pay station glanced at his name pinned to the folded coveralls. She smiled. "A red envelope for you."

"That's right," he said stiffly.

She pulled it from a file. "Congratulations," she said, checking numbers on the flap. She wrote in the date, June 21, 1957. "Going to Florida?"

"No."

"Would you wait a minute, please?"

Horton Beam leaned against the wall while she stepped into the supervisor's office. He heard her voice. "Beam. A weaver."

The supervisor came out and shook his hand. "Want to thank you for your years of faithful service," he said easily. ". . . company retirement . . . first of every month . . . always glad to have you return for a visit. . . ."

Mr. Beam endured it.

". . . small token of Mr. Corey's appreciation . . ." The supervisor extended a gilt box. Had Mr. Beam been a foreman, the mill would have sponsored a small supper in the Newton Hotel Dining Room, and the cheap watch plus a retirement medallion would have been presented there following some speeches about free enterprise and honor.

Mr. Beam snapped open the box and examined the timepiece. "Sure do appreciate," he muttered. He had never cared for wrist watches, which could not be put decently out of sight. Strapped there over the pulse, the hands on that dial seemed a naked measurement of a man's heartbeat. Wearing it would be like watching your life ebb. He said aloud, "Mighty nice." The supervisor shook his hand again.

"Good luck," said the cashier.

Mr. Beam went out into a summer's day. The heavy door closed finally behind him; he clanked down the steel stairway, crossed the asphalt drive, and walked onto the patch of green fescue right by the sign which said, "Keep Off the Grass."

He was repeating softly, "They can all go to Hell. They can all go to Hell."

Walking home, Mr. Beam stopped at the Atlas Café for a beer. In the front booth he waited, alert, for someone to ask about his retirement. Would he go fishing? Visit some kin? Varnish bird-houses?

And he would tell them: Not a thing. Not one solitary thing. No trip. No satisfying hobby. All his relatives were dead. He would do nothing. Nothing whatsoever. It was high time.

Time. Mr. Beam took out the ticking wrist watch. It was accurate; it bore the same inscription as a hundred others:

WELL DONE!
Corey Knitting Mills

(At one time the retirement watches had been larger and rounder and the engraving had read, "Well done, thou good and faithful servant," but that was in Old Man Corey's day. Young Corey had been to college in Raleigh and he felt that didn't have the right tone. He said the first janitor ever got a watch like that, they'd start getting letters from the NAACP. So the quote was shortened, but the janitors never got watches anyway. They got fruit baskets.)

Mr. Beam glanced around the café to see if anybody might ask him about his new watch. He knew no customers by name. Even the counterman was just a familiar shape, head to belt buckle. In all these years, they had never swapped a dozen sentences.

Mr. Beam paid for his beer and bought half a pint of frozen custard to carry home. "I got a new watch," he said.

"Great," said the counterman, slapping his change onto the thick glass.

Mr. Beam lived two blocks beyond the Atlas Café, on Helicks Street. The house was nearly as old as he was—sixty-five—and its white paint had yellowed and the green trim looked black. Once it had stood on a large plot of grassy land with an orchard and cow barn, a vegetable garden, oval fish pool, grape and rose arbors. Then maybe the man who built it died; and his sons sold off a corner here and a strip there, until a crowd of little houses and woodsheds began to nibble all around it. Now the outsized house looked awkward in its tiny yard. It had grown power wires and an oil drum while shedding some of the banister posts around the porch and sloughing off several bricks from the foundation.

Mr. Beam locked the front door behind him. The rooms were cool. He threw his tie into the front room in the direction of his bed. Then he contemplated the parlor, where Elsie's overstuffed furniture sat just as she had left it. Maybe he would sell it all and have that room entirely bare. Maybe he would hide the wrist watch under a chair cushion just before the junkman came.

He ate supper standing in the kitchen—crackers and sardines with frozen custard for dessert. He had spread the wrist watch on the table with its straps open, like something which might be cooked for a coming meal. It was his free time lying there, raw and unattached, and he did not plan to use it for any purpose at all. No, he thought, for years he had taken colored threads and crossed them with other colored threads to make a neat pattern. He began to grin. At last, he thought with delight, he had come to his raveling days! Still smiling he tucked the watch into the corner on the kitchen windowsill where it could run down all by itself.

The rooms had grown dark. Mr. Beam left the empty can and custard carton in the sink and went through the house turning off all lights except in his front bedroom. He looked aimlessly through a shelf of old books there, remembering the man reading in the toilet. Some people might retire to spend their time reading, he thought with a sneer.

He tried and abandoned Sherlock Holmes. He glanced at one book explaining the Holy Spirit, which Elsie had earned for Sunday-school attendance. Several books had belonged to their son John in his student days, and one of these fell open to a page which began, "When I Heard the Learn'd Astronomer . . ." Mr. Beam closed it quickly and yawned.

Usually he slept deeply and well. Tonight the chorus of summer insects was not restful. Drowsily he heard their noises blend until they turned into the roaring of Corey Knitting Mills. At last the sound thinned to that of a single motor. Mr. Beam was riding in some strange aircraft and stars were flying by its window like streaks of ice cream. Sometimes a dripping meteor of lime sherbet rolled sluggishly by in the dark. His aircraft dipped and looped among this flying brightness until its fins were wet and luminous.

He lay in his own bed, sorting out the dream from morning sunlight which lay at a bright angle on his bed. Bride of the Green Planet, indeed! But there was something wistful about that dream ride among the stars—going nowhere special, coming from no place remembered. It had been like a child's game, played for its own sake, without any winners and any rules.

Mr. Beam got a crazy idea. The more he lay in his bed and thought about it, the more he smiled. It was a shame he could not go back again to the mill washroom to hear that fellow ask what he'd be doing with all his free time.

"I'm going to be an astronomer," he should have said. "A learn'd astronomer."

He studied the book while he ate a hard-boiled egg at the kitchen table. Walt Whitman. Born 1819. Left school at an early age to learn the printer's trade.

Printer, weaver, what was the difference?

Paid to have his own first book published. Wore a large beard . . .

Horton Beam flipped through the pages until he found the lines and read them slowly aloud.

". . . heard the learn'd astronomer, When the proofs, the figures, were ranged in columns before me . . ." (He pronounced "ranged" as if it were the sound of yesterday's bell.) ". . . shown the charts and diagrams, to add, divide, and measure them . . ."

"Good stuff," said Mr. Beam, fingering his mustache. Silently he read the rest, then thumped the book shut on the table and made an angry face. Well, if that didn't beat all! Charts and lectures, applause in that room, and in the end all Walter could think to do was go look up in silence at the stars!

He turned the book to read its title. *Leaves of Grass & Other Poems,* it said. As if the grass had any leaves! It had grass, that's all, or grass-blades at the most. The whole thing turned out no better than what's-his-name in the mill toilet, always on the lookout for the story line. Fairy tales. Green planets.

Mr. Beam leaned back and made the chair teeter. That learn'd fellow was telling him something, and old Walter never even listened!

Me, I'm listening.

He pulled out his pocket watch. I hear this thing eating up my days. I'm listening to that, Walter. I hear my fingernails growing. And let me tell you about that hillside and them stars—I been there already. I have played out that story game. I have married and lived happy ever after, and I have worked hard for all the right number of years. And I am outside that story. It is going right on without me in it.

He slid the watch into his pocket. I am leaving you, Walter, out there in the dark. I am going back inside and study every one of them charts and proofs he was telling about.

Mr. Beam put his saucer of eggshells into the sink with the other things before he walked to the corner and caught the Transit Bus uptown to Newton City library. He had never been inside the library. The woman at the front desk looked like a twin of the bookkeeper at the mill pay window. He didn't plan to ask her anything. So Mr. Beam walked up and down the three rows of double shelves until at last he found the Dewey Decimal System explained on a pasteboard chart. He ran his finger down rows of books, looking for 520.

It stopped at *The Universe Around Us,* by James Jeans. This contained many photographs of nebulae, the Russell Diagram, a table of the stellar weights of binary systems near the sun. Hastily he put it back on the shelf. But nearby was a simpler book identifying major star groups like the Big Dipper, Dragon, Swan, North Star. Mr. Beam saw from the illustrations what effort had been required for someone to draw chalk lines among these random stars, trying to make some pattern. He ran his fingertips across the page and they tingled, as if the pictured spots were still white with their own heat.

When I learn all this, he thought, there won't be a single use for it. I can learn one shines east and one shines west, and nobody will ask me to move them. I'll learn how far away they are, and never want to go.

Let Walter go!

"May I help you?"

He ducked his head to the librarian. "This one."

She carried it to the checkout desk and showed him where to sign the new patron's card. With care he wrote: *W. Whitman.*

"The stars are beautiful these summer nights," said the librarian with a friendly smile. She pressed some numbers in his book with a rubber stamp.

What did he care for that? No use. No purpose. No beauty, either. He was just learning something for its own sake. He had retired from all the parts of that story; he had even . . . even abdicated.

"I hadn't noticed it," the Astronomer said aloud.

When the Astronomer got home from the library he found a young man sitting on his front step, chewing a piece of his hedge and spitting green pulp into his yard.

"Hello," the stranger called.

The Astronomer stopped at his own sidewalk and turned the book in his hand so its title would not show. "You looking for me?"

"Looking for Mr. Horton Beam. Heard you might have an extra room to rent."

"No rooms."

The young man did not move. "It's a big house for one person. I got money in my pocket."

"No roomers," said the Astronomer and stepped past him and went inside.

By lunchtime the young man still had not moved from the front steps. He had eaten one candy bar and thrown the wrapper into the yard. Not once had he looked over his shoulder at the front door which had been banged against him. Nor had he shifted his position, hunched, spread-legged, not even when sunlight moved up the sidewalk and reached into his face.

In the kitchen the Astronomer ate some old cheese which he found deep in the refrigerator. He chewed on the rind, frowned over his book and spun a new word 'round in his mind. Polaris. It was a clear and distinguished word.

He walked into the parlor and squinted through Elsie's curtains. Still there. Polaris to you. He looked at the dust which came off the ruffle onto his hand, wiped it against his hip pocket and opened the book to the beginning. He walked to the back of the house, reading in time to his steps. There was the Big Dipper. There were two pointer stars. These aimed at the north one. Its name was Polaris.

Most of the afternoon he restudied that first chapter, finding the dipper, veering off to the North Star. All this time the stranger sat on his front step, smoking cigarettes and flipping butts to smolder in his grass. The city bus came and went at the corner of Helicks and Martin streets.

The Astronomer rocked in his kitchen chair and studied the charts. There was Dubhe. There was Merak. And there, of course, just where it ought to be, blazed Polaris. Out front the young man minded his business.

When it began to grow dark the Astronomer went to the front porch and looked at the stranger's unmoving back. "You can't sleep here."

"You said that already."

"You live in Newton City?"

"Not yet."

He looked twenty, twenty-five, maybe even thirty. He had a face like a rat terrier, all eyes and bones. "You say you're working?"

He stood up, shaking his head. "I said I had money in my pocket. Tomorrow I'll be working."

A little man, with a wired-together look. "Know anything about astronomy?"

"No."

"You ain't from Corey Knitting Mill, are you? It's not some kind of joke the boys thought up?" The Astronomer shook his head in answer to his own question. Nobody on that shift had ever joked with *him*. And likely the men at machines on his left and right had never noticed Horton Beam was gone. He said, "Six dollars a week. Upstairs."

"All right."

"And it's dusty. My wife's dead." The Astronomer turned and walked inside to his own downstairs bedroom opposite the parlor. All that reading had tired him out. If the stranger found the bathroom, fine; if he didn't, that was fine, too. The Astronomer rubbed at his eyebrows, which seemed to be buzzing at the roots.

He had decided not to search for Polaris in the sky this night, not to hurry. There was no schedule, no time card to punch. Although he wore only his underwear to bed, the sheet was too hot. He pedaled lazily at it and worked it off. Maybe the stranger was a thief. Not much to steal, he grinned in the dark, except a wrist watch on the kitchen windowsill.

That word was like a live coal inside his head. He dropped low into himself and closed his eyes so he could look up to where it smoldered in his skull. *Polaris.* The Astronomer fell asleep still reaching for it.

Next morning when the Astronomer went to the kitchen he found six dollar bills folded neatly under the salt shaker. The house was quiet. He stuck the money in the window with the watch.

As usual, he boiled the coffee until it had spattered all over the range. The liquid was thick and very dark. Even when Elsie was living, he had made the morning coffee because he liked it strong. Sometimes, he remembered now, Elsie had used his leftover coffee in country-ham gravy, to make the drippings darker; and had always told him, "This stuff is strong enough to wake up the pig."

As soon as the first cupful was safely in his stomach, the Astronomer began to squirm and feel uneasy. At first he did not know why. He took out his pocket watch, put it back, washed the accumulated dishes. Looked out the window. Lined up all four chairs precisely around the table.

Then he realized he was only looking for work. His stomach, from habit, had waited for its strong coffee and now his hands were hungry, too. He turned them and examined both sides, wondering. The message of retirement had not reached them yet; it was still traveling somewhere toward them and they had not been told. Funny thing. He let his left hand rest on the refrigerator. Almost immediately it began to pick at a crust of something, a drop of food dried on the white wall.

It's a real habit, he thought. Liquor and morphine and work. Maybe I'll have to taper off. Fix a doorknob or something, to keep these muscles quiet. Break out of these habits one at a time.

And after that . . . after he had gone from inner box to larger box to even larger box, breaking out of all his virtues, then he would be free! He would be free to . . .

The moment hung over him, perilous. The end of that sentence almost fell in and crushed him. Free to be myself?

He covered his thoughts with a great clattering as he got out the long metal toolbox. The key was missing and he had to hammer his way in with kitchen knives and a rolling pin, and this took a long and noisy time.

By suppertime the Astronomer had dealt with every doorknob in the house, replaced some hooks on window screens, spliced some lamp wires, put a new washer in the kitchen faucet. When he settled into the wooden swing on his front porch, he saw that his hands were content to lie resting in his lap. Soon it would be dark, and he would teach them to point to Polaris in the northern sky.

He leaned forward and stared down the street. The man who had rented the upstairs room was coming back, and he had a woman with him. The two walked silently, wide apart. A boy on a bicycle could have passed between them.

The Astronomer leaned over the porch rail to make certain. Yes, it was the same man, not very tall, his muscles put together with knots. He was carrying a suitcase. The woman was taller.

Uneasily the Astronomer went into the parlor, where he hid behind his own door and watched the two come up the sidewalk, cross the porch, stop in the hall. "That you, Mr. Beam?"

He came out of the shadow and looked at them.

"I left your money in the kitchen."

The Astronomer began shaking his head. "I never said for two."

"She'll take no more room than me. It's a big bed. I'll even pay eight dollars."

"I never said two." All the time he waited for the woman to speak. She was not pretty. Her face was flat and her limp hair had the same surface as oiled brown floors in country stores. She looked like a refugee.

"I told you I was married," the young man lied. He waved an arm in which, the Astronomer saw, blood vessels grew very near the surface like a set of curling vines. He'd never liked men with arms like that. As if everything in them were pumped to the top and straining to push through.

"You ain't married," the Astronomer said flatly, looking at the woman with her stringy brown hair. Her mouth moved but he could not tell if that was a smile.

"I'm Fred Ridge." He put out his hand and the Astronomer looked at the set of blue cables which disappeared into his sleeve. High blood pressure. He won't last long enough for pensions.

"This is my wife, Eva," the man was saying. "I got in yesterday; she came on the bus. Had to find a place to live . . ."

"You ain't found it yet," the Astronomer broke in. He would not shake the hand.

"I got a job. You want two extra dollars?" Fred Ridge held out a pair of bills.

"Let's leave," said the woman. Her voice was weary. Perhaps she had been crying.

"It'll be dark before long and we got no other place to stay."

"Let's go, Fred." She didn't sound as if it mattered much. She was wearing a wedding ring but the Astronomer didn't think Fred Ridge had bought it. Not that he cared about that. He was outside that story.

"Eight dollars, then," he said. The woman looked surprised.

"And don't you worry about that room being dusty," Fred Ridge said earnestly. "My wife will tend to that." He smiled at her but her face did not change. "Won't you, Eva?"

"Goodnight, Mr. Beam," she said.

The Astronomer stood holding the crumpled dollar bills while they climbed the stairs and disappeared down the upper hall. Somehow the day was spoiled. He'd let strangers invade it, for one thing, and buy his privacy for two measly dollars. First thing he knew some real wife would be knocking on Horton Beam's front door asking after some little man with fat blood vessels; and he'd be standing in his own hallway trying to decide between yes and no.

The Astronomer shook his head to that. No, he would say nothing to such a woman except, "I've retired." And she would say something else and he would repeat it, "I've retired," until she really believed him and went away.

The sudden noise of overhead footsteps shocked him. It was as if the wind had whistled through tree limbs where no tree grew. The Astronomer turned up his face, mouth open, and the tapping sounds seemed to float down like flakes to lie upon his tongue where he could taste them. How long had it been . . .

Suddenly the woman's head appeared over the stair railing. "Mr. Beam?"

He snapped his mouth shut, too hard.

She called, "We'll soon have our own linen but I wonder . . ."

"Sheets?"

"And a few towels if you could spare them."

The Astronomer pawed through the hall closet where brown paper packages of flat laundry had been tossed, some of them opened at random, some empty. He pulled out sheets, two towels, two pillowcases. Eva Ridge came halfway down the stairs and reached for them.

"Thank you. I'll wash them, of course. And I wonder . . . a broom?"

Silently he fetched it from behind the kitchen door, thrust the handle upward into her waiting fingers. "Nobody's been upstairs for a long time," he said crossly.

"Thank you," was all she answered.

When she had gone, the Astronomer saw with relief that night had fallen, and he carried the library book into the back yard. He struck a wooden match, stared at the diagram and adjusted his position. When he blew out the small flame it seemed his fingers were still burning and sulphurous. He closed his eyes and made his own nightfall, and when they had adjusted to darkness he began to study the sky, frowning. One of the muscles in his neck complained. He swept his gaze across the sky, looking for patterns. If that was it, it was a queer dragon, he thought.

The front door of his own house slammed. He saw Fred Ridge walking rapidly down Helicks Street toward the bus stop. When the Astronomer swung his head to the lighted upstairs window, he could see the woman passing back and forth, throwing her image on the yellow shade. He watched the shadow stop; a set of fingers made a latticework at the mouth. She was lighting a cigarette. Then she began to march from left to right, right to left. Room's not big enough for pacing, thought the Astronomer, and swung his eyes to the dark vistas above, where the dragon shape was traced by stars thousands of miles apart. For a few seconds his eyes superimposed the lighted window onto the black sky. He blinked its shape away. Thuban, he recited. Al Tais. These were stars in the Draco constellation. He noticed the light from that window threw down a golden rectangle on the grass, and when the woman paced in the upper room a misty twin slid back and forth at his feet.

Thuban and Al Tais, he tried again; but it was no more effective than a list of Santa's reindeer. He closed the book and stalked into the front yard, where he could not see the lighted window but he could not see all the constellation, either. His neighbor to the right, Mrs. Blevins, was taking the cool of the day on her front porch.

"I seen you looking up," she called pleasantly. "Is there going to be an eclipse?"

"No," said the Astronomer.

"Not a cloud in the sky," she said, "and my petunias are bent over. Seems like spigot water's not as good as rain." When she saw he was moving farther away from her across the yard she raised her voice. "I see you've got company."

"Not for long."

"It'll be good to have some young people on the street." Mrs. Blevins stood up from her rocker, talking louder and louder. "Old people in old houses—it gets on my nerves. Is it kinfolk or roomers?"

"Roomers."

She cupped a hand to her mouth. "I might try that myself," she shouted. "How'd you decide what to charge?"

He said shortly he had taken what they offered.

"That ain't businesslike," called Mrs. Blevins. "We ought to set up the same rate for the whole street. Property owners got to stick together."

He withdrew even more, crossing his own front sidewalk to get to the far half of the yard.

"You want a piece of cake?" she screamed.

He shook his head and pointed to his own house. Then there was nothing to do but march up the front steps and go inside it, and straight down the hall through the kitchen and out the back door again. He turned his star map and matched the proper line with the horizon.

But since he had automatically held the page in the clearest light, he found he was standing right in the oblong cast from that second-story window. And even as he realized this a shadow crossed him and passed on, then came over him a second time.

Fuming, he gave up and went indoors to bed. It was a long time before he stopped hearing the steady footsteps of the woman in the upstairs room.

The Astronomer dreamed he stood by a culvert after a rainstorm, watching twigs and bottle caps and old letters with the stamps soaked off carried away on the dark water. When he woke the pipes inside the wall by his bed were roaring. Both dream and reality were a disappointment to him. Again the upstairs toilet flushed. Water bill's going sky high, he thought.

He started for the hall, turned back and slapped through the garments hanging in his closet. Once he had owned a bathrobe; he remembered it. Plaid flannel. It was nowhere to be found and again he heard water rushing down the pipes. He pulled on trousers and a shirt.

In the hall he leaned on the stair rail and finally decided to call out, "Everything all right up there?" Nobody answered. He reached for his pocket watch, then went back into his bedroom and found it lying on the bureau. Eight-thirty. Morning. Over his head he counted rapid thuds—bare feet this time, muffled. He found his own shoes and left the laces open while he shuffled toward the kitchen.

He was almost there when he heard the other noise from upstairs. The Astronomer made a face. "Is somebody sick?" he finally called.

After a silence the woman's voice said, "You're damn right."

He came back to look up the stairs. She was crouched on the top one, wearing a pair of jeans and what seemed to be Fred's oldest shirt. Her spread fingers were resting atop the uncombed hair.

"You by yourself?"

"He's looking for work. You got anything for vomiting? Seltzer?"

"Nothing but baking soda."

She shook her head. "All I need do is belch one time to bring my feet up out of my mouth." She closed her eyes and grunted.

The Astronomer turned away. "I'm going to make coffee," he said reluctantly. "Don't guess you're up to that."

"No." She frowned, rolled her eyes, then slapped her hand across her mouth and ran to the upstairs bathroom. He could hear her retching.

To the empty air he said, "You better go back to bed," and turned to the kitchen to start the coffee boiling. While it was thumping up and down inside the pot he blackened a piece of bread on the top burner of the oil range, flipping it over with a pair of forks. He chopped a piece of cold butter off the chunk in the refrigerator and tried to mash it around with the back of a teaspoon. Elsie used to melt the butter, he remembered, and paint it on toast with a brush. When a little song started inside the kitchen faucet, he knew the toilet had been flushed again upstairs.

Munching the toast, he looked inside the refrigerator again. Yes, there it was. He went to the bottom of the stairs and called, "Mrs. Ridge?"

She lurched out of the bathroom, one hand pressed to the middle of her body. "Everything must be tore loose from everything else," she mumbled.

"There's a bottle of club soda in the refrigerator."

"Why not? At least it'll be something to lose besides my stomach lining." She held the rail very carefully descending the stairs, and when she passed him the Astronomer drew back from her sour smell.

"I don't guess you need a doctor?" he asked her back.

Eva Ridge said she didn't like doctors. She got the soda herself

and snapped off the cap against the metal handle of a drawer.
"That's good," she sighed after the first swallow. "I hope it stays
down." She groaned very softly.

I hope it ain't catching, thought the Astronomer, putting the
table between them. "You better sit down," he said, and she did.

She took a swallow of soda and forced it back and forth in the
cracks between her teeth. A speck of foam appeared at the corner
of her pale mouth. "Last night when I ate that hamburger it was
pretty good," she said, "but it sure did rot while I was sleeping."

The Astronomer ran his tongue daintily over the roof of his
mouth. One of the troubles with women, he thought, one of the
many troubles, was the way they put everything into words and
spoke it right out. At how many supper tables had Elsie said
briskly, "Don't eat them onions. You know it gives you gas." And
once he'd been drinking tomato juice when she told how Mrs.
Blevins' grandson had his tonsils took out and something went
wrong and for two days the child's blood ran downhill in his
throat. That was the end of tomato juice for him.

Eva Ridge had been watching while he absently scraped toast
crumbs off the table onto the kitchen floor. "I meant to bring back
your broom."

"I warned him it was dusty up there. Used to have a woman in
to clean once a week but I let her go," he said, defensive. The
Negress had breathed in and out between gritted teeth—it was
that simple. He had fired her because he could not stand the
serpent's hiss in her dark mouth.

"Have you been a widower long?"

"Yes." He opened a cabinet, intending to offer her a glass for
the soda, and saw for the first time that every tumbler on the shelf
was cloudy. Surprised, he counted them: Five. Had there not once
been twenty or more, in a neat upside-down row to keep out dusty
air? He took the nearest one and ran a cloth inside. "You want a
glass?"

She nodded. "You ought to keep glasses turned the other way
unless you wash that shelf a lot. The rims get dirty."

"Elsie always kept them this way." He saw her wipe a finger around the edge before she poured in the soda, and he could imagine what duties that finger had been performing while she was sick upstairs.

Politely she asked if he had any children.

"I had two boys. Both dead."

Eva Ridge closed her eyes a minute. "That's hard," she said. "Losing children. That's very hard."

"Robert died in the war." On some hot Pacific island, Robert had rolled over a dead fellow soldier and been blown to bits by a booby trap wired beneath the corpse. For a long time afterward Elsie had hung the set of dog tags they received in the parlor window; and if these shook in the smallest wind she would stop motionless, and slide her right hand under her breasts and lift them slightly upward. When Elsie died, Horton Beam stored the tags in the bottom of a trunk.

The Astronomer said, "It was a long time ago."

"I've got two children," said Eva softly.

"Well, they can't live here! Two people is twice as many as I promised, and that's one place I draw the line! No children in this house!"

She stood, shaking her head. "There won't be any children in this house. I'm a little dizzy. Think I'll lie down." She carried the glass out of his kitchen.

With relief the Astronomer opened his book. The Dipper had seven stars. *Alkaid, Mizar, Alioth, Megrez, Phecda, Merak, Dubhe.* He could remember them because their initials traced the chronology of a day: A.M., A.M., P.M., Dark.

Or a life. He thought about Robert's life flying in spatters and droplets against the tropic air. All A.M. Robert never lived to collect on his afternoons.

But John—they had planned to outwit chronology with John. The war was still on when their second son finished high school, but Horton and Elsie Beam were determined John would not be swallowed up by it. Robert's G.I. insurance had been earmarked to send John to college. He would be exempt from army service so long as he took R.O.T.C. at the university; and there were signs the war might end before John would be educated enough or trained enough to go and die in it.

So in the summer of 1944—thirteen years ago—sophomore John Beam had been spending his vacation as part-time worker for Wicker Seed Company of Newton City, shoveling grain down the sides of a bin. And one day the wheat slid suddenly in upon him and carried his feet into the slot and buried him five feet under; and he smothered before the others could help.

At one time the very thought of it had made him suck in his own breath until his chest was hot with pain, but now the Astronomer only closed his eyes briefly. He had outlived Robert, and outlived John, and outlived Elsie; and finally he had outlived his grief for all of them.

With care he drew the Dipper against his closed eyelids. *Alkaid, Mizar, Alioth, Megrez, Phecda, Merak, Dubhe.* They made a set of mental stepping stones.

When he stood to rinse his coffee cup the Astronomer had begun to hum a popular tune:

> I've told every little star
> Just how grand I think you are . . . .

He knew only the tune and none of the words. It was a cheerful little melody, he thought. And almost instantly: Elsie never sang around the house.

He carried his book on stars to the porch swing. *I wonder why that was.*

Fred Ridge came swinging down the street before he had turned more than two pages. The young man was whistling. Found his job. Coming to brag.

The Astronomer called before he had barely turned in at the walk. "Mr. Ridge? Oh, Mr. Ridge!"

"Good morning, Mr. Beam."

"I'm telling you the same thing I told your wife—I'll have no

children in this house. I want that understood or you can take
your eight dollars and put it right back in your pocket."

The mouth that had been spread on a smile congealed around
the teeth, and Fred Ridge looked more like a terrier than ever.
Ready to bite. "She told you about the children?"

"I guess you wasn't going to tell anything till I heard babies
crying in my own house!"

"They're not babies," said Fred Ridge softly. "I never thought
she'd tell about the children."

"Well, I hope it's clear to you and you can make it clear to her.
I told her straight out: no children. But sometimes women hang
on to what they want; they don't argue but inside they're already
making their own plans."

"Ain't that the truth!" sighed Fred, and he massaged the back
of his neck with those wiry fingers. "I can't feature it. That she'd
talk to somebody she didn't hardly know."

"Well, she was sick," said the Astronomer.

"Sick? What you mean, sick?"

"Been sick all morning. I . . . ."

Fred Ridge pushed by him and started into the hall calling
Eva's name. The Astronomer yelled, "I gave her some soda water!"

"Eva?" he heard the young man call. "Where are you? What's
the matter?" When he bounded up the stairs the Astronomer could
feel the boards vibrate all the way to the porch. This house
couldn't stand young people living in it, he thought irritably. You
put two little kids in here and the paint would flake right off the
walls.

All that racket over an upset stomach. One good thing about
being sixty-five, he thought, so many upset stomachs have come
and gone that one's about like another. At least till the last one
comes. And this Eva Ridge; she's not the kind to die from some
little thing like that.

Lots of things I could tell that boy. I could tell him if a woman
gets up to any age at all she's hard to kill. Once her womb dries
up without serious trouble, she's over the hump; she gets solid.

She's got to wear out at the far end of ninety or else Death's got to come and murder her the hard way. Once a woman gets fifty, he's had his last good, clear chance; now he has to be sneaky. Death has to use all his skill to get old women.

Fooled Elsie, He did. She slid by pneumonia and childbirth, got over being flushed and queer by the time she was fifty. Then she turned to iron. Never even got a head cold. Carried all the furniture around on her back, moving it from place to place, always moving it.

So Death let her relax, let her get confident. Let her fall down all the cellar stairs and get nothing but a bad cut along one arm; and then He waited. Used it to strike her down. Blood poisoning. A chill, a fever, a breath that toothpaste could not clean, a tongue that water could not wet, a feeling of gloom, some sudden sweats —all the little symptoms. Guerrilla warfare she couldn't bring her strength to bear upon. She never even thought to go to a doctor till she'd lost a war she didn't even know had been declared. Septicemia, the doctor called it.

So there it was: one dead soldier, one bin of wheat, one little cut. I wonder what He's got in store for me.

The Astronomer lay back in the porch swing again and opened his book and began to pronounce the words. Polaris. Draco. Vega. Septicemia? What had made him remember the name of that little death? He clicked the others rapidly through his mouth: Pollux and Castor. Leo. Arcturus. Hercules. Hercules. Alkaid. Mizar. Alioth. Megrez. Phecda. Merak. Dubhe.

At last they lay overlapping and complete on the surface of his mind, like a set of shining scales.

Now there were three people living in the old house on Helicks Street. As soon as each began giving any attention to the other, a pattern and schedule developed.

First the Astronomer noticed the times Fred Ridge went out and came in again; he saw the upstairs lights go on and off, heard soft voices.

"Got a night job at a filling station," Ridge said at the end of the first week when he handed over eight more dollars. "Not much, but it's better than nothing. Little town like this, you wouldn't think any station would stay open all night."

"No, I wouldn't."

"You think Eva's all right? Me working at night, sleeping half the day. Hard to tell."

"I guess so."

Walking away the roomer said, half to himself, "She sure has got the blues."

The Astronomer had no idea how Eva was. The day she brought back the empty soda bottle and glass she asked if she could have coffee in his kitchen in the mornings. He told her he didn't care.

So every morning she would stumble down the stairs, heavy-eyed and silent, to pour herself one cup of his strong coffee; and at the end of that first week he found one of Elsie's measuring cups filled neatly and leveled off with eight tablespoonfuls of ground coffee. He figured Eva had bought at least a pound bag but would be doling it out to him one cup at a time. That way, he thought, we won't have fresh coffee but once a month.

Nothing was the way he had planned. Fred Ridge left the house at twilight and every night the Astronomer woke at 3:15 A.M. and heard him coming home. He knew suddenly how clocks—and pocket watches, and wrist watches—had first been invented. Three people living together in some cave had been enough to start it.

Some days the Astronomer did not see the young couple. When Eva drank her coffee he might be trimming the hedge, or putting a sheetful of laundry on the front steps for the truck to collect. He would be throwing the covers up on his own bed, or reading his book about the stars.

But most mornings she would come into the kitchen while he was still scraping the last hard egg white out of its shell. She poured her own coffee, said no more than "Morning," washed out her own cup. She was almost as comfortable as Elsie, the

Astronomer thought, except Elsie had never smoked cigarettes while Eva never seemed to stop.

One morning when she was late he went to the foot of the stairs, half tempted to call her. She came in sight just as he opened his mouth. He put a hand up as if he were grooming his mustache.

"I overslept," she said, and almost smiled. "What time is it anyway?"

"Nine. You got a clock up there?"

She shook her head. "Any coffee left in the pot?"

"Plenty." He followed her to the kitchen and ran his hand along the windowsill until he found the wrist watch which the mill had given him. "This thing's just rusting away in the window," he said. "Might as well get some use out of it." He held the watch out, face down, and she laid it in her palm and traced curiously the engraving on the back.

"Well done," she read. "What did you do well?"

He was not able to explain, later, the sudden closing of his throat. It felt as if someone had tied a fat knot in his neck. He shook his head, trying to loosen his own skin. "Not much," he finally said. She had combed her hair this morning and it was spread in an aureole about her head, as if she had lain in bed an extra hour, brushing it wide against the pillow.

"You mind if I wear it on my own arm?"

"I don't mind." He saw she was holding her wrist toward him and he took the watch and began to fumble with the strap. "It may not even run. If Corey Knitting Mill has finally give away something for nothing, it's the first time."

"Why for nothing? It says 'Well Done.' "

His face felt like a furnace. "Saying and doing is two different things." He buckled the strap and turned away. "I reckon you two worked it out about the children."

"Some things you can't work out," she said shortly. "Where's that coffee?"

He matched her tone. "Where it always is," he snapped, and left the kitchen.

He settled himself into the front porch swing, started it swaying. The sunlight came mottled through the vines and made bright patches on his skin and clothes. He would never get over this particular joy of being outside Corey Knitting Mill, this chance to lie in his porch swing in the daytime while his body grew warm and felt light and seemed to rise on his bones like yeast bread.

But this morning Eva followed him to the porch. "Thank you for the use of the watch," she said.

He kept his eyes shut. The way he was lying a circlet of sunlight fell just in the center of his forehead, and when the swing moved a golden ball rolled from one eyebrow to the other. "That's o.k.," he said.

He heard her go and come back again. "I brought you another cup of coffee."

He swung his feet to the porch floor, sat up, took the cup. "First time I ever saw you wear a dress," he said.

Covered with vases of blue flowers, the dress buttoned all the way up the front. Eva tugged at the belt. "Getting too tight," was all she said. She pulled up a wooden rocker and arranged herself in it carefully, propping her feet on the banister rail among the vines. Before they disappeared under green leaves, the Astronomer saw that her toenails were painted red. She had carried a second cup of coffee for herself and she rested it on the arm of the chair. Touching the watch she said, "You never did tell me what you did well."

"I kept my fingers from getting caught in the machine," he grunted. He felt like a nap.

Eva giggled. "That's not a bad idea. We ought to teach our kids that: Stand Back from the Machine! Be more sense than all the sermons."

Nosir, thought the Astronomer. If you're leading up to kids, nosir. He put a cushion under his head and stretched out again in the swing.

She said softly, "I miss my children," and buried her mouth in the coffee cup. He pretended to be asleep. "Mr. Beam?"

Nothing. Slow breathing.

Eva crossed to the porch rail and emptied the rest of her coffee onto the ground. When he heard her walking into the house and up the stairs he pulled his book from under the cushion and began to thumb pages. Parts of this new book he did not like. He skipped gravitational effects; he did not care about birthdays and star influences. He would not read the theories which tied Moses and the plagues of Egypt to some heavenly disturbance or plotted the course of a star over ancient Judaea. The word "relative," he had decided, was ugly in both its sound and its meaning. Had old Walt Whitman been able to leave that lecture and write his verses, he should have gone the minute that learn'd astronomer started explaining what was relative. Anyway he—Horton Beam, *this* Astronomer—had walked out on that whole discussion. Keep it simple, he told the book. Let the stars wheel by.

This was the book he used, at least his selections from it, all those summer nights of June. Some evenings he stood in his yard with a recently purchased pair of Army surplus binoculars, and verified what its pages said. He could see what he hoped were two of Jupiter's moons.

By the first of July the Astronomer had begun adding sums from his rent and pension money to see if he could afford to buy a telescope in time for next month's meteor shower. If Eva and Fred Ridge paid every week . . . if he ate less often at the Atlas Café . . . he could manage. Every morning he told himself while he waited in the kitchen for the sound of Eva coming down for coffee: *I'm putting up with all this just to get a telescope.*

In July, also, his binoculars picked out a cloud of stars in Hercules, like a little cancer on a giant. He thought about primitive man pointing skyward at such things, talking of divine signs. He knew it was only an expected star cluster.

But curiosity overcame him. The Newton City library checked out more books to W. Whitman—this time on Greek mythology. He stumbled through the strange words trying to learn how the constellation had been named. When finally he knew the story of

Hercules with his eaten flesh, and how he had climbed onto his own pyre and gone quietly to sleep in the flames, the Astronomer was disturbed. Such a stupid old story, not much better than *Bride of the Green Planet*. He regretted his curiosity. Of course he knew the little shadow west in the kneeling warrior was only a swarm of stars and yet . . . and yet he did not like the look of it. He could not rid himself of the feeling something unpleasant was about to happen.

Once Eva found him at the breakfast table muttering over the Greek stories.

"What now?"

He sounded the word carefully. "Myth-ol-o-gy."

"I thought you were strictly a star man," she said.

"I am."

She pointed to a drawing on the book's cover. "Texaco Gas?"

"Pegasus," he said, very carefully again. "He was a flying horse."

"Sounds like a kid's story to me."

It seemed to the Astronomer her mouth somehow laid children the way a hen laid eggs. That was all she could talk about. "I don't know any kids' stories," he snapped, strictly a star man himself.

Over her shoulder as she left Eva said, "I used to know a few."

He wondered about that. Had she known about Hercules? Or Bellerophon riding the winged horse to kill a three-headed monster? Or the woman who had snakes growing from her scalp and could only be killed reflected in a shield?

"If it wasn't for needing a telescope," the Astronomer said aloud to his coffee cup, "I'd throw them people out."

It was a Sunday night in July. The Milky Way lay north to south, halfway up over the eastern horizon, and the Astronomer was traveling it through his glasses when he heard the sound of angry voices.

The upstairs window was open to the humid night. Bits of their quarrel, like pieces of paper, seemed to swirl down and about his head. He glued the glasses to his eyes and stared blindly at Leo where the Sickle was going down.

"You damned fool!" Fred Ridge was shouting. "Oh, you fool!"

"Half fool," came Eva's slightly calmer voice. "You were there, too. You were right there and not in China."

Fred said he wished he *was* in China. "There's the money, for one thing. You know what they pay me at that filling station! And what about Sion? He's likely looking for us. We got to be able to move at a minute's notice!"

"We can still move."

"The hell we can. And when he does find out, he'll think that's why you left. You know he'll think that."

Her voice became a screech. "He can read a calendar! Lots of things wrong with Sion, but he ain't stupid! He can still read and he can still count. I tell you, I didn't know myself! Not till yesterday."

Something scraped across the floor, perhaps a chair. "I knew we oughta gone farther away. Newton City's too close. This is too much. Too much. We gotta move."

Eva sounded tired when she answered. The Astronomer couldn't make out all her words. Something about not being able to afford moving any more. "Damn right I know how much they pay you!" came the last of it, at top volume.

Fred said again, "You fool!"

Now Eva gave a harsh laugh. "It's no mental thing, Fred Ridge. Smart or dumb, makes no difference. It ain't in my *head*, you . . ."

He wouldn't let her finish. "You're glad—I can see that. By God, if I find you did this on purpose . . ."

"Setting you a trap?" The laughter started again, broke. "All you can think is *you*. Hard on *you*. Trap for *you*. All you see now is poor little Fred Ridge, the boy the rules caught up with!"

The Astronomer was gritting his teeth. He found he had focused carefully on a patch of black space, evenly between the flecks of light. My telescope, he thought. My telescope and Eva. He hardly caught himself thinking that second thing.

Her voice had run on. ". . . wondered how I feel since you walked into the room. I left a lot, Fred. Not just that idiot back there, not what went on around me seven days a week. I could spare that. But there's two kids back there and what the hell you care? All you care about is finding it's not as easy as it looked, and I knew that before you was even born!"

By this time the Astronomer, not stopping to think, found he had left the yard, hurried across the front porch and into the hall. Eva was still yelling. Her voice drew him up the stairs. He hardly heard Fred's angry words.

"Don't throw that up now it's too late! You knew when you came just what you got and what you left. . . ."

"You NEVER know!" Eva screamed. By then the Astronomer, without knocking, had banged open their bedroom door to find her drawn back against one wall, her features askew, and Fred with one arm raised taking his first furious step to where she stood.

"You cut that out!" the Astronomer shouted. Automatically he made his voice louder than both of theirs. He was almost surprised to hear his own words exploding. If he was surprised, Fred and Eva froze where they were. Their open mouths still held the last angry sound. Their faces, all except the eyes, stopped still as if a camera had caught and held their fury.

Horton Beam swallowed, looked at the arm which Ridge had flexed and lifted several words ago. "Stop that!" he ordered between his teeth. The arm came slowly down. If he touches her, the Astronomer thought, I'll kill him. It was a discovery. He looked at Eva to see whether he might have spoken that aloud. Her face showed nothing but surprise.

It's true, I'll kill him! Unable to stand that thought blazing in his head he added lamely, "I can't have all this noise!" turned, and fled down the hall for six long steps, leaned on the wall and told his heart: Slowly. *Slowly*. The tremble inside his chest vibrated outward in spreading rings as far as his fingertips. He looked down the staircase with wide eyes, as if some chasm had opened up before him.

Now he could hear them again inside the bedroom, quieter.

"What got into Beam?" said Ridge.

"You heard him. Noise," said Eva. Was her voice cautious? Was it veiled? Did it believe that clumsy thing?

"Was we making that much noise?"

She spoke as if her throat were lined with rust. "We were getting ready to." A pause. "You would have hit me, Fred."

"I never meant . . . Eva, I'm sorry. Coming the way it did. And you so calm as if you expected me just to, you know, grin about it."

"You've not seen me grinning much lately."

"You're sure it isn't . . . you're sure I . . ."

"Listen," she snapped, "Sion was careful. We had two kids already. You hear me? He was *careful*. I can draw you a picture."

"Goddamnit, I was careful, too!"

"Not all the time. He went to Charlotte—you remember that night?"

"Yes," said Fred softly.

"You can count it up if you want to," she said, her voice rising again. "I'll lend you my fingers and toes if you want to figure out the days! Oh, it's yours, all right. And I didn't have this piece of news before I left Sion. Yesterday I got the word, yesterday. You believe that?"

"Hell, what'll we do?"

At least I got him to that point, thought the Astronomer grimly.

Fred repeated, "What do you want us to do?"

"Not quarrel, for one thing." He could hear Eva pacing. Maybe she had put a palm to her forehead and spread the fingers into her hair, the way she did early mornings.

Fred was walking, too. Then both sets of footsteps stopped. Had he touched her? The Astronomer winced. He made himself remember his telescope and the coming meteor shower. Had no business in there. Leaving right now. Go watch the stars. None of my business. Not even interested.

"How long will it be?" he heard Fred ask.

"Early March," said Eva. It was as if she picked up some earlier sentence, editing out the whole quarrel. "Count back three months and add nine days, the doctor said. Maybe March eleventh."

March, thought the Astronomer in the hallway. The Sickle will be halfway up the eastern sky again. Orion will be bright; Cetus and Pisces going away . . . Fish giving way to Man . . .

Now he stumbled hastily down the stairs and wondered where he had dropped his binoculars when he hurried to her. He found them finally, hanging half on and half off the front porch, with one of the lenses broken.

"Goddamn." He sat right down on the steps, suddenly too tired to stand a minute longer, and began rubbing one finger back and forth on his mustache. It felt like toothbrush bristles. It's my house. Nobody can yell like that in my house for eight lousy dollars. Broke my binoculars. Goddamn.

He was still there, still stroking, when the two came quietly down the steps behind him. They opened the screen and stood on the porch at his back. He moved his forefinger one inch east, one inch west. He would not turn around. Ridge cleared his throat.

"Sorry about the noise."

"It wasn't anything, really," the woman said. "But it must have sounded terrible." The Astronomer stared into the street. Like the fur of an angry cat, the hairs above his lip seemed electric. He kept rubbing.

"They're broken!" cried Eva. She reached to take the strap of his fieldglasses from his other hand. "A crack. Can it be fixed?"

Fred Ridge offered quickly to have the binoculars fixed, as if in some way this would make things up to Eva.

"I'll do it," the Astronomer said. He still would not face them. Heavily he added, "I never meant to butt in."

The boards of the porch groaned as Fred Ridge shifted his weight from one foot to the other. "We was just going down to the café for a beer. Why don't you come along, Mr. Beam? This heat's been rough. No wonder we been yelling."

The Astronomer shook his head.

"Do come," said Eva. "We'll feel better if you come."

For the first time since the scene in the bedroom, the Astronomer looked into her face. No change. Nothing to show that 280 nights of stars drifting westward might add up to one unwanted child. Her face was open and innocent. For a minute, like Fred, he wanted to strike her. There ought to be some mark on her face, even if she had to settle for a bruise. Inside himself he cried, *I want that telescope.* And said aloud, "I'd like a beer. Thanks."

They walked three abreast along the dark sidewalk by Helicks Street, making conversation about Fred's job. "Them niggers come in after midnight to buy a quarter's worth of gas," Fred said. The Astronomer said if it wasn't one thing it was another, no matter where you worked. Or what you did, said Eva. She was the quietest of the three.

Politely Fred asked, "You studying stars out there?"

"Just something I got interested in. Passes the time. No time for things like that before I retired."

"What do you get out of it?" asked Eva. "You know, just finding the right one and giving it the right name?"

Adam gave names. "They're far away," he fumbled. "Different. You buy a dog, now, you get involved in the thing, try to read its mind, decide the animal loves you. Decide you love it back. You get to thinking it's the smartest animal in the world—you know?" He saw they didn't know. "Most things people do," he tried again, "lead to lying. You tell yourself it's important, or kind, or good to pass the time this way. First thing you know, you're in some club with other people full of the same lies."

"Never thought of that," mumbled Fred, showing by his tone he was not thinking of it now either.

"The stars are just out there. Facts. You find the right one or you don't. If you don't, you buy a lens with a higher power." He was glad to find himself talking again about lenses, objects, *things.* By August, he rushed on, he would buy a small telescope.

"It all beats me," said Ridge. "I don't like the way that makes me feel, space and everything." He waved an arm at the sky. "Like I was the size of some ant."

"We all are," said the Astronomer. "That's one of the lies stars won't let you tell."

"It would make me lonesome," said Eva with a shudder. The Astronomer changed the subject before she could get started on children. He talked about the kind of telescope he'd like to own.

Then they were in front of the Atlas Café, passing under an arch of neon and through the gray light to a booth. Fred and the girl sat together on one side; the Astronomer faced them.

"Three beers," said Ridge to the man at the counter. "Pabst and . . . ?"

"Budweiser," the Astronomer supplied.

"Two Blue Ribbons and a Bud." The man brought three cans, cold and wet to the fingers, and a set of glasses on a tray.

There was an uncomfortable silence. Fred asked where Mr. Beam had worked before he retired and the Astronomer said he had been a weaver at Corey Knitting Mill.

"He got this watch. I told you about that," said Eva. She was wearing it on her arm. " 'Well done,' it says on the back." She pointed to its face. The hairs on her arm were light and fine, as if she had dusted them with powder.

"They give them watches to everybody."

"How long ago did you lose your wife?" asked Eva.

Twelve years. And the children dead, too. He looked away from her when he mentioned children. And all the time the Astronomer answered these questions he found it hard not to stare at Fred's right hand. This was the hand which had been raised to hit her, in the eye, or perhaps across the mouth. . . .

"I lost my temper back there . . ." Fred said abruptly. Perhaps he had noticed the stare.

Eva interrupted. "Fred didn't mean it. I understand. I hope you understand it, too."

"I had no business coming up. I won't do that again."

The Astronomer's little sentence was like an open door they had been searching for, all up and down some winding wall. And into that opening which they had both invented, they poured the whole story. One would barely finish a sentence before the other would lift it up and rush on. They wove the way a loom weaves fabric out of threads. The Astronomer turned the beer glass—one rotation right, one left—watched bubbles rise from its bottom, studied the foam subsiding while they talked.

They told him how Eva had been married ("very young," she inserted) to a man named Sion Leeds, had two children, a boy aged one and a daughter nearly three. How Fred Ridge ("Always was a drifter till now," he supplied) had come to work for Mr. Leeds, selling used cars, spending his days on two lots. The front lot held the sale cars, clean and waxed and with mended upholstery, and behind a leaning tin fence was a sea of metal which catered to scrap dealers and teen-age boys rebuilding older models. ("Depressing," said Eva. "The way it looked. The nice cars in front and out back what they were going to be someday. Like reading the future.")

They told how Fred had eaten meals at the Leeds's house and watched her, how she had carried bag lunches to the car lot and watched him; how one day each had caught the other behind that tin fence. ("We just hung on," said Fred, sweating.) The Astronomer rotated his glass of beer.

They told of the days going by, their plans not to see each other, the accidental meetings, the near-accidental meetings. ("Skip all that," snapped Eva. "It sounds like an excuse.") Then they told him one day they simply walked away and got on a bus which would take them twenty-eight dollars' worth of distance away from that place, that man, those rusting springs. And the two children. Eva didn't mention them again but the Astronomer could picture them, suddenly, playing inside an old car behind the tin fence and beeping a silent horn.

All this they told him—Fred did most of the talking—but they did not mention the night in June when Sion Leeds had been in Charlotte and Fred had not been careful. They did not say Eva had walked away from home not suspecting that carelessness was growing inside her like Hercules' aggregation of stars. Or whether, that first morning she was sick in the Astronomer's house, she had wondered what day it was or what day it ought to be. They did not say she was five weeks pregnant now, and Fred had nearly hit her on account of it.

"We loved each other," Fred was saying. He wiped his wet face. "Nothing to do but go."

"Nothing," Eva echoed.

"It's not what you think." Fred took a long look into both their faces. "It's like being married. I mean it. Better or worse."

"Worse," sighed Eva to herself.

"End of the world. And everything."

"End." Eva looked as if any minute she would cry. She glanced once across the table at the Astronomer, rather timidly, he thought. When he turned his glass another time he was happy to find it empty. "Let's have another," he said.

They drank the second beer. Fred had put his hand atop Eva's and they lay, one covering the other, on the scarred table. The Astronomer was not sure what he ought to say. Haltingly at last, he tried to explain the coming meteor shower and what his telescope would find. The other two pretended to listen. Their faces were bored and lonely and disappointed.

It seemed to the Astronomer his former sharp focus was wearing round and blunt. One thing led to another, and that one touched some third unsuspected discovery. It was like taking a cup of water, one purposeful cup, and emptying it onto one selected spot; and then chasing off after undreamed rivulets and pools and tiny cataracts.

He should never have looked up the story of Hercules. That was his first mistake. Now he was toppling a row of mistakes like a row of dominoes, and moving in progression away from his earlier intent. Because of Castor and Pollux he had to find out about Leda. Cassiopeia took him into Ethiopia with other questions. Orion and his dog carried him over an old sea where the arrow flew. Diana's seven nymphs and the women who had nursed Bacchus marched in a sky the Astronomer had meant to keep austere.

He had allowed for only fact and observation. Now these were being pressed into the mold of old and human stories; and when he watched the distant constellations drift westward he began to see quarrels and loving and sudden death.

He thought he would halt this process by concentrating on something real and specific. He gave up the plan to purchase a telescope, which he could do quickly with mere money, and began to construct one himself. This was a problem worthy of a man's retirement years, even if it did mean bringing home another book from Newton City library.

One convex lens, some cardboard mailing tubes, tape and glue, the problem of finding how long the lens's focus was . . . he piled tools and objects about him on the parlor floor. The task kept him too busy for coffee with Eva in the mornings. He worked slowly. He would barely nod she called "Good Morning" from the hall.

But sometimes he might look up from his work after she was out of sight behind the kitchen door. See? I can *build* a telescope! I'm not dependent on you for anything!

With care the Astronomer painted his homemade spyglass black. All day its surface dried atop Elsie's favorite marble-topped table. In the evening when he tried it on the steady moon all he could see was a glare of light. The main tube was shortened, tried, shortened

again. He carried his coffee daily into the parlor and left a series of
pale rings on the furniture. One morning he found a new measuring
cup of ground coffee left on the kitchen counter. Another day the
rent was there, weighted with a spatula.

He tried the telescope again. Now he could see the moon had
holes and hills, although his glass gave it a strange color; and he
was sure of the moons of Jupiter and an occasional bright nebula.

These things the Astronomer studied so he need not see Eva's
face. But sometimes he focused on a star field and as it began to
come in sharply it would round to the shape of her eye, or string
out like a wisp of her hair in the wind. This caused a pain in his
head behind each eye.

Late summer nights the Astronomer would lie in his bed with
his hands crushed into fists and strain to hear sounds from upstairs—sounds like the legs of the bed vibrating on the floor above,
or a sigh dragged out. And sometimes he did hear things. All
windows were open and the ceiling was thin. Sometimes he did.

They have to get out of my house, the Astronomer would think
in the darkness. He has to get out of my house.

Daytimes he worked to build an altazimuth stand for the telescope, using a piece of wood and three broom handles. When it
was done he found it inconvenient to use and moved the stand
into his bedroom, where he stumbled on it every night. After that
he decided to buy concave mirrors to make a reflector, but his
hands were clumsy and refused to join things properly. Finally he
counted the bills he had been tossing on the kitchen windowsill,
endorsed his last mill paycheck and his first retirement voucher
and bought himself a small telescope. By that time, it seemed
permissible to buy one. Already he had demonstrated what he
could do, by will power alone, if necessary. He found a storage
place for the homemade spyglass and the cumbersome telescope
stand inside the hall closet.

It was because of his new telescope the Astronomer was still
awake and sitting on the front steps quite late when Ridge came
home one night. The sky had been crowded and cloudless. He had

lost track of time. Must be 3 A.M., he thought. Eva's asleep by now.

"You're up late," Ridge grunted.

He held out the new telescope. "This is it," he said. "Want to try?"

Fred took the tube without much enthusiasm and glanced through it at the sky. "Makes things big," he admitted, and handed it back.

"Want to sit down?"

"Might as well. Everything smells greasy when I get out of that station. Takes me awhile to sleep. I wash and wash, and it still smells."

"Hot, too," said the Astronomer. "Humid."

"Terrible. Every drunk in town wanted me to wash his windshield. You find something good up there tonight?"

"Been looking for the meteor shower. Sometimes it's so easy to see what I'm looking for that I don't even trust it." Gently he closed the telescope. "Thought I saw a meteor fall from Perseus but the book said it would. Who knows if I saw it or just expected to see it?"

None of this interested Fred a bit. "Eva ever come out and look at these things?"

It was casual. Wasn't it casual? "She goes to bed early," the Astronomer grunted. "I hardly ever see her."

"She's sleepy these days." Ridge stretched. "I feel like somebody painted me over with dirt that'll take scraping to get off." He lit a cigarette.

"Maybe you oughta look around for some other job."

"I never finished high school. There ain't a lot of jobs I can do."

"What's wrong with selling cars? Some people can sell and some can't. If you're a good salesman you can find work anywhere."

He shook his head. "Stay in car sales and make it easy for Leeds to find us? Nope. No thanks."

The Astronomer looked through his telescope down Helicks Street as if he could see Eva's tiny husband coming from far away, with an even tinier child tucked under each arm. The Astronomer said, "Gas station's not too far from the car business."

"I wonder if he's even looked." Fred drew on the cigarette. "He's funny. Quiet. Never could tell what would have any effect on that man. What would make him laugh, for instance. Most jokes didn't. Or what would really make him mad. Maybe he's not even looking."

"Two kids? I think he's looking. He may not even be sure she wasn't kidnaped."

"You're right about that. Wasn't much about her he *did* know."

The Astronomer made his voice light, offhand. "Fellow about your age?"

"Older," said Fred. In the dark the Astronomer smiled. "Bigger," Fred added. He stopped smiling. Fred stretched out his legs, flipped the cigarette away. It swooped through the dark like a miniature star, curved, was pulled to its death by gravity. "Well, she can't go back now, that's for sure," said Fred.

He let that go by.

Fred said, "If it hadn't been for this, I think she might have gone back. I wasn't sure she'd come away at all—she kept changing her mind. One of the kids would get a splinter in his foot and right away she changed her mind."

Against his will the Astronomer said, "You never changed yours?"

"No."

He tried a new subject. "Maybe you could get a job in the next town, with better pay. Come back and forth on weekends. Separated a lot like that, you two might be harder to find." He wiped his forehead. By this time of night you wouldn't think the air would be so hot.

"No," said Fred simply. "I couldn't be away from her. Not now." He stood, walked a few steps into the yard, turned and came back. "Good of you to want to help. Appreciate it." The Astronomer made some noise, almost a growl, for answer.

Fred propped one foot on the second step. "There's no help for people anyway. They do just what they want to do. Nobody listens to anybody else."

"Well . . . sometimes . . ."

"Listen, she don't even listen to *me*. She never came because I had some good arguments for it. She might say so, but it's not true. People do what they want. That's all."

"At my age, I ain't sure."

"That's all I *am* sure about."

"Some people," he offered, "try to do what they think is right."

Fred shook his head. "Big lie. You want to do anything bad enough, and it turns out to be right."

"Yeah!" said the Astronomer, suddenly excited. "That's what I said before! About the meteor falling from Perseus!"

"Huh?" said Fred.

"Nothing."

"I got to go in," Fred vaulted the steps to the porch. "She'll be looking for me. Gets about three o'clock, she starts striking matches to see that watch in the dark."

"She better be careful with matches," was all the Astronomer could think up to answer.

"What you said about doing what's right . . . you mean anything special by that?"

"No."

"Maybe you think she oughta go back. Maybe you been telling her that?"

"She never asked me," he snapped. "I think she misses the two kids, if you want to know what I think."

"Yeah," said Fred, looking off into the sky. "She does. That's why I've never been sure . . . I'll never know if maybe on purpose . . ."

"Both my boys died," said the Astronomer thoughtfully, "and Elsie never let go of them. Not for a minute."

Now Fred turned on him an accusing stare. "You do think she

oughta go back. Carrying my baby to that man. That's what you think."

He let the word slide out between his teeth. "Maybe."

"Beam, you're a funny man," said Fred Ridge. "You want in and you want out."

The Astronomer, with dignity, pulled his telescope out to its full length and trained it overhead. Suddenly Ridge gave a loud laugh. "I thought of something."

"She's striking them matches, looking at the time," he said tersely.

"It was your name done it. Beam. Horton Beam. Beam. Just popped in my head from way back when I used to go to Sunday school. Don't ring no bell with you?"

"No."

"Well, I know it's in the Bible someplace. Didn't you ever hear the story about taking the mote out of somebody else's eye before you even take the beam out of your own? Get it? The *beam* out of your own?"

"What's that?" The Astronomer hated quotations. They had come out of Elsie the way rain comes out of clouds.

"It's in the Bible," chortled Ridge, opening the screen door.

"Not no Bible I ever read!" He heard the young man, still laughing, bound up the stairs to Eva.

The Astronomer slid the segments of the telescope, one by one, inside each other. He rolled the compact tube between his palms and stretched a cramped foot with lazy calm. But all the time his mind was skittering. Nervously his mind chattered: Whose eye am I in? Whose eye?

The Astronomer held groceries against his chest and waited in line for the cashier. The woman ahead of him, as if she were stocking an ark, had taken two of everything in the store. His own purchases were few—bread, canned beans, vienna sausage, crackers, cheese, mustard.

Nobody spoke to him. He glanced around but saw no one he knew. Just after Elsie died parades of women had come in and out his house with casseroles and homemade cakes, but during the past twelve years those women had moved away, or died themselves. Mrs. Blevins still lived next door. Mrs. Eames and Old Lady Rives were directly across Helicks Street from his house. None of the three was in the grocery store.

The aisles were crowded with young women in twill slacks and knee shorts, their heads weighted with steel and plastic curlers. Toddlers rode in the shopping carts and screamed at one another.

He lined up his jars and packages at the checkout counter. If he paid for his food through a bank account, he thought, this crisp young child might eventually learn his name. She totaled his order without lifting her eyes from purple prices inked on each item. When he paid in cash she did not glance beyond his money or the flat of his palm on which she spread the change.

If I had a car, he thought, this boy who carries out grocery bags might someday learn which one was mine.

"I'll carry it," he said. The boy looked as far as his elbows and forearms, and placed the bag into his grasp in such a way that most of his face was hidden behind the crackerbox.

Back home he carried his packages inside and almost fell over Eva, who was down on her hands and knees scrubbing his kitchen floor.

"Now don't say one thing!" she ordered when he stopped in the doorway. "I was going crazy for something to do and I cleaned that upstairs room till the wood wore thin. So don't you fuss."

"I'm much obliged."

"I hate housework," she said, puffing slightly to the rhythm of her arm, "except when everything's in such a mess to start with you can really see some progress."

"Like my kitchen?"

"Yes." She grinned. "It's dry by the sink. You could put that bag down."

He did so, stepping carefully and recalling that first day of retirement when his own hands had been hungry for tools. From where he stood on a dry patch of linoleum by the sink he looked down on her back, and he had a great longing to place his hand between her shoulderblades where the bones might feel like the edges of wings. He turned away and began to set out the groceries.

"You must get tired of being cooped up," he said. "You could go to the picture show at least."

Eva wrung the cloth into a pail. "I guess so. They quit making the pictures I liked. South Seas. Jon Hall. Technicolor."

"You like the radio? Books?"

"Magazines," she said.

"They got lots of magazines at the library. Might even have a book you'd like to read."

She said coldly, "I took a business course. After high school. It's not that I'm dumb."

"I could bring you some books. Or maybe you'd like to go with me next time."

She was standing, stretching her arms. "I might. But none of them star books. All that's over my head, in more ways than one. I never even read Flash Gordon when he used to be in the funny papers. Or that other one—Rogers. Buck Rogers."

"It's not like that. Besides, I look up other things."

"What things?"

He stacked food in the cabinets. "How constellations got their names. You remember that flying horse. Things like that." Things like Ariadne, Daedalus, Neptune's dolphin. The tale that Pan had died on the night of the Nativity. Side issues he had not expected to study and would never use. More and more these things impinged upon the simple stars. "One thing leads to another," he added, frowning.

"Ain't that the truth." Eva poured water down the kitchen drain and scrubbed porcelain. "First kitchen I ever saw without any cleanser."

"Cleanser?"

"Scrubbing powder. Comes in a can." Above the gurgle of water going slowly down the drain there came another sound.

"Somebody's at the door," said Eva. He saw that her hands had frozen into claws.

"I'll get it."

"Nobody's come to your door before. I been listening. Nobody's been at that door since we moved in but you and me and Fred."

Her fear made him peevish. "I guess you think I don't know a soul in this whole town. I guess you think I got no life of my own whatsoever!" He stalked across the damp floor toward the front.

Outside stood a young man with a big smile, a leather case, and a certificate that said his encyclopedias were the best any student could use.

"No students here," said the Astronomer, shaking his head.

The young man discarded that paragraph and talked about expanding the mind. The world, to hear him tell it, was full of wonders. And learning was a natural process—the brain had to learn the way lungs had to breathe. He happened to have here . . .

"I ain't interested in learning a single thing," the Astronomer said, and sent him on his way.

"Just a salesman," he told Eva in the kitchen. "Encyclopedias."

Once more she began to wipe the sink. "Nothing but a salesman. I keep expecting . . . I don't know. Somebody. Somebody to come after me. He's got, maybe, my wedding picture in his hip pocket to show to people. Goes up every sidewalk and knocks on every door. And sooner or later . . ."

The Astronomer asked with a shrug what could really be done if she *was* found?

"That's likely all he'd have to do, just find the face that matched what he carried in his pocket. I think that would ruin me." Suddenly she grew cheerful. "Listen, I'm tired eating uptown," she said. "Can't I fix lunch for you and stay here today?"

He wanted to tease her. "I reckon so, since you cleaned my floor."

She eyed him to make certain he was not serious about that. It seemed to the Astronomer people all his life had looked at him twice to make sure he was kidding. He said brusquely, wiping away his smile, "There's luncheon meat in the refrigerator. I got eggs and bread. Cheese."

"Got mayonnaise? I could fix deviled eggs."

He found the jar at the back of the cool shelf. "What else you need?"

"I'll find it."

"Be back in a minute." One square of sunlight fell through his bedroom window and showed where the rug was wearing thin. The Astronomer closed the door to his room behind him, scratched the bare place with the toe of one shoe.

Standing there where the threads were separating at his feet, he thought over his flat attempt at humor. Fred makes her laugh. Sometimes I can hear her all the way downstairs. And he remembered the many times he had tried to work up nerve enough to introduce himself to people saying, "I'm Horton Beam. Just call me Hor for short."

Well, he had never managed that. He decided to change into a short-sleeved shirt. He stepped into the patch of sun, took off the shirt, and glanced at himself in the mirror. The bright light made his undershirt look dirty.

Apollo in the sun. No Greek god by a long shot.

He put on a clean shirt. I could tell Eva about that nickname, he thought. Just for a joke. I bet she'd laugh. No, she might think I meant something by it. Some kind of insult to her.

Even filtered through the glass, the sunlight became too hot. He walked away, working buttons into their holes, knowing he would not tell Eva the little joke about his name.

Too many jokes about it already, he thought sourly, remembering Fred and his Bible verse.

"Now show me that new telescope," Eva said. Lunch was over and the last dish washed and put away.

"Nothing to see with it now." The Astronomer was full, satisfied, and happy.

"That's all you know. Houses up and down the street. People. Cars and license plates. Trees, maybe a bird."

"I left it in the swing." He followed her to the porch, smiling at the way she bounced from one step to the next. Each part of Eva's body seemed in conspiracy with every other part. When she unscrewed caps from jars, her waist turned; once when she bent to a low kitchen shelf he had watched her torso flow toward the level of her fingertips while the strands of her hair floated down across her face.

Still, she was not pretty. Her hair needed something done to it—a cut, bleach, permanent, maybe only a comb and shampoo. A woman would know. She did not shave the hairs from her legs. Around her middle . . . yes . . . the curve was already too shallow. Or did he imagine that?

Eva sat on the porch rail and fixed the glass to her eye. "Land ho!" she said with a giggle. He watched her from the swing. "I see a pigeon on that roof."

"The white house? Mrs. Eames lives there."

"What's she like?"

"Why . . . Elsie knew her. She's all right. Grows strawberries in the back. Used to bring us preserves."

"Some woman's on the next porch. Playing solitaire on a card table."

"Old Lady Rives," he said. "Lived there as long as I can remember."

Eva chuckled. "She cheats. You don't say a blessing when you eat?"

"What's that?"

She was swinging the glass toward some other yard. "At lunchtime I noticed you never asked to say grace. Thought you would."

"No." Almost defensively he added, "Elsie did. I don't put much stock in religion."

"I taught my kids to say grace. You know—God is great; God is good; Let us thank Him for this food. Roberta can say that all the way through. Timmy just mumbles."

Now he had names to go with those children who, in some junk-
yard, played world travelers in a rusted car.

"I figure people might as well say it," Eva went on. "For luck. I
can see the bus coming way down the street. Transit Bus Line.
Driver wears glasses."

"I never thought about saying any prayer for *luck.*"

She shrugged. "What harm can it do? I got used to praying.
Growing up with the nuns."

He was surprised. "You're Catholic?"

"I'm not anything." The bus came growling by and stopped at
the corner. She read aloud several advertising posters she could
see through its dusty windows. "I lived in a Catholic orphanage till
I was nearly eight."

"Your parents were Catholic?"

"Beats me," she said in a bitter voice. She handed him the telescope and looked after the disappearing bus. "Pavement's in bad
shape. Must be a good telescope. Shows up every crack."

Not until this minute had the Astronomer thought to use his
telescope for examining his own neighborhood. He studied, curiously, the parched grass in his own yard, Mrs. Blevins' wilted
petunias, then—to his shock—the face of Mrs. Blevins herself,
flattened against the pane in her side window. He jerked the lens
away from his eye as if somehow the woman had been looking
through the far end of the tube at him and Eva.

"I got adopted," Eva was saying. "Farm couple with no kids.
Seems like I barely got through the door before she started having
babies, one after the other. Like they was stored up. An avalanche
of babies." Eva laughed. "I brought her the luck of the saints, I
guess."

"Sometimes it happens that way."

"She used to say I was a big help with *her* children. As if I fell
in some other department. Maybe her sister or some cousin. She
was right mad when I married Sion. One kid wanted to be a nurse;
one wanted to go to beauty school. I could have worked awhile and
helped all six of them. But I didn't. Sometimes I wish I had."

Again he looked through the telescope. "That street does need repairs."

"Fred's got a thing about streets," she said.

"Holes like that are bad on tires."

"Fred's been nearly everywhere, you know. He was even in the Coast Guard once. Used to own lots of sea charts, with little bitty numbers written all over the ocean along the coast. How deep it was, I guess. He left them behind when we . . . left."

"I've never seen the ocean."

She was really surprised. "At your age? Never rode down east just to see it one time?"

Stiffly he said, "I'm not so old. I got plenty time to see it. If I ever decide to see it."

"Fred's been about everywhere," she repeated. "That's why he's so hipped on roads. Which state has the best highways. What's the quickest way between two towns. I know that's what he does all night at that filling station—reads them road maps."

Still angry the Astronomer said, "But this time you think he'll stay put in one place?"

"I don't know," she said softly. "Sorry about talking so much. I get lonesome."

"I like to hear you talk."

She reached for the telescope and trained it on something far away. "Everything turns into a map for Fred. There's just one way to travel, one shortest, easiest highway. The widest, blackest line on the paper. That's how Fred lives. That's how I'm living." Her throat was moving up and down.

The Astronomer remembered the story of Daedalus and the labyrinth; two nights ago he'd read that one. Fred might be right. Anyway, that might be the only question worth asking: whether my life was mapped out before I came, or whether I blaze some trail as I go along. It made the Astronomer irritable to think about Daedalus in the daylight. He managed to say, "Don't let things worry you. Won't do any good."

"Because people wind up doing what they want to anyway? That's what Fred says. Everything else is sidestepping."

"He might be right."

"I see a bird nest. Nothing in it, though. Maybe you never saw the ocean, but you and Fred got certain other things in common. I talk and talk, and neither one of you talks back."

And that had been Sion's trouble, he guessed. "I'm talking," said the Astronomer. "Out of practice, that's all. Been living twelve years by myself." I did talk to you, Elsie, didn't I? *Didn't I?*

As if she read his mind she said, "Women do it better."

"Oh, women talk a whole lot. I'll not argue that." He grinned.

"That's not it. Women friends—and there ain't many, don't mistake me—but real women friends talk into things. Men talk out."

The Astronomer said that just wasn't so. "Women don't stick to the subject at all. Already we've been from table praying to road maps to what's wrong with men."

Eva threw back her head and laughed. It was the first time he had ever made her laugh. The Astronomer was delighted.

"See there?" she roared. "I been talking into it and you're already *gone!* You have done left it!"

Something had gone. He ran his mind backward over their talk. "Fred and the road maps . . ." he said frowning. "He thinks like a road map?"

She laughed even harder. "There *you* go, thinking like a road map!"

"Hand me that telescope. I think I better look at that bird nest."

She put it into his hand. "What if you can go fifty roads? What if back before you even remember you promised somebody you would? Or what if you go north ten miles and I go the same ten miles, only I travel six inches off the ground? What difference does that make?"

"Damned if I know," said the Astronomer. Damned if he knew anything.

"Or look," she said earnestly now, "say you're a woman and I tell you what's worrying me. Now a woman tries to deal with the worry, as straight-on as she can. But you or Fred, you'd be interrupting when I got halfway through to point out what was wrong with my thinking. You never would get down to what was wrong with *me*."

Now he began to find his way. "That would be fine. Because in the long run, you'd have to deal with your thinking, with where it let you down. See that?"

"You think it's that simple?" She looked confused. "Maybe that's all that makes *men* unhappy, the way they think. That would sure explain a lot."

"This ain't even thinking," the Astronomer said grumpily. "This is talking but it ain't thinking."

"Listen, if I acted in bed the way Fred acts in conversation, he'd be long gone. I know that much."

"You got to quit telling me private things. I don't like it." The Astronomer turned his furious face away. "I'll talk about the ideas. But you got to have more decency about your private life."

"Decency!" Eva threw up both her hands, and her body did that little trick it knew; the hair and eyebrows and shoulders seemed to fly up alongside. "Damn if you don't do the same thing Fred does. I talk about me, and him, and he talks about ideas. I talk about babies and he talks about money. I tell you I'm lonesome and sometimes I pray for luck and you ask if I'm Catholic. I give it up; I quit. If I try every man between here and Singapore, it's not going to get any different."

She rose from the porch rail and said she was going in the house.

"And listen," she said through gritted teeth. "Don't you dare thank me for cleaning that kitchen floor. Not now."

He had planned to thank her, and for the lunch also. "I won't," he said instead. She slammed inside the house. Trying to help he called after her, "You can look through my telescope any time you want to."

He thought he heard her laughing on the stairs.

It took the Astronomer a long time to find the clipping. He had to guess at the date—between June 10 and June 20, he thought— and then guess at the town. Newton City library didn't even keep files on all the nearby newspapers in piedmont North Carolina. So it was more luck than anything else when he found it, page 1, the *Monbury Gazette,* June 18, 1957. (I was at work that day, he thought. I never knew she was in the world.)

MRS. SION LEEDS DISAPPEARS was the headline, and in smaller type, Husband Fears Foul Play.

He cut it out with his pocket knife and carried it home in his wallet to Eva. She let out a snort when she saw the part about foul play. "He knew better than that. He knew Fred left. He knew I'd been crying for two weeks straight. He can add two and two." Where the clipping lay in one palm she slapped it with the back of her other hand. "Listen, stupid ain't the problem." She glared at him.

"Read the rest of it."

He could tell by the sag of her jaw when she came to the part about Timothy Leeds, age one, and Roberta, three, who had been taken to live with Mr. Leeds's sister while their mother was being sought.

"Well I reckon Christine had herself a party!" Her voice was choked. "It's no more than she ever expected. She warned him I didn't have background. I reckon she had herself a big I-told-you-so party, and both my kids ate cake."

"I shouldn't even have brought it home."

"Was there anything after this? Police search? Something about Fred?"

"I couldn't find anything else."

She held the fragment of newspaper flat to one cheek as she paced the floor. "Oh, Sion knows! He may not know why, but he knows," she said. "Christine, now, she don't know one thing her own self, but she can play back what other people know like some phonograph. I reckon my kids are hearing a whole lot of interesting things from their Aunt Christine." She crumpled the clipping and threw it on his parlor floor. "I wish I'd never seen this thing!" she cried, and ran upstairs to her room.

For a while he left her alone. Then the silence bothered him and he tiptoed up the steps. Her door was open. She lay on the bed, eyes closed. He could see the streak where tears had run into the hair at her temples and dried.

"Eva?" he said softly.

Perhaps she was asleep. He walked into the room and stood by the bed looking down at her. This time, he thought, she can talk to me as if I were some woman friend. He put out one hand to touch her lightly on the shoulder.

She drew a shuddering breath and her breasts quivered under the thin dress. His hand, all by itself, curved in the air into a cup. He saw how rough it was near her younger cheek; the skin looked like a plowed field.

"I'm sorry, Eva. Don't cry any more," he whispered. It took all his strength to get the hand pulled through the clotted air and thrust into his pocket. "Don't cry," he said again. He walked hurriedly from the room and closed the door quietly behind him. That right hand hung in his pocket the way a sash weight hangs in a window.

The next day there was a man in a brown suit standing on the other side of Helicks Street, just reading the news at a place no buses ever stopped.

By noon he had disappeared, but a tall man in a baseball cap was sitting on the curb half a block away. The Astronomer studied him through the telescope. He looked bored and harmless. He seemed to be counting the tarred-over cracks between the two gutters. Eva did not come downstairs for coffee but sat upstairs on the floor at the hall window and watched. The Astronomer had no way of knowing that and yet he did know it; one look at the ceiling seemed to tell him where she was. Had he stood on a chair to touch one certain spot overhead he knew it would be warm to his hand.

By suppertime the brown-suit man was back, but this time he called at all the houses over there and seemed to be selling something intangible. Magazine subscriptions, perhaps. He carried a notebook. Maybe, thought the Astronomer, he's got a wedding picture in his hip pocket. The man did not get to their side of the street before sundown. He caught the last bus uptown.

That night when Fred Ridge came in from work Eva was sitting halfway up the stairs. The Astronomer, sleepless in his bed, heard her go running down to him. He could even hear the sound of their clothes rasping together and the squeak of fingers intertwined. It was terrible—feeling heat through walls and hearing the noise of a single seam stretching. Two pulses made a great din in his ears.

"Hottest summer I ever saw," he heard Fred say. "Let's sit on the steps."

"I can't go out. They're watching the house. I'm sure they're watching. It's somebody Sion sent. . . . Maybe the kids are sick. . . ."

"Imagination," Fred began. Words trailed upward as the two mounted the stairs. The Astronomer could have listened but he brought his energy to bear; inside his head he added up forty-five years of accumulated mill whistles and set them blasting at once. The scream was almost as good as silence. After a long time he fell asleep.

No one was on the street next morning. Eva came downstairs showing by her puffy face and vacant eyes she had not slept. Coffee was ready. He had placed her cup and saucer across from his own. The Astronomer heard her shuffle into the kitchen but he would not look up from his new book, *Design of the Universe,* in which he had already read three times the sentence, "All straight lines are in fact curved," without being any better off. If it had been a different morning, he might have read it aloud. "What's that do to Fred's road map?" he might have said. He could tell by Eva's face this was not the day for it.

"Morning," he said.

"It was morning all night long. By now it must be afternoon," she said in a cross voice.

"Coffee's on the stove." When she had poured it and half fallen into the chair he said, "Nobody's out there."

"It's early yet."

"Coincidence. Coming right after that newspaper clipping . . ."

"Don't mention that." He stopped mentioning it. "Beats me how you can concentrate on a book first thing in the morning."

"I can't. This stuff gets harder and harder. I'm in too deep."

"Yeah," she said. "Me too."

He thought it might help to change the subject. "Did you know all the stars I looked at this week might not even be there any more? This is how they looked some two hundred years ago. It took that long for the light just to get here. For all I know, every one exploded last century and the sight of that explosion is still flying toward us through space."

Eva said that was a helluva thought to open her day. She stepped to the kitchen window and examined that part of the street. "What time is it?" She remembered the wrist watch, glanced at its face, wound the stem. "If I had the strength to laugh it would strike me funny, wearing WELL DONE on my arm," she said.

The Astronomer poured his second cup of coffee, meanwhile scraping back through the pages he had just read, looking for something else to tell her. "Bad enough I'm messed up in Greek stories without the stars being two hundred years old."

She was still staring at the wrist watch. She said nothing.

Nervously he flipped a few pages. "It says here if I took one spoonful of this coffee and dropped out three of its atoms every second, I'd have to sit here fifty billion years just to empty this spoon."

"Oh, stop that!" Eva snapped. "Who the hell cares?"

He took up the spoonful of coffee into which he had been peering with a thoughtful face and poured it—too hot—down his throat. "Sorry," he croaked.

"I'm waiting for that doorbell to ring."

"He was probably selling magazines. Or insurance. Or tickets to some ball game. He probably never heard of you."

She slapped her hand on the table. "Oh, I can't *stand* you this morning! If you want to be a speck in the universe then be it and shut up; but let me alone!"

Hurt, the Astronomer brooded. It's not that I want to be a speck. Fred Ridge might think so. People do what they want. Maybe they *are* what they want. Want to be little and you're little. Want to be old and the years are gone. Damn Fred Ridge. He ought to write a book. He could call it *The Power of Negative Thinking.*

"I'm sorry," Eva said. "Today I wish they'd find me and get it over with. I got the blues, like Fred says."

"That's all right."

"We talked all night. I've got to go back."

In a twinkling his mind whisked her out of his house and into that car with the playing children. He saw himself, every morning, drinking his coffee all alone. "All right," he said with effort. He put a third child into that rusting car, with raised blood vessels in its chubby arms. One big happy family.

"How can you say that! No, I can't go back. You know that. It wouldn't help." She placed both palms to her temples as if she might wrench her head from her neck and grind it to a fine powder in her hands. "You got any aspirin?"

For some reason, he kept the bottle in the breadbox. She swallowed two tablets with her coffee. "Up to a point, Fred's right. I guess it's no sweat to pick between very good and very bad. Or what you want a lot and don't want a little bit. Dogs and cats do that." He took the aspirin bottle and put it on a shelf before she could ask him why he kept it in the breadbox. "Sometimes everything you do would be wrong. Sometimes there *ain't* no nice straight roads on the map."

"You're absolutely right!" the Astronomer declared, believing for the moment that she was.

"If I went back to Sion, Fred thinks that would mean I chose Sion over him. One more case of doing what you want and making the right excuses."

"Maybe," he heard himself say in a voice suddenly sly, "maybe you wouldn't have to choose either one of them. Maybe there's a third thing to choose."

She had not even heard. "What if you do something you can't excuse? Fred can't imagine that. I can imagine it."

The Astronomer tried to imagine it. I rob a bank? I must have needed the money and had no other way. Even if I murdered somebody, I'd probably think there was a good reason. Unless I was crazy. Crazy people don't make excuses for anything they do. He started to ask Eva about crazy people.

"I don't know why I feel so lousy," said Eva. "Fred says it's physical. My stomach's half sick all the time. My face looks ugly in the mirror. Fred says I'll soon be feeling better but I doubt it."

It was the closest she had ever come to saying she was pregnant. He didn't want her to come any closer than that, no matter what it excused. "How's your headache?"

"You ever feel," she said dreamily, "there might be some deed just waiting out there for you to do? Lying ahead somewhere with your name on it? The one you can't excuse? And it might be coming at you, like a ship in the dark. . . . Fred thinks I'm going bats," she finished crisply. "He'll be glad when the moon changes." She snickered. "Is that two hundred years old too? The moon we see?"

The Astronomer said he didn't know. "I guess I could look it up," he said reluctantly. Eva said she had enough troubles, thank you.

For some days after that Eva did not come downstairs at all. The Astronomer even wandered up and down the second-story hall studying cracks in the plaster and checking the light switches. Finally he was forced to catch Fred Ridge when he left for work at 6 P.M. to ask him how she was.

"All right."

"She's not sick?"

"I don't think so." The man looked worried.

"I thought if she was sick . . . there was a doctor that tended my wife. Of course he might be dead now, but I could find out. There's a telephone next door. Mrs. Blevins . . ."

"I don't think she's sick."

He could no longer hear her footsteps overhead or tell where she was. She fixed peanut-butter sandwiches in her room and ate them, alone, while Fred slept his daytime sleep. At night when the Astronomer took his telescope outside, he found her window dark.

He bought three magazines at the café and left them in the upstairs bathroom. Another time he brought home library books— a novel about British royalty, an antique book, a Chinese travelogue, and left them propped against her bedroom door. He found them one morning at the foot of the stairs and, though he turned each page carefully and looked for clues, he could not tell whether she had read a word. A few times he carried the whole coffeepot to her room and rapped on the door.

"Brought you some coffee."

"Not this morning, Mr. Beam. My stomach's upset." Her voice was muffled through the door.

Her absence threw him off schedule. Mornings, with Fred asleep and Eva not moving anywhere he could tell, the silence kept him from reading. He decided to imitate the habits of his boarders. He drowsed, sweating, in his bed most of the day. It was only to give him more time with his telescope at night. Only for that.

So in early August he was often awake and on his front porch when Fred came home just after 3 A.M. At first they swapped a few words about the weather, the present condition of the sky, a knee the Astronomer had which ached before rain. A few times Fred went upstairs and came back down again with the news Eva was asleep and the room too hot for him. The Astronomer found an old fan in the cellar for them to use.

Finally it became habit for Fred to sit half an hour on the porch steps before he went indoors, and after a few nights of this he took to bringing home two cans of beer he picked up on the way. One night Fred paid; the next night the Astronomer would send him out at 6 P.M. with the price of refreshments.

Fred talked about being in the Coast Guard, the sea off Hatteras, how a car salesman managed to pad his prices.

Then the Astronomer would say he was strictly a mill-town boy, had joined the Army in World War I but never left the States. By the way, was Eva seeing a local doctor?

Korea was supposed to have been a hellhole, Ridge said. When he had been only fifteen he had worked part time in a mill himself as a sweeper. She wouldn't go back to Dr. Morrison, he added offhand. She was taking his calcium pills. But she never went back to his office after that first visit when he told her she was pregnant. Of course, she wasn't due for another checkup till late in August.

The pregnancy, now, was in the open. But the Astronomer skirted it at first, saying his son Robert made spending money as a sweeper once, long before college and the wired box which blew him up on Guam. She was planning to see a new doctor maybe? Anybody he knew?

Hard work for little pay. He'd been too young for Guam. Said she was changing to a doctor named Brock. An old man. Had an office down on Fisher Street. Somebody recommended him.

Fisher Street? That was . . . wasn't that way down . . . wasn't that over the railroad tracks and next to niggertown?

Fred guessed it was. Eva kind of liked that street. Said it was on the very edge and that was what she was on herself these days.

She ought not to go way down there, the Astronomer said.

Listen, what could Fred do? These days she flew off the handle over anything.

Yeah, but Fisher Street . . . Look, if somebody came to Newton City to draw some line between the sheep and the goats, Fisher Street would be as good a place as any to draw it. Lots of bad things took place on Fisher Street. No place for Eva.

Fred said he had already told her she was bats.

Fellow down there had to be a bad doctor. Maybe sold dope on the side. That's how things were on Fisher Street.

All Fred hoped was this new baby would make up for them other two. Never would understand how two kids that were part of a man who bored her to hell and back could make that much difference. Wouldn't she see Sion every time she looked at them?

Women weren't like that, the Astronomer said. Send her back to that first doctor.

And them kids was little—one and three! Not sitting home crying for their mama. They'd already forgotten. She ought to know that.

You got to get her off Fisher Street.

She didn't have to come if she didn't want to. But she wanted to, all right. Now she was looking back and looking back.

All women do, said the Astronomer. Lot's wife did.

Fred didn't remember Lot's wife. Eva said Fisher Street was exciting. She said people got tattooed and robbed in those buildings. She said you could buy a drink for a quarter and colored women for a handful of change. Probably exaggerating.

The Astronomer said it was the gospel truth.

Eva said she liked to look at the faces of all those people. Was it true you could mark a baby by what you looked at before it was born?

Not true, he said.

Because if this baby was . . . well, not right . . . he thought Eva would go crazy.

Yes.

Thanks for the beer, Mr. Beam.

Goodnight, Fred.

He listened to Fred going up the steps, down the hall. He heard the bedroom door open and close. He smashed the beer cans, one at a time, between his hands and then folded the two ends together. It took him a long time.

This was one of the nights when he did not wait for Fred and the beer but, yawning, went to bed soon after midnight. The Astronomer had been sleeping down deep where his dreams were, fleeing some enemy down a dark street, when there came a great banging on his door. He sat bolt upright in bed and stared at the door behind which that Enemy stood.

Wildly the Astronomer thought, He has got in my house!

Then his fingertips began to remember the surface of the sheet and his feet knew the frayed rug when he put them onto it. He knew he was awake and that someone was yelling, "Mr. Beam! *Mr. Beam!*"

He clicked bits of reality into place on the way to the door. A Monday night. August, 1957. Couldn't smell smoke. Voice was familiar. He jerked open the door and Fred Ridge almost went on banging him in the face.

"Where's Eva?" Fred yelled.

"Well, she's not in *here!*" he heard himself answer. The tone, he thought, sounded half guilty.

"She's noplace upstairs. And it's three o'clock in the morning!" Fred's fist was poised in the air halfway between himself and where the door had been.

"Not upstairs?"

"Not in the bedroom. Bathroom. Doesn't answer. Nothing to show where she's gone, not a note or anything. You seen her tonight?"

"No. I don't know where she is. She was there when I went to bed."

Ridge slumped sideways. "You never heard her go out? Maybe she came down the stairs . . . the front door . . . ?"

"Nothing," said the Astronomer. He looked with wonder at the doorknob in his hand. "I've been asleep!" he told the hand accusingly. "Sound asleep!"

"Oh God!" said Ridge. "She's gone back to him!" He turned away and took a step in no direction at all.

"No, no." He followed Fred into the hall. "She would have left a note. You know she'd not go back without even a note."

Fred's voice was dull. "But it's three o'clock in the morning. Where could she go?" They looked at each other, blank.

"It's hot. Outside in the yard? Some air? Fell asleep in the porch swing?"

Ridge ran outdoors with the Astronomer close behind. Not even a small breeze stirred the swing. Fred clattered down the steps and started around the front yard to the right.

"I'll meet you," said the Astronomer quickly, taking the other side. He searched the grass and shrubs for some figure which might be sitting in the dew. But all the time his real search was for something prone, for a lost shoe, for a woman used up and crumpled and thrown away in his grass.

He stamped on every shadow as if he might shake her loose. There was nothing.

When he rounded the back corner of the house and saw Fred Ridge coming too—alone—his lungs seemed to fall in like pricked balloons, and he let out a held breath. "Uh," he grunted, and stopped in his tracks.

Both of them knew the yard was empty. Yet Ridge ran to him. "You find her? Anything?"

"No." His whole body was taut with alertness. He could almost hear grass-blades touch. The boards of his house expanded and contracted like thunder in his ears. He heard the whistle of stars passing overhead. If she was anyplace here, I'd know about it, he thought. If she rolled her eyeballs once, I'd hear that noise.

He heard himself saying, "I told you to send her to some other doctor."

Fred raised his white face. "You think? You got some reason to think she's gone down there? Maybe got sick and set off by herself to see her doctor?"

"I'd hate to think," said the Astronomer, "that she's on Fisher Street at three o'clock in the morning."

"I'm going to see." Fred had already turned and was trotting toward the front.

"You wait," the Astronomer ordered. "I'm coming too." He glanced at his torn pajamas. "One minute. A minute can't make any difference now." And he passed Fred running, ran through the yard and across the porch and to the closet in his room, unbuttoning as he went.

All the time he slapped on a shirt and stuck a belt through part of the trouser loops he felt he was wasting time, so he bellowed Eva's name twice in the empty house. Then he was running again in shoes with the laces clumsily tied. He caught up with Ridge on the sidewalk just beyond the Blevins house.

He was puffing. "Bus station. Closest. Pick up a cab there. Too long to walk."

"You think she walked?"

Who could tell? Fred lengthened his stride and they hurried down the dark street without talking. It was not unlike the dream the Astronomer had been having, except they were the pursuers. The two of them seemed to flow along the streets, with houses and trees passing them silently on turfed conveyor belts. Not a car passed. They stepped from one yellow streetlight to another in seven-league boots.

In front of the bus station they shook a cab driver awake.

"Any special place on Fisher Street?"

"Dr. Brock's."

It was like driving over the horizon into daylight. Fisher Street was wide awake and noisy. Lights blazed and blinked and flickered; signs clicked on and off. There were no crowds, yet plenty of people sauntered by the store fronts as if they had all the time in the world, Negroes and whites, a drunk, a woman with a magenta mouth and eyelashes like a carpet sweeper. There was an elevator boy in crimson pants, some soldiers, a beggar, a handful of people neither black nor white who had pale eyes and brown but frizzy hair.

The two men got out of the cab. Juke music was playing in two opposite cafés; it met where they stood in a hash of sound. The Astronomer paid taxi fare. Fred was already onto the sidewalk staring up at a set of dark second-floor windows.

"Nobody there," he said, when the Astronomer was standing by him. "I don't know where else . . ."

He barely listened. He was tuned to the noise of Fisher Street. In a minute his ear would tell him where Eva was. "She's got to be here," he said, and he turned on Fred Ridge an angry look. She's wasted on you, he thought. "Down this way first. We'll cross over and walk back up the other side. There's noplace else for her to be. We'll find her." I'll find her, he thought.

So they began to walk. Together they went into eating places, diners, shelters where sandwiches and coffee came out of coin machines. They pushed aside curtains in tattoo parlors. People swore. They eyed the girls who would either dance with you or take off from work the rest of the night if it was worth their while. The Astronomer was not sure why he looked so closely at each of those faces. They were all strangers.

Pawnshops were closed. The man at the tin hot-dog stand was leafing through *Photography Annual;* he had seen no one, he said. The air smelled like an old carnival which had been at the same stand for years, adding each season a new layer of sawdust, rising higher and higher and brighter by degrees.

The Army-surplus store was closed. A shoe repair shop was dark.

The first help came from Madame LeMann. She sat on a folding stool under a huge painted hand of benediction, and she had read the palm of a woman who sounded very much like Eva. Hours ago, she said.

"I told her long life and happiness," said Madame LeMann. Her face was brown under a mop of orange hair. "Nice girl," she added, "but quiet. So what else could I tell her?"

At the shabby funeral parlor two men were sitting on the steps. The doors of their long black car stood open in case they should want it in a hurry. When Fred asked them, they said they never watched people going by.

The man who took Photos-While-U-Wait had not seen Eva. Nor had the clerk at the desk in the two-story wooden house which called itself the Fine Hotel. A Negro cab stand yielded up one wary man who had not seen anything all night, anything at all, or anybody.

Fred and the Astronomer crossed the street and started down the other side.

The basement All-Nite-Spot had served lots of beer to white men and colored ladies, but no white ladies. Not tonight. And there were servicemen inside the pinball-machine arcade getting their names and addresses stamped on circles of aluminum, but no Eva.

Least crowded of all was the small Salvation Army building, although three men were singing "Leaning on the Everlasting Arms," under a sign which said beds upstairs were fifty cents a night. The trio stopped in the chorus right between "Leaning" and "Jesus" to consider the problem, but they had not been there very long. Fifteen minutes at the most. They had not seen the woman Fred described.

Then they found her. In a niche between buildings a set of dark stairs led up to offices. Eva was sitting on the bottom step, looking out of her shallow cave at who went by. The Astronomer saw her first. *"Eva!"* he called.

But Fred Ridge brushed by him. He stood in the alleyway, shutting her from view, and laid his two hands on her shoulders. "You've scared the life out of me!" he said, and shook her lightly.

The Astronomer, cheated, stayed behind on the sidewalk. He could not hear Eva say anything. There was an old movie poster buckled against the brick wall. Not about the South Seas, he noticed.

"You all right?"

He heard Eva ask what time it was. She's pawned my watch!

"Mr. Beam? About four o'clock?" called Fred.

"Four-fifteen," he said, putting his pocket watch away. Now her gaze took him in, too. Slowly she got up from the step. She was still wearing the wrist watch, he saw. Forgot to wind it, maybe. She came out of the dark into the lighted street.

"I never meant to stay so long," was all she said.

The Astronomer stepped to the curb and waved until the cab left its stand and drove up beside them. Fred said to her quietly, "Now we're going home."

He even owns the *house!* the Astronomer thought bitterly. The three climbed into the back seat. Eva's face was pale. She put her head against the upholstery and closed her eyes.

"You're not hurt?" Fred shook her shoulder. "Eva?"

"I'm tired," she said without opening her eyes.

In front of his house, the Astronomer came around to open the door. But again it was Fred who took her by the arm and led her up the walk. He was saying things to her in a low tone.

"Fifty cents," said the driver. The Astronomer paid. His legs were aching from the long walk in the middle of the night. He had a flat taste in his mouth and doubted he would be able to sleep.

They were on the porch when he caught up to them and said to Fred in a very loud voice, *"You owe me for the taxis!"*

"What?" Fred acted as if he could barely hear him. "The taxis. Yes. I'll pay you tomorrow."

The screen door squeaked; they went inside. He heard them going slowly up the stairs.

The Astronomer stopped on his own porch with his fists clenched. At least he could have *thanked* me!

Lying alone in his own bed through the remainder of a sleepless dawn, he was sure that was the reason he was so angry.

It was almost noon before he made it to the kitchen. Eva was already there; his cup was on the table; she was nearly through cleaning out his refrigerator.

"You'd never guess the stuff I found way in the back!" she said cheerfully. "Even the mold finally got old and died and something new was growing to eat *it* up!"

"You're mighty bright this morning," he said, not feeling very bright himself.

She prodded him toward the open refrigerator. "Just look at that. Isn't that better?"

The shelves were clean, neatly arranged. "Is that all I got in there?"

"That's all was left when I threw out what was rotten."

"Appreciate it," he mumbled, starting on his first cup of coffee.

She began scrubbing the outside of the door. "It was nice of you to get out of bed and come looking for me last night."

"Fred was in a state. Thought you'd gone home to Monbury. Or been kidnaped."

"I shouldn't worry him," she said.

He saw he would have to ask her. "We thought maybe you'd gone to see your doctor? Brock?"

"I was just walking around. Did me good to get off by myself. I used to do a lot of walking."

"Next time you ought to walk up and down this street. That's not a safe neighborhood at night for a woman by herself."

"It's all lighted up. Busy. There's something to look at."

"It's not a good place," he insisted.

She rinsed out the rag, stood on a chair and swiped off the refrigerator top. "I never spoke but to two people—a fortune teller and the nurse that works for Dr. Brock. Just happened to see her outside his office. We had a good talk."

"A good talk?"

"I wanted to ask her something. After that I just walked around. When I sat down to rest I remembered I was sleepy. Just went on sitting." She laughed. "I was half asleep by the time you came. Guess I didn't make much sense."

"No," he said. "It doesn't."

"If you're going to the library today, I'd like to ride along. I never did thank you for bringing me those books."

"You're welcome. We could catch the next bus?"

"I'm nearly done here." She rinsed out his coffee cup while the Astronomer collected *Design of the Universe, Bullfinch's Mythology, A Primer for Star-Gazers*. They walked to the corner and stood waiting for the Transit Bus. Eva picked blobs of tar from the telephone pole. "You ever chew this stuff?"

He made a face. "No."

"I did. Roberta does. It's got a funny taste—tastes the way the coal burners used to smell in the orphanage. Ever chew peach-tree gum? Eat wild locusts?"

No, he never had. He was glad to see the bus coming.

As soon as they had taken their seats, the Astronomer began to feel uncomfortable. It seemed to him the other passengers were staring. Even men behind newspapers and women minding children seemed to send watchful glances—at him, not at Eva.

Eva said, "That fortune teller said I'd have a long and happy life. My hand is good." She held both out, palms up. "The left one is your potential, did you know that? And the right one, since you use it so much and wrinkle and change it with so much moving, shows what you're doing with your potential. I never knew that."

The Astronomer slid his eyes to one side and stole a glance inside his right hand. The surface was like shattered glass.

"I think she was lying," said Eva. "She wanted to make me feel better."

They left the bus at the square. "Just down this street," he said.

"Wouldn't it be something if everything was really written in your hand? And all the time you thought you were choosing something there wasn't a choice to make? So you got nothing to feel proud about or guilty?"

He kept his face turned aside. Already he felt if she looked squarely at him she would read something written not in his hand but in his features, something which had been spelled out for the other passengers on the bus. They must have been able to see the way his skull and cheekbones were set in angular capitals: L-O-V-E, perhaps, or even F-O-O-L.

The library was a remodeled funeral home with red velvet draperies at the front windows, urns of ivy by the steps. GROSS COUNTY LIBRARY SYSTEM, said the sign. As they went up the steps he said to her softly, "We can't talk inside."

"Listen," she roared, "I told you already I'm not dumb. I got through high school and even took a business course! I been in as many libraries as you have!"

The shelves of books made useful fences. Sometimes the Astronomer caught glimpses of Eva in this book-lined passageway or that.

Once he turned into an aisle and came upon her kneeling at the bottom row. "Excuse me," he said nervously.

She selected some Agatha Christie, Harnett Kane, F. Van Wyck Mason, Faith Baldwin. The Astronomer got Edith Hamilton's *Greek Way*. He hesitated before he signed it out as Walter Whitman, scribbled quickly, slid the card across the desk underneath his palm. Eva did not see.

At the drugstore they had a Coke; Eva bought a new lipstick. He had planned to tell her not to go back to Dr. Brock on Fisher Street, but he was afraid it would spoil their only outing together. Of course nothing had happened: an old man and a young woman had ridden a bus to town and would ride it back again.

Yet, while he held his waxed cup high to mask his telltale face, the Astronomer boiled with happiness. All he wanted was that this one morning in his life might be prolonged.

The next four days were good ones. Eva was light-hearted, and it was no longer hard to make her laugh. Fred often brought beer in the old way; he was unusually friendly. They had been allies on a difficult night. The weather was cooler. The zodiac made a low arc in the southern sky while star showers fell from Aquarius almost with nonchalance.

Yet the Astronomer was not really surprised the night Eva disappeared again.

It was early in the evening, not yet seven. Fred had left for work an hour before. The Astronomer had his head in his closet, looking for a sweater to wear into the cool air when he watched the stars. He stopped with his head thrust among jangling coat hangers. He could hear her. He could hear Eva tiptoeing from her room and down the flight of stairs.

That was what stopped him, even when he got his hand around the knob of his bedroom door. Even louder than the sound of her feet was the sound of how secretive they were, and with what stealth each followed the other. He pressed his forehead against the panel of his door, more to keep himself from flinging it open than anything else. The front screen squeaked as it closed behind her.

Only then, also tiptoeing, did he move to the parlor and stand by the window to watch Eva walking down the street. She looked calm; that was the most he could tell. The Astronomer sat on one of Elsie's parlor chairs while he tried to decide what to do.

He knew Eva was going to Fisher Street, but not why. He thought she would probably come home from Fisher Street all by herself. Between those two things stretched the chasm of all he did not know. Systematically, the Astronomer began to swear in a whisper.

Fred would not be home for eight more hours. He could telephone; Mrs. Blevins would let him telephone and he'd say . . . "Eva's gone for a walk?" He thought about Fred saying Horton Beam wanted in and wanted out. He'll never know what I want. He's not even built for knowing that.

He decided to wait. He took out his pocket watch and laid it on the marble-topped table.

By seven-thirty he was tapping his foot. He started upstairs, to see if this time she had left some note on the bureau. Then he was afraid Eva would come back and catch him snooping in their room. He decided to do his waiting in the yard, with his telescope. At least he would be able to look out through two centuries to where old meteors were falling. It would give him perspective. He carried the folding glass into the back yard.

The Astronomer paused with his head upturned and his telescope fixed on a patch of cloud. Of course he could go after her himself, right now. He would be able to find her. He had found her the first time.

But she slipped away. She *sneaked* out of the house.

He gave up astronomy for the night, went to his room and arranged himself on the bed and began doggedly to smoke and read. He read about Perseus at the wedding feast, and how he had forced Phineus to look upon Medusa and be turned to stone. He read of the Graiae, who had been old from the day of their birth.

After he finished reading about Theseus and the labyrinth he put down his book and simply smoked cigarettes and watched the ceiling. That's all I really want to know. I want to know whether life is really a map, where you follow the trails marked out for you, or whether it's a labyrinth.

And that was a lie. What he wanted was to know what Eva was doing this very minute. What is it that draws her back to Fisher Street? The same thing that made her come away with Fred Ridge and get so little joy from it?

He drove himself back to the book. Wasn't it true that, at sixty-five, he had at last broken out of the map? Retired? Abdicated? And now he was wandering around trying to trail a string or chop a mark on every tree he passed? And maybe he was wrong. Maybe being with Fred was one joy after the other, and Eva had no regrets.

His watch said 10 P.M. He carried the book to the porch, where it was far too dark to read. Nothing wrong with being on my own porch. When she comes up the walk I'll say . . . I'll say . . . Have a nice walk? Hope it don't rain. She had on that thin dress, the yellow one, with the little jacket that comes off.

About marking a trail, now, chopping each tree—that would be backward. If you turned around to follow the trail you'd made, it would only take you back to where you started. Wouldn't be a bit of help in knowing what lay ahead, over the next hill.

That's it! That's what I'll say when she comes up the walk. I'll talk to Eva about the road map and the maze. I'll get her to talk about Fred's single road and Eva's one hundred. She'll see I understand her!

I'll tell her Fred on his turnpike won't ever know what's off the beaten path. Good phrase. I'll use it just like that. The beaten path. But I don't think I'll tell her about the Minotaur. Not to-night.

The lights were beginning to go out in the houses on his street. He fixed himself a sandwich and made eight circuits of the kitchen table while he chewed it up and got it swallowed. No, he'd leave out the Minotaur. But maybe he'd put in Ariadne, who had helped Theseus in that labyrinth. Eva would probably like that part.

He went back to his room and began stubbornly to read again. If he finished this one, he would go upstairs and borrow one of Eva's books. With her four and his one, he could outread the clock till she decided to come home.

By 1:00 A.M. he was reading one word at a time, pulling it off the page where its meaning was glued and misshapen. Some paragraphs he had to reread three and four times. Just after 1:00 he heard the tapping of heels on the sidewalk in front of the house. The Astronomer got off his bed, plodded barefoot to the hall. He could see her through the screen. She walked as if she were exhausted, her right foot going each time a bit farther right than was needed. She came up the front steps in a crooked line.

He stepped behind his own door. Won't move or speak, he thought. If she wants to tell me tomorrow, she will. Two hours till Fred comes home. He doesn't need to know.

Eva crossed the porch; he heard the screen door close. She stopped and pulled off her shoes in the hall. He could see her nylon foot step on the first tread.

Then, to his joy, he heard her call softly, "Mr. Beam?" He could hardly believe the sound of his own name. He waited one minute too long before he moved, and she had gone up the flight several more steps before he turned on his bedroom light and put his head out the doorway.

"You all right, Eva?"

"I thought you'd be asleep."

"Just came in from the porch," he lied. "Thought I'd go back and smoke one more cigarette before I went to bed."

"Mind if I join you?" He saw she was leaning heavily against the rail.

He took the pack from his pocket and waved it toward the front door. "I'm feeling fine," said Eva as she passed him in the hall. He caught the smell of whiskey but it was not very strong.

"Glad to hear that," he said.

He followed her into the darkness and took one of the big rockers. Eva perched on the banister and accepted a cigarette from his hand. "The reason I called you," she said, bending to his match, "I wanted to ask . . . please don't tell Fred I went out."

The Astronomer blew out the flame. So that was it. "All right."

"I really am fine. There's nothing wrong."

"I said I wouldn't tell him."

She puffed rapidly on the cigarette. Each inhalation sent a red circle of light around her mouth and nostrils. "And I was wrong—about something bad waiting to be done. The ship that would run you down in the dark and all that?" She waved the cigarette around in the dark. He heard her laugh.

His own had gone out. The Astronomer lit it again.

The glowing jewel was back at her face. "Because nothing happened. It didn't make a bit of difference. And I don't feel a bit different. Fred's absolutely right and now I'm all over being bats." Again she gave the high laugh. "And I'm not drunk, if that's what you're thinking. I didn't give myself any built-in excuse like that."

"It's late," said the Astronomer, "and maybe my mind ain't working good, but I can't figure out a thing you're saying."

She threw the cigarette away. "Too strong," she said. "I'll have one of my filters." When he stood to light the second one, he saw Eva's face more clearly by the flame of the match, and he stood without moving till his fingers burned. She wore no lipstick and her hair was in tangles. He saw the yellow skirt looked as if she had wadded it up in her hands. He could not stop himself.

"Eva," he said sharply, "what have you done?"

She turned her head. Shadow slid over her face again. "I told you, it makes no difference. You and Fred are right; I give in; I'm going to start a map collection of my own. People can excuse anything they want to."

"Excuse what?"

"Maybe it's in the palm of my hand that on one day I'd run away with Fred Ridge. And on another day I'd do something else.

And something else. But there's nothing in there about punishment. Me and the nuns made that up. I been feeling bad for nothing."

"Eva, what . . ."

"I even made it up about feeling bad. You could go on and on. And not feel bad."

He knew his voice was going to be hoarse. "Eva? What have you done?"

"I tested it out—that's what a man would do, what you and Fred would do. I changed my way of thinking. Tested it out."

"I think you are drunk," he managed to say.

Still she would not face him, though her voice was fast and confident. "I mean, you just say to yourself: Okay, so I'm a whore, and it doesn't make any difference. You're not even there. You're off somewhere watching. It's such a little thing; it's all over so fast. Sure enough, you can't see what the fuss was ever about."

Now, of its own accord, the Astronomer felt his right hand drawing back in the air. He made it wait, unmoving. All the way down from his shoulder the muscles, one by one, contracted.

She gave him no time to speak, or to bring his fist rushing through the air.

"How can those few minutes change anything at all? Zip-zip, and you're exactly what you were before. Not any better, not any worse. No trouble living with that. . . . I don't think you even have to live with it. It sort of falls off, you know? It's so small it falls away and you leave it there. By the time you've walked a block, you can hardly remember a thing about it!"

The Astronomer moved across the porch away from her, dragging his hand out of the air. It was shaking. Eva tossed her head, drew again on the cigarette, flipped it into the yard with a gesture that was very wide and very free.

"So I feel good. From now on I'm going to feel good and stop worrying."

"Good?" he groaned.

"Good! Damn right! Because there's no problem! Nothing's waiting out there but you, yourself; and by the time you get there, everything's perfectly natural. Everything's been arranged!"

"Go to bed, Eva," he said dully.

She stamped her foot, rose from the porch railing. "I'm not afraid any more! Why can't you see that? I'm tired and I'm not much proud, but I'm not scared, either! I don't think I'll ever be scared again."

"Go to bed, Eva, before I hit you."

"Why can't you understand something so simple?" she hissed. She ran inside. The Astronomer was left with that right hand wrapped tightly around the cold chain of the swing. He turned his mind away from what Eva had said and it fell gratefully on something he had been reading. He knew suddenly what it would be like to look upon Medusa and feel flesh turn to stone.

He might have stood all night where she had left him, like a statue, but Fred would be home at three. He did not want to see Fred.

He dragged himself indoors to bed, where he lay like a piece of dead granite, no—like a worn river rock. No, worse than that. Like a heap of gravel.

For two days he and Eva would not speak. She thought this was a great joke. Indeed, she carried her laughter like a beaker of acid, pouring it everywhere. They passed in the kitchen; he turned his face; she snickered. She came in from the café swinging a bag of hamburgers, saw him in the swing. He lay with his eyes shut while she went giggling by.

On Friday, when Eva paid the room rent herself, out of money brought home that night from Fisher Street, the Astronomer burned the bills at the oilstove flame. Eva almost fell down laughing.

Fred was so relieved at her new good humor the Astronomer had not the heart to speak to him. He felt lonely and afraid, and the stars whose names he had forgotten came and went in the night sky.

The morning she tried to pay the rent was too much. He walked

out of his own house and would not go home till nearly midnight.
He read area newspapers in the library, beginning with that day
(August 23, 1957) and working backward. It seemed to him
the pages were full of accounts of embezzlers being found out,
husbands putting ice picks into erring wives, suicides, runaways
from prison being ultimately extradited back to North Carolina.
The only thing of interest he found in the latest *Monbury Gazette*
was an ad for Leeds Car Lot, promising overall price reductions.

In the afternoon, thunderstorms broke out of the gray sky. He
sat through two hours of Dead End Kids and Boston Blackie in a
movie house. He ate supper at the Atlas Café, stayed to watch box-
ing on television. It was past 11:30 when he walked the damp
sidewalk home. The white oaks growing alongside shed their last
drops on his head.

When he turned in his walk, the Astronomer saw that every
window was dark. Eva must be asleep, perhaps dreaming some
scene in which black ships reversed course and sailed the other
way.

In the hall, he stood at the foot of the stairs and looked toward
the second floor. He did not go up. There was no need. He knew
Eva was not there. He sat on the bottom step awhile. The last time,
she had come home about 1 A.M. A little over one hour from now.
Nothing to worry about.

Yet no hope stirred in him. At midnight he called her several
times, louder and louder. There was no answer. He went to the
kitchen cupboard, where he kept cheap bourbon he rarely drank,
and poured himself half a glass. Ward off colds, he told himself.
I was in the rain today.

At one Eva still had not come home, nor at two. The footsteps
he heard soon after three belonged to Fred Ridge.

The Astronomer was waiting at the bottom of the flight of
stairs. His joints had grown stiff sitting in the damp air from the
open door. Fred came in and stared at him. "She's not here," he
said.

"Not here?"

The Astronomer shook his head.

"You know when . . . ?"

"I've been uptown. When I came at eleven-thirty she was gone."

"You look for a note?"

"No."

Fred took the stairs three at a time. The Astronomer heard him slamming around the bedroom. He came down slowly. "Nothing." Fred crumpled beside him. Neither of them spoke.

After a while the Astronomer put his hand three steps up, took the bottle of bourbon from behind one of the stair posts and handed it to Fred. He looked at it blankly, took an absent pull.

"I better go after her," he said without much enthusiasm.

"Not this time." But he doesn't know about that second trip. Or does he? He looked into Fred's face, trying to decide.

"She might get hurt," said Fred.

"Think we could stop that?" He tried to put more kindness into his words. "When she's ready she'll come back. There's nothing to do but go to bed and sleep till she comes home. Then it won't seem so long to wait." He put a timid hand on Fred's shoulder, for suddenly he sympathized with the young man. "I'm going to bed. I just waited up so you'd know. As for Eva . . ." He swallowed. "Eva can take care of herself."

"I don't think she can," said Fred.

I don't think she wants to, the Astronomer thought. He made himself say, "Lately she's seemed happier. You think so?"

"Sometimes," Fred growled, "I think I don't know one thing that goes on in her head. Sometimes I get right sympathetic with old Sion." He turned to go back upstairs.

The Astronomer held out the bottle. "Take it with you," he suggested. "Help you sleep."

"Guess so," Fred muttered, but he went up the stairs without remembering to carry it along.

The Astronomer sat with the silly bottle turning in his hands until he heard the plumbing roar and the door to the bedroom close. He placed the bourbon three steps up again, brought himself two pillows and a bedspread from his room, and tried to get comfortable on the angled stairs.

It was impossible to relax. The board that fit under his neck with some comfort had a twin that cut sharply across his spine. He had begun to sneeze. Never a car went by on Helicks Street that he did not hear, and hope. Sometimes he catnapped.

Once he dreamed Eva swam in a swollen sea, and he could not get to her. Rents of lightning showed some huge, shadowy thing that was going to run her down—a whale, or an iceberg, or a pilotless ship. Most of his sleep came in scraps too small to make dreams.

The last half hour or so of darkness, the Astronomer was wide awake. Through the screen he watched the black dilute itself until he could make out the dim front of the house across the street. The roofline came first; then squares of doors and windows. Corner streetlights went off automatically. Yellow and blue began to wash into the grayness above the trees, and he could see the whole front of the Eames house and the silhouette of a pigeon on one of its lightning rods. The milky light appeared on his own front walk and crept up the porch and filtered into the hall; and still Eva did not come home.

The Astronomer sat watching Saturday come where Eva had not. Daylight eased down the front hall toward his feet. When the tips of his damp shoes began to seem faintly gold, he gave up waiting and carried the bedclothes to his room. He lay across his own bed with his face pressed in the sheet. Doctors say rest is just as good as real sleep, he told himself.

He was numb with weariness. His nose was stuffy and he thought he had begun to run a little fever and feel queer. The Astronomer sent a wide-eyed gaze one inch away into the white weave of the sheet; dizzily he could see through that and padding and spring and rug and floor and even earth. There were caldrons deep inside the earth. So, with his eyes fixed vacantly on the core of Hell, the Astronomer rested, and coughed, and waited for Eva to come home.

Saturday passed. Eva did not return.

Fred Ridge came noisily downstairs early in the day, as if he were certain Eva would be waiting over coffee in the Astronomer's kitchen. Without a word, the Astronomer handed him a full cup. Fred held it in both hands.

"I borrowed Mrs. Blevins' newspaper." He passed half to Fred.

There was nothing about Eva. There were no accidents, no unidentified patients, no women with amnesia. No victims of rape or mugging. No riots on Fisher Street. The news was all about men who had to pay back taxes, criminals captured at long last, non-swimmers drowned on fishing trips.

"Something might have happened after they printed the paper," said Fred. "I could call."

"Is she carrying identification?"

"Yeah. I made her tear up all the old cards. Wrote out new ones the day we moved in here. Mrs. Fred Ridge. This address."

"Wait awhile, then."

"Sounds like you caught a bad cold."

For lunch, the two opened a can of pork and beans. The afternoon dragged. The Astronomer wondered what Corey Knitting Mills would do if police should notify them they'd found a dead woman wearing a mill retirement watch. Well, they'd never think of *me*. Some of the young bloods, maybe. But never me.

Late Saturday afternoon Fred, unable to stand any more waiting, went to Fisher Street. Nobody had seen Eva. Dr. Brock's office was closed. A note on the door said he was out of town for the whole weekend. The palmist was no longer sure she had ever seen Eva, but she offered to read Fred's palm.

He was so desperate he let her. She told him his love had gone on a journey, but would soon be back. She said he must be careful of rivals. She said he must beware of work done in the sun; there were outdoor accidents carved into his palm.

"What about Eva?"

"You are her own true love."

"What good is that?" Fred grunted.

At six that evening, Fred decided he might as well put in his regular shift at the filling station. He did not much want to go. He did not want to sit waiting, either.

"If she comes," the Astronomer said, "I'll let you know. I'll go next door and call you."

Fred wrote down the number. "I keep thinking about police. . . ."

"I know it. I'm thinking, too."

"But I figure they'd put two and two together and come up with Mrs. Leeds. She's in their missing persons file. They'd find Sion right quick, but I don't think they'd look very hard for Eva. They'd figure any woman that leaves one man might haul off and leave another."

"Yes," the Astronomer said. "I thought of that. Give her a little more time."

When Fred had gone, he walked through all the rooms of the house and back again, and through the rooms and back. *Let her come home tonight!* he told the faded red rug and the kitchen chairs and the neglected telescope. It seemed to him they sat with their atoms spinning, paying no mind to him. He could not pass a window without staring through it, left and right, up and down. *Let her come tonight!*

Long after it was dark he smoked cigarettes, coughed, rubbed the outside of his raw throat. He walked to the center of the street and looked both ways, stared up at the sky, which now and then dropped a blazing star as if from carelessness. He tried to read.

Rest is as good as sleep, he thought again as he lay stiffly on his bed. And so Saturday night also passed, and still Eva did not come.

Fred did not work Sunday. He did not sleep much, either, but at least he was in his room till nearly noon. "I'm going to eat at the café," he said. "In case . . ."

"You can make a sandwich in the kitchen if you want to."

Fred nodded his head. "Good. Thanks."

By 1 P.M., the two men could hardly stand the sight of each other. They paced the house, trying to choose different areas. It *is* my house, thought the Astronomer, after he had collided twice with Fred. And he could read in Fred's eyes: None of his business.

The Astronomer was trying to brace himself for the possibility Eva might never come back. She might be home by now, claiming her two children from Aunt Christine. Or she was the most popular girl in the cathouse, and customers liked to hear her laugh. She had been run down by a black ship, careening across dry land.

Fred made a second hopeless trip to Fisher Street, but on Sunday most doors were locked. Behind curtained windows people were getting over Saturday night. The man at the funeral parlor said Dr. Brock was often gone on weekends; in an emergency, he could be reached at home.

"Where's that?" said Fred, getting out a pencil.

"You don't know?" The man became uneasy.

"If it's in the phone book, I can find him."

"Brock's got several houses; I don't know where they are myself. People that wants him, they usually know. They don't need to ask."

Fred tracked down Dr. Brock's office nurse, but she was not in her rooming house. A landlady said she was off on a trip and would be back Monday morning.

When the Astronomer saw Fred's face, he did not need to ask if there was any news. "It's suppertime," he said. "Let's scramble some eggs."

"I don't know where else to try," said Fred. "You think she might have gone back? To her husband?"

"You ought to know better than me."

"I don't think she'd carry my baby home to him. I don't think that."

"They're burned on the bottom," he said, dishing up the eggs, "but eat 'em anyway."

Fred ate very little. He was jumpy. "What's that?"

"Car horn."

"I better go see."

"Fred, it's a block away."

The young man could not sit still. He kept jerking his head toward every sound, making him look more than ever like a rat terrier with twitching ears. "I think I'll try the bus station," he said over his half-empty plate of eggs. "A ticket. She could have bought a ticket. Some cab driver might remember her. Something."

The Astronomer was glad to see him leave. He scraped the dishes and stacked them in the sink. Now he had the house to himself, just as it had been in May and early June before anybody asked to rent a room. He listened to the whir inside the refrigerator, the creak of his chair, the drip of the faucet. The house was like a shell on the beach with all the life gone out of it. He could think things like that, couldn't he, even if he'd never seen the ocean and Fred Ridge had?

He carried his coffee to the porch, sat in a rocker, sat in the swing, sat in the rocker again. Waited. Dropped the cup, by accident, over the rail into the yard. Left it there. Plucked off leaves from a climbing vine and chewed them. Lit one cigarette, coughed his lungs all the way up behind his teeth, threw it away.

By midnight he had given up on both Eva and Fred. They were both gone. Fred had got drunk, or bought a bus ticket himself, or headed straight for Monbury to see if she was in that car lot, or followed some other woman home. And Eva was dead, or she was lying in a four-poster bed with her husband while her children breathed lightly down the hall, or she was in some other bed watching Sin sail by without crashing her down.

The Astronomer stamped through the house and into the kitchen and washed the damn dishes. So they were both gone and he was here. By next Sunday he would not be counting minutes, only the flecks of light falling down between Cygnus and Draco. . . .

He stopped with his hands wrapped in the towel. He had heard

. . . A second ago something . . . The Astronomer turned to the kitchen doorway. Somebody was in the house.

It seemed for an instant his heart closed into a small red seed and fell for miles in the universe beneath his ribs. He threw the towel onto the floor and ran. When he got to the parlor he could see her standing just inside the front door, leaning against the wall with a light switch jammed into one cheek. Her face was white as frost. Even in the dimness and from across the room, it looked as if all the bone had come through to the outside and frozen there.

The Astronomer ran and took her in his arms. She turned her cold face into the front of his shirt and her voice seemed to crack its way up through layers of ice. "Well," she said. "That was it. That was it. *It.*"

The Astronomer patted her brown hair. "Hush, hush," he said. She shivered in his arms.

"I did it," said the strange voice, "and that was *it.*" She rubbed her forehead back and forth against his chest.

For some reason the very motion made him realize his arms had gone out to her like a lover's. But Eva had merely leaned on whoever might be there. His ribs ached where her head was pressing. Who felt the coldest then?

"It's all right, it's all right," he murmured to her, and the heart in him went on down and down, like a cinder. "Eva, it's all right."

"Sick," she whispered. "Sick. Dear God."

"I'll get you to bed. Can you make the stairs?"

She raised her head and twisted her neck to see them. "No," she answered, and put her face back into the gap where his heart had been.

The Astronomer lifted her. She was heavier than he would have guessed. He staggered and lurched hard against the newel post. "I've got you," he puffed. "It's all right. Everything's all right."

"You lie," she whispered.

He floundered on the stairs, letting his left side strike the rail so he could lean from time to time and catch his breath. "Don't talk."

"Heavy," she crooned, "but lighter than I was, Lordy Lou." She had not been drinking, yet there was some smell. The Astronomer frowned. Some medicinal smell.

"When she talked about it, it was okay. God in Heaven-oh. How easy she did talk about it. . . ."

The Astronomer made the last two stairs. "Hush!" he ordered, his breath ragged. "Hush your talk." He kicked open their bedroom door.

He stopped for a minute and let his back rest against the frame. "Wearing yourself out," he said sternly. "Just hush."

Her voice was like a thin singing. "Even then it was the same at first. Long way off. Long way off, and watching. Like your telescope." She began to moan. "Sick. Oh Jesus."

"You got to vomit?" He lowered her heavily onto the bed and nearly fell himself.

She seemed to tear the laugh loose and throw it away. "Not enough vomit in the world." She closed her eyes.

The Astronomer slid off Eva's shoes, little things; he could not have squeezed four of his fingers inside the toes. The jacket of her yellow dress came off easily. It was a sundress with thin straps; he saw he would have to roll her on one side to reach its zipper in the back. "Don't worry 'bout nothing," he managed to pant, catching her shoulder and easing her away onto her side. He worked the zipper down and began to pull the dress toward her shoulders. Then he saw the stains on her white slip. He held her poised like that while he stared.

His first words were soundless. He tried again. "Eva? Eva! I'll get a doctor."

Little pauses had crept into her singsong voice. They fell between phrases like hiccups. "I've had a doctor. Can't you tell?" The pauses speeded up and began to overtake her words until she was crying jerkily, but without tears. "*I* can tell! Lord Jesus Christ, *I* can tell!"

Tears poured down her face and she began to shake all over and make a strange wail below the level of language: "OOH-wy! OOH-wy!" over and over again, rising higher and higher until it broke and dropped and then started the same shrill climb again.

Gently the Astronomer laid her back on the bed. He sank to the floor. The awful noise kept him from thinking. "Eva?" he tried. "Eva?" He put an arm across her so his hand curled round her farther shoulder and he squeezed. Each time the wail rose up he squeezed. He did not know what else to do.

Nearly an hour passed before she began to wear herself out. Then she seemed to drop off the edge of consciousness from time to time, climb back with her terrible "OOH-wy! OOH-wy!" as if she had caught onto her pain by her fingertips.

"Sleep now, Eva," he ordered every time. "Sleep, Eva." Her hold would relax. She would drop into the dark again, then drag herself back and begin to cry out louder and higher.

"Sleep, Eva," he droned, grasping her shoulder. "Shhh . . . Go to sleep." By 2 A.M. she finally fell too far. She lay somewhere between sleep and stupor. Sometimes her breath was deep and even. Sometimes she seemed to gasp for it. Her wrenched-out wail was ringing only in the Astronomer's skull.

He eased his hand from her shoulder. The fingers seemed permanently curled. With his other hand he forced them straight and rubbed his face, which was wet with perspiration and some tears he did not even know he had shed.

He drew up a sheet and placed it gently under her chin. "Uh," she said once in her sleep. He raised a window. The air on his wet face was almost cold. He stood there a minute, observing that all the stars were still in their places. He could hardly believe it.

The Astronomer staggered into the hall. He held the rail with both hands while he worked his way downstairs. On the bottom step, where one full night he had waited for Eva to come, he sank and dropped his face into his hands.

When Fred Ridge came banging in at 2:30, the Astronomer had not moved. His head was too heavy to lift; the arms which had carried her were aching. He slipped the two hands apart so they held his temples instead of his cheeks, making a hole through which he could see the knees and thighs of the man in front of him.

Fred was excited. "I've found a cab driver who picked up Eva and some nurse on Fisher Street but can't remember . . . Mr. Beam?" Fred lifted his head and looked beyond the Astronomer, upstairs.

"Eva's home," he said wearily. "I think." Fred almost fell up the flight of stairs.

From where he had been knocked slightly askew as Fred went by, the Astronomer braced himself to hear her awful cry again, but Eva must have been asleep. He was glad of that much, anyway. No one should ever have to hear that sound.

Just before dawn the Astronomer made the second-floor climb again. He stood in the doorway watching Eva sleep. Fred Ridge sat motionless on the floor beside her bed. *Just as I sat.*

"She's still asleep," Fred whispered, not looking up.

The Astronomer had already rehearsed the harshness to use in his voice. "She's had an abortion."

Fred wiped a hand across his eyes. "I know that," he said. "I took off the rest of her clothes."

"Maybe she'll die. I don't know about such things. What's normal and what's a hemorrhage. Do you?"

"No."

He went on without remorse. "God knows under what conditions this was done. The chance of infection . . . Have you realized yet she might die?"

Fred nodded.

"Tell me one thing. Did you ask her to do this thing?"

Fred closed his eyes and groped blindly for Eva's arm. "No! No!" Then he added, "We did talk about it once, when she first knew about the baby. We were quarreling. I didn't really mean it. Eva couldn't stand the thought. I never mentioned it again."

"She couldn't stand the thought."

"One time I said it, that's all. One time. She knew I never meant it."

Before he could stop himself, the Astronomer gave a high-pitched laugh. "You didn't have to draw her a map!" he charged. "Did you think you had to draw her a map?" He went off into gales of bitter laughter.

The noise woke Eva. Her eyes flew open but she did not cry out. She looked as if she could not remember this room or those voices.

Fred got to his knees and bent over her. "Eva? Eva?"

A spasm, something like a whirlpool, moved across her face and settled in a corner of her mouth, twisting it down.

"It's Fred. You're home. Everything's all right," he babbled. "I've been sick worrying about you. . . ."

Eva announced in a high clear voice that there had been a great deal of blood.

Fred rolled his eyes toward him. "Mr. Beam?"

Shaken, he came into the room and looked down on her white, deserted face. "I think a doctor. Right away."

"Eva," said Fred, "it's all over now and you're home again. Do you have much pain? Can you tell me when . . ."

"We need to call a doctor, Eva," the Astronomer interrupted. "A good doctor. You might be very sick."

"Will I die?" asked Eva.

Fred said of course she would not die; he would never let her die; he loved her. She lifted one hand to his face. "Poor Fred," she sighed. She rested that way a minute, leaning her hand against him. Then she looked at the Astronomer. "No doctor. If you're worried about what might happen, I'll go to a hotel." It seemed to wear her out, saying that.

"God, no!" he exploded. He wanted to stumble to her bedside and move her hand onto his face, where it belonged.

"I don't care if I die," she said. "I don't care a bit."

Fred told her not to talk that way. "It's my fault, all of it. I had no business mentioning . . . I was the one said you ought to . . . ." He choked. "I could bite out my tongue."

Eva giggled shrilly, then snuffled down the scale to a sob. "That's all you can spare, Fred? After *my* operation, that's all you can spare?"

He grabbed her hand and pressed it against his cheek. "It's going to be all right, Eva. Soon as you're strong again. We'll do just what you want. . . ."

She took her hand away and looked at it curiously. "I know you will," she said. The Astronomer saw it was her right hand, the one the palmist said revealed what one did with potential. Eva closed her eyes. Her body began to rock slightly from side to side. Spasms hardened her diaphragm and a faint keening rose in her throat. All her tears were being cried on the inside, out of sight, by organs meant for other things.

Fred groaned. He tried to hold her with his hands. She rolled away from him and pulled the sheet over her face.

"Maybe she'll sleep," the Astronomer managed to say.

"I've got to do something."

The Astronomer wondered: How can anybody dry those tears? He thought of Niobe, mourning.

The two men stood side by side, watching the sheeted form on the bed. Sometimes the white folds quivered; the hands were thrown about. Eva's shoulders beneath the cover would tremble until she put her hands to them, crossed, as if she might shake herself. Slowly the movement quieted as she cried herself back to sleep. She never made a sound.

Monday and Tuesday Eva stayed in bed. The Astronomer fixed canned soups and juices and lopsided poached eggs, balanced them gingerly on a bread board, and carried them up to her. Mornings and afternoons Fred looked after her. Often he accepted the meal at the bedroom door.

"How is she?"

"I don't think she's worse."

"Is she any better?"

"She won't say so."

Eva ate very little. Something in her face reminded the Astronomer of an old house where nobody is home, or is ever expected home. She seldom heard questions. Even less would she answer anything spoken to her. If Fred was out and he put food by her bed with cheerful remarks, she went on looking through the far wall. Many times Fred spooned soup into her open mouth. She let it accumulate in one cheek.

"Swallow now, Eva." She swallowed.

The Astronomer guessed from her rigid neck that she was always close to tears. Sometimes, even when he and Fred were in the room, her eyes would spill over. The wetness ran down her face with no more volition than soup ran down her throat. If the Astronomer tried to take her hand in his she would jerk away and lie stiff as an ironing board.

Monday she could not keep down her food. Fred asked for a basin or even a pail. By midafternoon she could only hang her head over the bedside and heave without effect.

Before he left for work, Fred made her take a little broth. Inside an hour the Astronomer was upstairs, emptying the basin again. Soon she had lost the broth and was again straining to spew up a thin white froth. Once, between gagging, she groaned, "It goes on making me sick, but it won't come up."

By Tuesday the food stayed in her stomach. She lay curled like a horseshoe. A few of his questions she would answer in a leaden tone: No, she was not hungry. No, there was no fever. Yes, she had slept a little.

That night while Fred was at work, the Astronomer tiptoed twice an hour into the bedroom to see how she was. Once, very quietly, she said out of the dark, "It would be better if I died." He did not know whether she knew he was in the room, or whether she was talking to herself. After that he stayed with her, crouched on the floor in a corner by the bureau. He felt better being close, whether Eva knew it or not.

On Wednesday she slept less; she answered him in sentences. Fred went to the drugstore for supplies. The Astronomer, taking dishes from her bedside, said, "You won't always feel like this, Eva. People aren't built that way. The truth is time does heal, and you have to hang on till it does."

Eva looked at him with contempt. "Everybody's not alike," she hissed.

"Three people I've buried. Time and grass cover it all."

"I never buried anybody before," she said, "and I don't want to talk about it."

"I only want to help."

"I don't want to live, feeling like this."

"You won't. You'll feel a little less like this, and a little less, and finally not much."

"That's awful," she breathed, and she looked at him with surprise and horror. "That's just awful."

"It's true."

"Then keep it to yourself."

He wanted her to begin letting go her guilt. And when she became abnormally quiet, when she went on watching him with that look of shock, he wanted the Guilt to let go of her.

Fred talked to her a lot. He could hear the earnest murmur of Fred's voice, absolving and promising, disregarding and foretelling. Fred hardly slept at all. Sometimes during the day he would nap on the Astronomer's bed, but mostly he sat with her and then worked all night in the filling station. He brought her gum, magazines, cigarettes, candy bars, a handful of gladioli taken from a park, a black nightgown, slippers with puffs on the toes like rabbit tails. "You feeling better?" he would greet her.

"Go to hell," she sometimes said.

Thursday morning Eva said she would like a pen and a tablet of lined paper, so Fred went running gratefully to buy them.

"Of course I'll stay with her," the Astronomer said.

"She's . . . she blames . . ."

"I know it."

He found Eva flushed and intense. "Come here!" she said urgently, as soon as he entered the room. She caught at his hand

and twisted it. "Mr. Beam," she begged, her voice broken, "will you forgive me? Forgive me?"

The Astronomer smiled at her. "Eva, of course I forgive you," he said heartily.

She searched his face. A certain fear seemed to grow in her eyes like a prick of light, very cold and very brilliant. In a shocked voice she whispered to herself, "That isn't it!" She let go his hand and fell back against the pillow. A tremor passed over her body.

"Eva?" She was staring at the ceiling. She did not even feel his fingers at her cheek. "Eva!" Suddenly she bared her teeth. He jerked his hand away, certain she was about to bite it. "There's nothing left to forgive, Eva," he said anxiously. She glared at him, her mouth spread on a silent growl. He retreated to a chair.

When Fred came bringing the notebook and a cheap fountain pen, Eva's eyes were closed. Fred said, "Look! She's smiling in her sleep!"

"She's not smiling," said the Astronomer.

Eva slept the rest of the afternoon, stirring, whimpering occasionally. At six when Fred left for work he called at the Astronomer's room, "Mr. Beam?" He ran to the bedroom door. "She's sleeping, but restless. Would you mind . . . ?"

"I'll keep an eye on her."

"Look," said Fred, his face uneasy. "I know this is tough on you. Two people you hardly know. We're imposing; I know it; if there was anybody else . . . You want to raise the rent?"

I'm not going to hit him, the Astronomer thought with care. But anger was in his voice when he said, "What do you think I am?"

"Well. Well, thank you," Fred stammered.

By now the Astronomer had it worked to a fine schedule. He smoked three cigarettes; then it was time to walk softly upstairs and stand in the doorway of Eva's room. Sometimes she lay on her back, arms spread, open to anything. Once she was on her stomach and, against the pillow, one small fist was clenched as if she had been beating feathers. Between trips, he sometimes walked rapidly around the yard, alert for any cry through her open window. He seldom looked at stars.

He had made his last check and gone to bed just before Fred came home from work at three. As soon as the screen door closed, he heard Eva calling, "Fred? Is that you? Fred?"

"I'm coming!" he called, vaulting the stairs.

And, without listening, the Astronomer knew Eva was waiting urgently, that as soon as Fred approached the bed she would catch hold of him with eager hands and search his face and ask if he could ever forgive her.

As clearly as if he, himself, had been upstairs, the Astronomer knew what Fred would say. Fred would be relieved. His face would relax; his tone would indicate *Is-That-All?* Happily he would tell her, "There's nothing to forgive!" He would be unprepared for the growing horror on Eva's face. The Astronomer screwed up his own face, just thinking about it.

Wincing, the Astronomer pulled his eyebrows over his squinted eyes. No, Fred would not be able to do it; he had not been able to do it. That prayer, *Forgive me!* was from Eva to herself; and Eva was not willing to grant Eva any forgiveness.

Friday she hobbled about upstairs. Her abdomen was very tender, Fred said, but he thought the vomiting had something to do with that. She combed her hair for the first time. Once or twice she flipped through some of the magazines Fred had brought. She was weak and unsteady, but the nausea had passed. There was no fever.

Downstairs the Astronomer began to relax. There was no infection. The rest would heal in time; she would recover. She would recover even from her grief; that was how people were. For a long time there would be this inner dialogue: question and answer, blame and excuse, guilt and reason. It would act like a bandage. Under her inner questioning, the wounds would grow together before she even knew.

When he went upstairs to bring down empty dishes from her lunch, he told Eva he might go to the library while Fred was resting downstairs. "Bring you something?"

Her forefinger drew a little circle on the sheet. "Bring me a Bible," she finally said.

He tilted the tray and a glass thumped on the rug. He had to crawl half under the bed to get it back. "Bring you what?" he finally said.

"A Bible."

"I got a Bible downstairs."

"Then bring me something else. Something about it."

He was confused. "Sunday-school lessons? Bible stories?"

"No. Something that says what it means."

He carried the dishes to the door, apprehensive. "I ain't sure anybody knows what it means."

"Well, everybody claims to!" she said with sudden anger. "If it's that much trouble, forget it."

"I'll see what they got," he muttered. When he reached the head of the stairs, she called him back. "Could you bring me your Bible to read while you're gone? Pass the time?"

"All right."

Before he left the house the Astronomer left a pitcher of ice water, matches for Eva's cigarettes, the large red Bible inscribed in pale brown signature, ELSIE KNOWLES BEAM. AGE 20. FIRST CHURCH.

At the back door, the thermometer read 91 degrees. The Astronomer could not understand it. He felt chilly and his hands were damp. Must be taking another cold.

When he arrived home with the books, Eva asked him to sit with her. "Not to talk," she said. "But can't you read here as well as downstairs?"

He tried not to show his pleasure. He pulled an armchair near the window. Eva, wearing a black cotton housecoat, began thumbing the books he had brought. She lit one cigarette after another.

Absently the Astronomer turned pages in his own book. It dealt with the stars at the time of Moses, how the heavens might have caused the flood of Noah, how celestial activity might explain the plagues of Egypt. He had selected it deliberately, having avoided that theme for weeks. Now he was ready. If Eva began talking about the Ten Commandments, he wanted to be able to put Sinai in perspective. If she talked of nuns and adultery and murder, he would burn out her fear with stars and comets.

But she did not talk about anything. With an angry frown, she plowed through the books, moving her lips, grimacing, blowing through her teeth. Suddenly she heaved one book at the foot of the bed and it fell off to one side. By turning his head the Astronomer could check its title, *Peace in God,* by Billy Graham. Bending, he took it off the floor and laid it on a table.

"They get you where they want you," she stormed, "and then you're supposed to buy the whole bag of tricks!"

He did not answer, but he kept his face attentive. When Eva is well, he thought, she'll remember I never lectured; I never asked her for anything. I listened and tried to help—she'll remember that. Where Sion failed and Fred failed, I'm going to be what she always needed. For the first time in days, he wanted to smile.

"I thought you might not like those books, so I picked out some others. They're downstairs. A murder mystery and . . ."

Eva interrupted. "They tell you *what* but they never tell you *how!*" She leaned back on the pillows. With one hand she rubbed her brows. "I don't know why they bother to write books about it," she said crossly, closing her eyes, stroking her forehead. The Astronomer watched the irritation ebb from her face. Underneath that glaze there was nothing but—could that be right? Yes. There was nothing but hunger.

Wearily she said, "Hand me another book." She did not mean the murder mystery he had saved downstairs.

He passed her another volume from the library's sparse "Religion" section, feeling she had sent him out for bread and he had only brought her stones. He had not known whether to bring her works with a Catholic or Protestant slant, or whether she really wanted philosophy and ethics. He had asked the librarian to tell him which works were most popular. Maybe that had been his mistake.

This book was by Edwin McNeill Poteat. Five minutes after she began it, she was riffling the pages and frowning again. "They start too far ahead," she said, accusing the Astronomer with her glare.

"Ahead of what?" he decided to ask.

"I'm not ready for Jesus yet. Not nearly ready. Don't they write any books at all for people who are where I am?"

The Astronomer felt like a clumsy waiter. He should now carry Jesus away from her table, a steak which had arrived before the soup was served. Besides, he didn't know exactly where Eva *was,* much less if it was the right place to be. He twisted in his chair. "Now, Eva," he began carefully, "you don't want to go off the deep end. I know you've had a bad experience. It's natural you should feel . . ."

He was stopped by the welling of tears in Eva's eyes. She grabbed at one of Fred's handkerchiefs on the table, blew her nose.

"I want to go off the deep end," she said intensely. "I want to go head first. Hand me another book."

He was reluctant. "Maybe this is something easier to talk about than read about," he said. "I'll try to understand if you want . . ."

"I don't," she said. "Let's have the orange one."

It was *The Screwtape Letters,* and held her attention longest. When she finally looked up from it, her face was still resentful. But she said vaguely, "I may come back to that one. In a year or two." She lay quite still and counted the buttons on her robe, up and down, from hem to throat and back again.

He got to his feet. "You're ready to sleep awhile."

"It's bad sleep," said Eva. "I dream."

"Right now you need sleep, the strength it brings. And it will bring strength." He was so earnest he believed she was bound to be convinced by his sincerity. "Nobody stays down for long, Eva.

Or up, either. You go back to the middle. Not black, not white.
Nearly everything is gray. . . ."

"I never cared for gray," she snapped.

He thought her husband Sion might be gray, gunmetal gray; and
Fred had looked, for a while, like something in white armor. And
abortion was black. And if Sion was gray, she could reject that
forever; he'd even help her do that much. "Forget about that,
then," he said quickly. "But let go a little. Relax. You're making
yourself miserable. Working at it." And again he did not know
whether he wanted Eva to let go, or guilt—Black Guilt—to ease
its hold on her. Whichever would listen first, he thought.

Half an hour later when the Astronomer came back to listen
at her closed door, Eva was speaking aloud. He knew it was none
of his business. He flattened his ear against the wood. No voice
was answering hers. Yet she droned on as if to some attentive
listener. After a while he could make out her words.

". . . so You are there because I say so. . . . You have to be
there because I cannot stand it if You are not there. And I'm not
going to worry now about where You were all the other times I
needed help; that's gone. And since that's settled I can ask You:
Please. Forgive me. I can't live if somebody doesn't forgive me and
nobody here can do it. . . . Can't be taken back or undone,
forgotten or anything . . . can't lose it or hide it or wear it out,
but can't live with it—either! . . . So You've got to be there or
everything's lopsided the wrong way, and too heavy, and tipping
over, and I will fall down forever . . . can't stand it and can't
be rid of it so will You forgive me? Please? Forgive me, God.
Only me and only this and nobody to forgive me . . . God?
Forgive me, God. . . ."

The Astronomer jerked his head from the panels of the door as
if the wood were hot. The hum of Eva's words was steady and
quiet and long—like a chain, and each insistent link was the same
unbroken circle behind another circle: forgivemeforgivemefor-
giveme. And on the end of that chain hung the heaviest, biggest
anchor of them all. To bury itself in mud, or fall in the sea, or hook

on? Would it drag Eva away until she was pulled down forever? Or had she done more than that already? (He thought of her saying she wanted to go off the deep end, head first.) Had she stood already on that edge and turned her back on gunmetal gray, facing away from the middle of everything, and taken one grand, free leap in the direction of the heart of that darkness?

Maybe it's a map, after all. This particular map. Or this particular labyrinth. The Astronomer tiptoed away into a house that seemed suddenly strange, and invaded, and not his. Whenever he turned a corner, he was surprised that No One met him. He was glad to be gone from Eva's door. The one thing he could not have stood was to hear a second voice.

Fred said, "Will you explain it to me? Why she goes on acting so funny?"

He didn't want to talk about it. Helplessly he waved one hand.

"What's done is done. I tell her that. Okay, so it's rough. But you have to go on. We can have a good life, just the two of us. She acts like she killed off the whole human race."

"I thought you was fixing her some toast."

"I am, I am." Fred turned his back. "Nobody can go back. Boy, I got things I could brood about if I tried. Everybody has. But it's over; you accept it."

Yeah. If you can. Aloud he said, "Eva told me once that when you said 'accept,' you really meant 'excuse.' "

"That's silly," grunted Fred. "I guess I know what I mean. I mean 'accept.' " He put the toast into a saucer. "I never said it was easy. Some things take longer. But what you can't change you gotta leave behind."

"Eva's going to be all right. If you feed her."

"I said I was fixing it! Where's the butter?"

The Astronomer pointed. He knew how Fred felt, being off the road map. Rocks. Briars. The thing is, maybe it *is* a map—all of it; maybe it's Eva's map, and you have to get to someplace like Eva got before . . . well, he didn't know before-what.

"This all you got?"

"How much you need for two pieces of toast?" Suppose that was right. And suppose it took different things to get people in that place, to break them, more or less. Maybe some could think themselves into it. Or lose their tempers once. Or kill an unborn child . . .

He did not notice when he began to speak aloud. "If that's how it comes about, that's mean. That's *wicked.*"

Fred had turned from the open refrigerator to stare at him. "I swear, you're bad as she is!"

"For God's sake!" the Astronomer burst out, then thought cautiously: No. Not for that. "For Pete's sake, Fred," he started again, "I'm tired! I've worried with you and Eva and listened to your problems and run your errands, and finally I got plain tired. You think I never got anything on my own mind?"

Fred smeared butter on the toast and stood at attention. "Pardon *me.*"

"Well, it's my kitchen and if I want to talk to myself . . ."

"Pardon me, I said. Won't bother you any more."

The Astronomer got angrier and angrier. "I was all set to retire and here you come, down the street, like all this time I been waiting for you to come live in this house. And do you want to know what I got out of it, besides the worry? One lousy telescope I ain't got time to use! One telescope that might as well be back in the store."

Fred said through a tight mouth he appreciated the butter and the two pieces of bread; Mr. Beam could add it to his rent bill.

When Fred had gone up to Eva, the Astronomer slammed the butter onto a refrigerator shelf and banged the door.

Well? Was that It? I was mean when I didn't need to be. Lost my temper. Jumped all over the boy. Was that it?

The Astronomer frowned at the lightbulb suspended just above his head.

"Well?" He finally said it aloud. It was *his* kitchen. "Well? Are You there?"

And the lightbulb and the ceiling and some dead flies and a cobweb were all there, just like yesterday.

Fred Ridge went to the café for supper before time to go to the gas station. He slammed the front door going out and did not call his usual goodbye.

At seven the Astronomer looked in on a sleeping Eva. He saw the cloudy milk glass and a few crusts of toast left on the saucer by the bed. He tiptoed across the rug to collect them. Alongside, he saw, Elsie's old Bible lay open to the end of the book of Hosea in the Old Testament. Eva had marked several parts with the pen Fred brought her from the drugstore. He glanced at her sleeping face, bent forward to read.

Above one chapter, Eva had marked an introductory summary: "Wherein the Lord commands Hosea to love and marry a harlot, to illustrate how He continues to love all that is unlovable in His people Israel."

He glanced at her still face again. He was glad he had never told her about his funny nickname.

Also marked were sections in a different chapter: "I will love them freely: for mine anger is turned away from him. . . . They that dwell under his shadow shall return; they shall revive as the corn and grow as the vine. . . . I am like a green fir tree."

The glass which rested in the saucer rattled briefly in his hand. He stilled it. Eva, he saw, slept quietly. Maybe without the dreams. He was glad for her rest, yet he was angry. He had soothed her when she cried; he had carried her in his arms. That awful moan had been heard by his ears alone, and he had loved her.

Looking down now upon her quiet face, he felt himself cheated and deprived. Oh, he thought bitterly, I *could* have forgiven her! If she had let me!

With every passing day, Eva grew a little stronger. She said she did not believe she could manage the stairs, but she practiced walking in the upper hall. From supper to bedtime every day, the Astronomer kept her company.

It was silly to call himself that name in his own mind. He was seldom out of the house; there was dust inside his telescope. The sky was something he heard described in books. If the Perseids had been a shower of August stars he had no way of knowing. Besides—he said, excusing himself—they were far away and long ago.

He was more interested in reading Eva's face. As complex as a zodiac, it seemed equally far away. He was content to give up the night and the constellations and settle for this little room. Meanwhile, her own mind was out beyond the curvature of space.

She was so quiet that once he said, "No need for me to sit here. I might as well be a chair."

Eva looked surprised. "Why do you say that? I'm the one asked you to sit here, even if you did nothing but read. I feel comfortable when you're here."

Yeah. Thanks a lot. But he continued to bring his book, or some cards for solitaire. He could not concentrate, but Eva could. She read through one stack of volumes after another. If he glanced up he would sometimes discover her with a book neglected on her lap, her gaze intent. The Astronomer would search her face. And Eva—whose face was she searching?

Eva was preoccupied; Fred was worried; the Astronomer was tense. Some mornings while he drank his coffee, he could hear Fred pacing in that bedroom, explaining something in a loud voice. Once or twice Fred left the house in the middle of the afternoon, his jaws clenched.

Another time the Astronomer carried a star chart to the porch swing; studying the diagram he did not glance behind him and almost sat on Fred, prone and furious. The Astronomer grabbed at the chain to catch himself and Fred shot upright with both fists clenched over his head. "*Jee*-sus!" he exclaimed, "and I thought she was bats *before!*" He almost ran down the street before the

Astronomer could get entirely disentangled from the swing.

He mentioned it to Eva, keeping his voice mild. "He seems right unhappy."

"Fred always said nobody could help anybody else," she said rapidly, as if she had been working out this answer well in advance of any question. "He's just now getting the chance to learn it's so."

In spite of these incidents, the Astronomer began to feel hopeful. Eva's health was improving; she ate well and spent less time in bed. Fred said he was getting a raise at the station. ("I can handle your debt on Fisher Street," he said, and all the way outside through the window the Astronomer heard her rising question, *"My* debt?") Nobody had come to knock at the front door to show any wedding picture.

Everything's going to work out, the Astronomer decided. I think I'll have the upstairs painted. Eva can pick the colors.

The night of September 5, he even planned a little celebration. He waited till Fred had gone to work, then carried the derby-shaped bakery cake with its pink candles upstairs to her room. Outside her door he lowered the cake to the floor, struck a match to the candles, carried it in, twinkling over his head.

"What's that!" cried Eva. She turned from the bureau where she had been brushing her hair.

"Celebration," he said, hoping he sounded calm. "You and Fred came to live here in June. The summer's over. It's in honor of a new season."

She rested the hairbrush on one shoulder. "Seems like a hundred years."

"It was June twenty-first when I retired, and Fred came to see me next morning. He spent that night of the twenty-second here by himself. The next day you came." The Astronomer cleared his throat. "Sorry I missed Fred. Meant it for everybody, of course."

She said softly, "It's very nice of you."

He put the cake on her bedside table and fished the knife out of his pants pocket where he had carried it upstairs. "The forks are in my shirt," he said, "and there's a stack of napkins under the cake. You want to blow the candles out?"

"You do it."

Feeling silly, he puffed out the tiny fires and served them cake on napkin squares. "Not bad," he said. "Listen, when you feel up to it, maybe you'd like to fool around in that kitchen. You said yourself it needed tending. I never even think to buy cleanser."

Eva had a mouthful of cake.

He rushed on. "At first I thought about painting the upstairs, but the more I turn it in my mind, the more sense it makes for you and Fred to take the downstairs. Like an apartment, see? I could keep kitchen privileges, if that's all right. More space down there than one man needs. We could fix it up a little. Fred and I can do most of the work on weekends." She could not guess how much that cost him. But he would take Fred if there was no other way. Anything to keep her here.

She was struggling to swallow and interrupt.

"Any moving to be done, I could do that. If you like this bedroom furniture better, we could even swap it. Take a Saturday, maybe. Some of this stuff wouldn't be so bad if it was painted."

She had begun to shake her head. He raised his voice.

"And out back—I never showed you—out back Elsie used to grow some flowers; you interested at all in flowers? Things that came up every spring—the yellow ones and the little white ones with orange in the middle. It's about choked with ivy now, but fall's a good time to clean it out."

"Mr. Beam," she finally said. "No, Mr. Beam. Please don't."

"Lots of people just don't care for flowers," he said quickly. "Never paid much attention to them myself. . . ."

This time she stopped him by laying one hand on his arm. There was a smear of chocolate on her thumb. "I'm going home," she said. "Soon as I'm able, I'm going back to my husband."

With all his talking the Astronomer had barely tasted his cake. Now he knew he never would.

"Home?"

"There's nothing else to do. I'll be going soon."

"You can't decide that now, before you're well."

"If I don't decide it," she said in a flat voice, "I'll never *be* well."

"When?"

"Soon as I'm stronger. Maybe next week. Fred thinks I'll change my mind."

"I hope Fred's right. Don't do this, Eva. Don't go back."

"I've got to."

"And what about Fred?" He did not dare say, What about me? Neatly she dusted her crumbs into the wastebasket. "Oh, Fred will think it through. Sensibly. He won't be able to change it so I guess he'll be stuck with his own advice to accept it and go on." She wadded up her napkin. "Before long there'll be another woman and I think he'll marry that one."

"You love him?"

"Yeah," she said. "Ain't that crazy?"

He was desperate enough to try anything. "And don't you owe Fred something? Because he does love you. You know he loves you."

"That's even crazier," she said.

He leaned forward carefully and dropped his whole piece of cake into the waste can. Eva said, "Love . . . I wanted it to drown me."

Drown, big ship in the dark, great leaps into chasms . . . he jerked the candles out of the cake and threw them away. "You could stay here with me," he blurted.

She never even considered it, not really. "I couldn't do that." She didn't need to think it over even once. That hurt him most of all. Grimly she added, "It's not as if I'll drown at home, but I've got to try. And there's Timmy. There's Roberta. I must have been out of my mind to think I could just leave them."

He leaned back in his chair. She never once really thought of staying here, with me.

"I loved Sion once, I guess," she was saying. "I've been trying to remember how that went. I'm going to be that way again." She smiled. "In the orphanage, there was this special club. It was hard to be a member. They had to pass on you; you couldn't snitch or cheat or have bad teeth, lots of things. Then when you passed all the tests, you learned this routine to get into the club meetings. It met in a hole in a privet hedge; and before the officers would let you in you had to come from the building with exactly twenty-seven steps, and hop on one foot, and say a couple magic words; you ever in a club like that?"

"No," he said. There were lots of things he had never done and —he saw now—would never do.

"Well, when you got the motions right you could come in. And when everybody got in right the meeting would start. Anyway, that's how I'm going home—to do that routine. I'm going to hop on one foot for Sion and stick out my tongue and roll my eyes and take the same twenty-seven steps, and he's going to let me in. And after a lot of meetings I'm going to know how to love him again."

"You're out of your mind," he snapped. "All you want to do is pay through the nose. You think you're guilty of something, so you're serving a life sentence."

"Always I been letting things happen. Fred happened. Getting abandoned, and getting adopted, it all happened. Marrying Sion wasn't much different. Now I'm going to make things happen."

Before he could stop himself, the Astronomer said, "Look what you made happen down on Fisher Street."

"Get out," she said.

"Eva, I'm sorry."

"Out and take your damned cake with you." She got to her feet and picked it up as if she might throw it, vaudeville style, into his face.

"I didn't mean that. I'm worried. I know you won't be happy. I didn't mean what I said."

"I'm going to *make* happy. I'm going to call it and look for it and drag it out. You hear me?"

He took the cake from her hand and put it back on the table. "I said I'm sorry. Eva, what makes you think he'll take you back?"

"Maybe he won't. I got to go see."

There was so little left. "You can always come back here, Eva. Any time. Next month or next year."

She sank into a chair. "Thank you, Mr. Beam. I'm sorry I yelled."

"If you owe any money . . . if Dr. Brock . . . maybe I could . . ."

"I'll get that paid."

How could he reach her! "You don't think your husband will pay a debt like that?"

She said stubbornly she would manage it.

"You mustn't go." Now that he had made the flat statement it was all he could think of. He stood and clasped both hands behind his back where each controlled the other's trembling. "He'll divorce you, and it'll be an ugly divorce. He'll take the children. If you're looking for punishment that's what you'll get, and in the end you won't get anything else."

"Don't talk to me about ugly. I have seen ugly. I have been there! And have I got the children now? Is any of that worse?"

He continued to stride. "He might even hurt you. He might pull out a gun and shoot you down. How can you tell?"

"How can *you* tell, who's never seen the man at all?"

"Send somebody else first. A lawyer, family friend. Find out what you'll be getting into. I'd even be willing . . ."

"No. I don't want to know what I'll be getting into." She stared at him. "Can't you understand I want to take that risk?"

He could have shaken her. "It's a big gesture you want to make, that's all. Like conscience money. You don't want to think about the long-range consequences. You refuse to think this through."

"You and Fred!" Eva laughed. "I thought it through before I came with Fred in the first place, and you tell me what good it was! Could I have sat there in the car lot, planning to get pregnant and then picking the best abortion to have? Could I have measured out the shame I might feel?"

"We said we wouldn't talk about that."

"This time I'm just thinking through the part I can use—me. How I'll be. What I can do. If I'd thought that way before, I'd have known there were some places I couldn't stand to be, road maps or no road maps. And not because of all the things people said. Because of *me*."

"Road maps again!" he said in disgust.

"Damn right, road maps!" she yelled. "No more of this clear direction, thought-through, plain road. Nosir, you and Fred go right off on it! Me, I'll think about *all* the roads at once. And what I'd be like if I happened to be on them!"

The Astronomer stretched out his right hand, palm up, fingers spread, hoping perhaps she would see what all he was offering her in that empty hand with its network of lines. "You can't change what's happened."

"I know that."

He folded his fingers. "Have I got to blame all these books? The library? Me for bringing them to you? Is this something some God said you had to do?"

She shook her head. "I don't know that much. All the time I'm praying I keep taking back my prayers."

"Not got a thing to do with it?"

"I wouldn't say that."

Now he was really angry. "Boy, you women do fool yourselves. And you're really no different from Fred; I don't see how you can miss it. Because you're doing just exactly what you want to do, Eva, no more and no less. And you're excusing it in a new fancy way. That's all it is. You're doing exactly what you say he's doing —leaving behind what you can't change. It's not a damn bit different!"

"No," said Eva thoughtfully. "I never could leave anything. That's what's wrong with me."

The rest of that cake was never eaten. And after that night the Astronomer hated to see Eva improving and gaining her strength. The first day she walked down the stairs alone he stood in a shadowed kitchen corner and hoped for her to fall. Yes, and if I could pray—he thought—I'd pray for a broken leg.

He tried to decide whether Fred knew her decision. Was that why the man was so withdrawn and irritable? If he spoke to him about it, what would he say? But more important was the question: Can Fred keep her here?

He tried drawing Fred out. "Now that Eva's getting better, you could take a daytime job. Live a more normal routine."

"Normal," said Fred. "That would be a change."

"I been talking to Eva about changing things around. Me taking the upstairs. You two having a real apartment down here . . ."

"Yeah," Fred sneered. "And what does she say to that?"

So Fred knew. And he was accepting it. Would he do nothing? Let her leave without raising a hand?

The Astronomer decided he was the only one left to fight for Eva. And he knew at last whom he must fight. It was not Fred and it was not Eva. It was not even Sion and two little children. It was that little God running amuck in her head.

But if it had saved her sanity? If he could prove it false, would Eva . . . The Astronomer's head felt full of bees.

He did make a few brief attacks. Harassment.

"You tell me why some Being with this whole universe to play with should care for you? And, mind you, I been learning some things about this universe. I mean, you can spread out a million miles into space or go down a million miles into little space, with the germs and the atoms. All that He made; and He's still got time for you and a few cells that hadn't even turned into a baby yet?"

Eva said she didn't even know. "When I think about it, I think that's crazy. I think that doesn't make any sense. I don't know why I should care for Fred or him for me or you for either one of us, either. Here's a big world, so why should we spend the time? And not even saving the love for the few people that deserve it. I think that's pretty nuts."

"What if you made Him up? You needed Him and you made Him up and when the need is gone your prayer is just going to float up there with every one of them two-hundred-year-old stars! All by itself!"

"It might happen." Eva stared at the wallpaper. "Yes. But He ought to be there. He still feels there. I'd rather run this risk than the other one."

The Astronomer grew impatient. "And you can't see this is what Fred said all along, believing exactly what suits you, with no regard for whether it's true? Excusing it? You can't see it's the same?"

"Maybe so." Eva did not seem to care. "I worry most about getting over it—that's something *you* said, not Fred. That people can't keep things. They're set up to heal over and outlive and outlast. And that I'll heal and then decide He wasn't ever there."

He began to nod. "That scares you, does it? That this thing, so quick and so convenient, is going to pass? Already you half expect it to pass."

She stopped him with an uplifted palm. "I don't mean that— that's not exactly what scares me. *This* is what scares me—I'll recover, and there I'll be, not believing again. And everything going smooth. And then what will He do to prove Himself? What terrible thing will He show me next? Something worse than this? Can He take me down someplace more terrible than this? That's what scares me. That scares me a lot."

"You're just stampeded. If you'd wait awhile . . ."

"I don't dare wait. I'm convinced, mostly. And mostly you're not."

Impatiently he asked, "Well, if He's there, why should it be so hard to convince anybody? I've got an open mind. I've had griefs before. Why doesn't He come and convince me?"

"Not just convinced. Committed."

The Astronomer snorted. "I knew it was a mistake, bringing you all them fancy books."

One night Fred volunteered, "The day she goes, I go." It was the first time he had admitted Eva would ever leave him. "I don't know when it's going to be, but I'll come home and find her gone. And I'm just going to pack up and start out."

Accept it and go on. "Start out where?"

"Who cares?"

"After her, maybe?" he asked with a flicker of hope. "To bring her back?"

"Back here to Newton City? With its Fisher Street?" He untied a shoe and dropped it onto the front porch. "She'll never come back here. No, when she goes she goes. And I'm next."

"I thought you loved her."

"LOVE HER GOOD GOD!" Fred yelled. He dropped the second shoe with violence. "Tell me what you know about it? You remember how it feels? Would it help if I cried? Yelled more? Kidnaped her, busted her one in the jaw? Stuck a knife in her ribs? Don't talk to me about loving her!"

But the Astronomer was every bit as bitter. "You could beg her," he said in a harsh voice. "You could get down on your knees and beg her."

"I couldn't do that."

"I knew it," he said with distaste.

"What you mean by that?"

"You're not able to do it. That's all."

"Don't tell me about being able! Don't tell me about loving! How would you know!"

Too angry to answer, the Astronomer turned and went inside his house, inside his room, banged the door hard.

Because I can't do it either!

He opened that door and slammed it shut again, as though one more slap of noise would cover those words and scatter them;

and never again in all his life would they come together for him
in just that terrible order and clarity.

These conversations should have prepared him. But he had not
stopped hoping. When he sat brooding on his porch on the evening
of September 10 and a taxi pulled up to his curb he barely noticed.
Wrong house. With one toe he pushed himself slightly in the swing.

The sound of footsteps in the upper hall and on the stairs froze
him with that toe arched out absurdly like a ballet dancer's. "Mr.
Beam?"

He had to start twice before his throat would make a sound.
"I'm out here, Eva."

She closed the screen carefully behind her. "Just a minute!" she
called to the cabbie.

The beautiful arguments he had mustered this past week dis-
solved. "Eva," he said, "not now. Not today."

Her crooked mouth was meant to be a smile: "Time to go."
Only the fingers scrambling about the handle of her pocketbook
showed she was nervous. She wore the same brown dress she had
worn the first day he saw her. There was no luggage.

"I wrote Sion I'd be coming. I mustn't miss my bus."

"The first day you came," he heard himself say, "I thought you
looked like a refugee."

"Yes. Well . . ."

Awkwardly he got out of the swing. It thumped him in the legs.
"Eva, you know . . . you know you can come back. Any time.
If things . . ."

"I know that."

"What time's your bus?"

"Seven-fifteen." She began to fumble with the strap of the wrist
watch.

"You keep that," he almost shouted. "I mean it. I don't want
the thing."

"Oh, I couldn't . . ."

He kissed her on the forehead. "Tell him an old man gave it to you. Retired. I don't think he'll mind. . . ."

"This will be the least of the things he has to mind." Her voice was husky; two drops began to swell in the corner of each eye. "You are a very good man," Eva said, "and a good friend."

"No," he said, glad to be telling this much truth.

She ran to the cab. The Astronomer turned his back as if he were going into the house so he could only hear the motor waning as she rode away. Three fingers he held in a small cup at the mouth which had finally kissed her face. He could not hold in the warmth of her skin. That was already gone.

He hardly looked aside from his pocket watch until the hands said 7:30 and the bus should be well on its way to Monbury. Then he walked to Mrs. Blevins' house and used her phone to call Fred at the filling station. Mrs. Blevins was excited to see him.

"You've not been in my house in I don't know how long!" she raved.

"It's an emergency. I'm in a hurry."

Fred answered on the first ring. "It's Horton Beam," he recited. "She's gone."

There was a silence, then one long let-out breath. "Okay," said Fred. The Astronomer heard him tell somebody he was quitting just before the phone clicked in his ear.

In an hour Fred was home, mildly drunk, not talkative. He grunted as he came in, walked by him up the stairs. The Astronomer stayed in the swing. Only once did Fred come down to call from the front screen, "She take a taxi?"

"Yes."

"How could she call a taxi?"

The Astronomer didn't know. "Maybe next door. Maybe she told them in advance when to come. What difference does it make?"

"Uh," said Fred and went back to their room. His room. Almost my room again. No. Never that.

At nine Fred came downstairs carrying a cardboard box and a large paper bag. "She didn't take her things," Fred said.

"No. She had on that brown dress."

For a minute Fred's mouth looked almost as crooked as hers had looked. "He bought that one for her."

"Did she have enough money?"

"I think so. Reminds me, I'll pay through this week . . ."

"I don't want it."

Fred raised one brow. "We're leaving without notice. . . ."

The Astronomer shouted, "For God's sake don't give me any *money!*"

"All right." A car passed slowly on Helicks Street. Both of them watched it, leaned slightly forward, stared until it made a right turn and disappeared. "Well," said Fred, "I'm going to hop a freight if I can. Don't know where. Maybe I'll let you know where I am, just in case."

"In case she comes back?"

Fred shrugged. "You never can tell." He looked embarrassed. "I . . . I thank you for everything." The two men shook hands.

It was all right to watch Fred Ridge out of sight. The paper bag, propped on one shoulder, was the last thing to fall down the hill in the growing dark. Carries it like a sea bag, he thought.

When he started indoors the Astronomer tripped on the sill and nearly fell. Can't even find my way in my own house. There's a labyrinth for you, your own furniture and door sills after all these years! Just moving down the hall, he strewed the air with echoes.

The cabinets and white refrigerator looked ghostly in the kitchen, but he was not anxious to turn on any lights. They seemed to float in the corners like clouds. Even the air about the house was still. Not one mockingbird was singing.

In a little bit, I'll fix something to eat.

He sat at the table. The whole summer, gone for nothing, all because somebody on Fisher Street charged Eva a couple hundred dollars to take out a flap of flesh that could have been nothing but trouble to everyone. And if she needed forgiveness for that, why wouldn't she take forgiveness from him, from Horton Beam? I could have done the job cheaper for her, yes, and better too.

All she had to do was stay. That's how cheap my forgiveness comes.

Maybe Fred was right, and these last weeks Eva had been a little bats. Because right now she was riding away on that Greyhound bus, thinking Something had put a hand into her life and stopped it cold at a certain point.

Listen, he thought, if it's just needing forgiveness—I've plenty to be forgiven for! I could use lots of forgiveness, and Nobody says anything to me! There was Elsie; I always let her down. I was too hard on the boys; they thought I was a cold fish. And then there's plain disbelief—you'd have to be forgiven that.

He turned rather nervously to the refrigerator, which looked so much like a floating phantom, and banged it with his fist. Yes, it was solid. It was just what it seemed, just what it had always seemed.

I could have begged Eva to stay. She didn't mind begging for what she wanted. I overheard her doing that. Came right out with it, begging first just to have Him there. Forgive me, she begged. I could have begged her the way she begged Him. It might have worked.

Well, I couldn't beg and she could, and she's gone. And gone without being sure of anything at all. Yet that kind of doubt was enough to send her back to something bound to be hell, at least in the beginning. What kind of iron doubt is that?

Here he was, Horton Beam, sixty-five and retired, in this house of thunderous silence. The Astronomer hurried—no, ran—from the kitchen and down the back steps into the yard, where he turned his face upward. Pegasus was galloping over the east. From near Capella a small torch skidded down the sky.

Listen! The Astronomer sent his thought desperately beyond those stars. Listen! *Say* something to me!

$\mathcal{V}$OICES OF THE $\mathcal{S}$OUTH